Fox Forever

MARY E. PEARSON

SQUARE
FISH

Henry Holt and Company

New York

For my precious Ava—
The future is yours.

SQUARE FISH

An Imprint of Macmillan
175 Fifth Avenue
New York, NY 10010
macteenbooks.com

FOX FOREVER. Text copyright © 2013 by Mary E. Pearson.
All rights reserved. Printed in the United States of America by
R. R. Donnelley & Sons Company, Harrisonburg, Virginia.

Square Fish and the Square Fish logo are trademarks of Macmillan and
are used by Henry Holt and Company under license from Macmillan.

Square Fish books may be purchased for business or promotional use. For information
on bulk purchases, please contact the Macmillan Corporate and Premium Sales
Department at (800) 221-7945 x 5442 or by e-mail at specialmarkets@macmillan.com.

Library of Congress Cataloging-in-Publication Data
Pearson, Mary (Mary E.)
Fox forever / Mary E. Pearson.
pages   cm.—(The Jenna Fox chronicles ; [3])
Summary: Before he can start a life with Jenna, seventeen-year-old Locke, who was
brought back to life in a newly bioengineered body after an accident destroyed his
body 260 years ago, must do a favor for the resistance movement opposing the
nightmarish medical technology.
ISBN 978-1-250-04005-3 (paperback) / ISBN 978-0-8050-9639-2 (e-book)
[1. Medical ethics—Fiction.   2. Bioethics—Fiction   3. Biotechnology—Fiction.
4. Government, resistance to—Fiction.   5. Science fiction.]   I. Title.
PZ7.P32316Fm 2013   [Fic]—dc23   2012027677

Originally published in the United States by Henry Holt and Company
First Square Fish Edition: 2014
Square Fish logo designed by Filomena Tuosto

10 9 8 7 6 5 4 3 2 1

AR: 4.8 / LEXILE: 740L

I am fearfully and wonderfully made.
—*Psalm 139:14*

The Favor

I stare at my gravestone. Locke Jenkins. They paid too much for it. More than they could afford. I wonder what slick salesman talked them into it. I reach out and run my fingers over the recessed letters. The *L* is nearly as weathered away as the life I once had.

Closure. That's what I came for, but now that I'm standing here, I think that letting go of the past doesn't come in a single moment. Maybe the past has to fade away slowly like letters in granite. Worn away over time by wind, rain, and tears. Maybe that's why they did it, ordered a ridiculously expensive gravestone for a small urn of ashes. Maybe that was their way of letting me fade away slowly.

I look at their graves to the right of mine. I wish I had brought flowers for them. What kind did my mother like? I can't remember. Did I ever know?

I know it's normal to forget. That's part of letting go, but my memories are all I have, my only connection to the original me. On a daily basis, I search the details of my life, the conversations, the routines, the fears, the small in-between moments that connected one day to the next, all the voices that have come and gone in my life, still whispering to me. Everything that might help me to understand who I am now. A man, a boy, a something. I promised Jenna I would find out.

I glance up at a shadowy figure fifty yards away. He's been following me ever since the train station. He stoops like he's visiting a grave. He thinks that fools me? Watching my back has become second nature. But I play his game. Maybe he plans to mug me. That wouldn't be a good idea. If he's smart he'll reconsider.

The phone tab in my pack vibrates, but I ignore it. I've had to wait for this world for so long, now the world will have to wait for me. My parents deserve that much. I keep waiting for a feeling that doesn't come. A realization. Maybe even a message from the universe. I only hear a graveyard full of silence. Not even the sounds of grief. I know they cried plenty for me. I never got the chance to cry for them, and now it seems too late. The world has passed me by.

I fill the void with my own message instead, a whisper to my parents. "I'm okay."

After 260 years it's a pretty pathetic offering, but I know that's what they'd want to hear. Or that I had just been elected president. I smile at the thought, remembering all the things they hoped I would be. They never would have guessed that I'd end up like this. My dad, at least, might be impressed, in a horrified sort of way.

Yeah. I'm okay. For them, I have to be.

I look up. The stranger who was following me is gone. Maybe he really was visiting someone here, his good-byes too late, just like mine. I head for the main gate of the cemetery, weaving my way through tombstones and memorials. The cemetery looks like it's been abandoned for decades, the grounds in disrepair, weeds and rubble filling spaces where grass used to grow, but I suppose the dead don't really care.

My phone vibrates again. Miesha's called three times today, Jenna once, and Kayla once. Who's next? Allys? When I—

"What the hell do you think you're doing?"

I spin but my feet are already flying up, my pack sailing from my shoulder, a kick at the back of my legs sending me sprawling to the ground. I roll, but he's already on me, his knee on my chest, rage in his eyes. His weight is nothing. I could toss him, smashing his skull into the stone cherub just feet away.

"Back off, man. I'll give you three seconds. And then I'm going to seriously hurt you." And I will. I've learned that giving people second chances can lead to disaster. Gatsbro taught me that.

He grins and that's when I recognize him. A scar slashes his face from his temple to the corner of his mouth. In an instant a blade is at my throat, no time to react or push him away. He presses it against my skin with precise pressure. "*Lesson one:* Never give the enemy a warning." He pushes away from me and stands, shaking his head. "Get your miserable ass off the ground and let's go."

I stand, brushing the dirt from my coat. "I'm not going anywhere with you. I'm on my way to Manchester next. I've got business there."

"You were told to go directly to Boston. Not here or anywhere else. You promised a Favor."

"I don't always do like I'm told. You better get that straight right now." I walk over and retrieve my pack from the base of a tombstone. "I have things to take care of," I tell him. "I'll make good on my promise in a few days. Maybe less. It won't take me long to find what I need to know in Manchester."

Disgust fills his face. "I knew you were the wrong person for this." He turns and walks away.

"Wait a minute!" I call and follow behind him. "Wait!" I yell again. He doesn't stop. I double my stride so I'm walking next to him. "It's only a Favor. What difference does a few days make?"

He stops abruptly and faces me. "Don't bother showing up in a few days. By then he might be dead."

I stare at his face, trying to read it. He's exaggerating. He thinks I'm just a stupid seventeen-year-old kid. He doesn't like me. I'm not sure he likes anyone. Except maybe this person he wants to help. When I agreed to return the Favor the Network had done for me, they didn't tell me who the Favor was for or what it was they wanted me to do, but I assumed it was something small. For God's sake, they don't even know me. *The Network thinks you have some special abilities that could do the job.*

Just how much did Jenna tell them about me? Do they know? Is that the look on Mr. F's face now? Revulsion? Am I making his skin crawl because of what I am?

"What's your real name?" I ask. "I need to know that much."

"For now, it stays Mr. F. You'll know more when you need to know more."

And he's scared. This is more than just a Favor. Way more. What have I agreed to? I could back out right now. He'd let me. Probably even be glad if I did. To him, maybe I'm even less than a Non-pact. There's always a pecking order, no matter how lowly you are.

"Let's go," I say.

And I walk away with an asshole who I'm not sure I trust and who's way faster with a blade than any Non-pact should be.

Alias

The train ride to Boston is silent. I'm traveling as Nate Smith these days, courtesy of the Network. I presume Mr. F has a fake ID just like I do—otherwise, a Non-pact could never get on a train, but then, fake IDs are his specialty. When I try to bring up the Favor, he shakes his head. "Later. Not here." I don't try to talk about anything else. He's on some kind of power trip, and I decide he can trip out all he wants. I'm not here for him, and he'll find that out soon enough. I'm only here to return the Favor I owe. How long will it take? A day? Two?

The last time I helped a Non-pact, it took about thirty seconds flat, but it stuck with me for days. All I did was get him a fair price on a loaf of bread from a greedy baker who was ripping him off, but it felt like I was saving the world. It felt good, unexpected, and right. That was a power trip in itself. After 260 years of being powerless, I sucked up the power like it was air.

The train pulls into the station and Mr. F stands without speaking, expecting me to follow him. Kara called him Mr. Friendly. She was always quick at sizing up people. I walk cautiously behind him, noting that his limp, which was quite pronounced when we first met, is now gone. Was it all an act? I try to stay focused on him and watchful of the strangers I pass, but the minute we step outside the train station, I find my gaze wandering, recognizing street corners, landmarks, and buildings. I feel the remnants of my past reaching out to me, and I almost feel like the Locke I used to be.

Boston.

Home. *My home.*

Sure, it's changed. A lot. After 260 years, I wouldn't expect anything else. I already saw some of the changes when I was here with Kara, but we only stayed for a single day and I was too busy running or hiding most of that time to really notice the details. A lot of the shops have been converted to housing. Except for food, apparently no one goes to stores to buy things anymore. Tourism seems to be the only thriving tradition of the past—trinket and tourist shops crowd near busy corners. I note that the newer buildings are colorized with a white reflective surface, which explains why the city looked like a glowing geode in a bird's nest when I first viewed it from a distance. Paved streets have the same reflective color. Is this their attempt to counteract urban warming? Even though it looks like they've tried to keep the architecture historically accurate, details like this scream that I'm not in the Boston I once knew.

But there are still touchstones, vague ghosts of the past that float in and out of view, streets I walked with my parents, a corner café where I hung out with Jenna and Kara. And then, unexpectedly, a more recent ghost—the alley where Gatsbro beat me up. I've changed since then. It won't happen again.

I'm expecting that we're headed for the abandoned boarded-up buildings to the south of Boston, the outskirts where proper citizens never venture. That's where the Network hid me and Kara the last time I was here. Instead he seems to be on a steady course toward the Commons. It's getting dark now, and as we head down the center path of the Commons, I lengthen my distance behind him. Something about this doesn't seem right. Non-pacts don't congregate in public places. Where's he leading me?

We're only a short way in when he loops around and doubles back the way we came and heads down Tremont Street. He walks with his head lowered, not looking at the occasional passerby. I keep my head up. I'm not afraid and I want to know who I'm passing. A few look at me, quick glances perusing my appearance—or maybe they're only noticing my coat. I'm still wearing my freebie government issue. Proudly. Let them think what they want. The black fabric billows and snaps in the breeze.

Mr. F turns at King's Chapel and walks along its dark unlit side, then slips into the recessed doorway of the weathered building opposite from it. I don't remember this building being here before, but I follow. It's dark—very dark—which is the one thing that still makes me freeze up, but I don't let him see my weakness. I strain to see and I do. I feel the rush behind my eyes, and the dim red outline of something begins to take form. I can see more than Mr. F can, I'm sure, and as we walk down steep steps, I know before he does that someone is waiting at the bottom with a bat poised to strike.

"Stop," I whisper. "There's someone there."

"There better be," he answers. "Or we'll all end up dead."

The Team

I sit at a table with a woman, the man with the bat, and Mr. F. They stare at me curiously, maybe suspiciously. I'm getting better at reading faces but it's hard to read theirs, because the lighting in the room is very dim. They lean back in their chairs, capturing the shadows over their faces like they've done this before, accustomed to guarding their identities. We're waiting for another man. The basement is damp and smells of mold. I hear water trickling above, maybe through old leaky pipes.

Mr. F grumbles something under his breath, almost in a dialect, mostly unintelligible. I catch enough to know that he's annoyed with the waiting, but then, he seems to be pretty much annoyed with everything.

A light flips on, and they squint against the brightness over the table, looking away.

"He's here! Welcome, Locke!"

A man strides across the room and holds his hand out to me. "I'm Carver." I stumble to my feet and reach my hand out to him. His handshake is firm and I note that detail in the same way my father would have. He's well-groomed, not rumpled like so many Non-pacts are. His clothes are cheap but laundered and curiously pressed like he's meticulous about his appearance. He looks directly into my eyes. "Sorry to keep you waiting. I didn't know exactly when you'd arrive. I see you've already met your team."

I look at the three still sitting around the table and then back to Carver. "My *team*? Uh, no, we haven't met yet."

"No?" Carver looks at Mr. F.

Mr. F shrugs.

Introductions are made. Livvy, Jake, and Xavier. *Xavier?* I offer the tiniest smirk to Mr. F on hearing his name.

I turn to Carver. "I don't know what you mean by team. To be honest, I don't know anything about this Favor. Father Andre only said—"

"Please, sit down. We'll tell you all the details soon, but first we need to know everything about you. And I mean everything. If you haven't guessed already, this is no ordinary Favor. A lot's riding on it, and we don't have much time. We need to know all about you and everything you can do—*and* everything you can't. Then we can begin your training for—"

"Hold on just a minute. No one said anything about training. I can't be here that long. I need to get to Manchester."

"Please." Carver leans across the table. "Whatever you need in Manchester we'll have others take care of it. Jake here, for instance. He's my behind-the-scenes man. Good at details like that."

Right. I already witnessed how good he was in a dark corner with a bat.

Carver straightens, rubbing his palms together. *"Please,"* he says again. "You have my word we'll take care of it. But we need you here now."

His eyes are as desperate as Mr. F's were earlier. I sit back down.

"Everything," Carver repeats. "No detail is too small."

I look them over. Perfect strangers, and sketchy ones at that. How much detail is really safe in their hands? I glance at Mr. F. Petty criminal or not, he did hide Kara and me in a basement and give us new IDs that allowed us to escape.

I remember what I'm here for. My friends, Dot, Bone, Kara— and me—each of us trying to escape from a world where we have no value or rights. Kara and Dot will never get that chance for Escape now, but that doesn't mean I can't make it happen for myself, Bone, and others like us. I don't want to be hiding and running for the rest of my life, and I have a very long life ahead of me. If I live the full six hundred years that Gatsbro predicted,

I'm not going to spend it on the fringes like a stray dog. I don't even want to wait ninety years for change the way Jenna had to wait. I want it now. I'm just not sure these people are the ones to make it happen.

I lean back in my chair. "Okay, you asked for it." They have no idea how much detail I've held on to. I tell them everything, and I start at the beginning because I don't know where else to start.

I tell them how I grew up just a few blocks from here. I tell them about my parents and their high expectations for me because I was the only good student in the family. I tell them about my brother and sister and the trouble they got into. I tell them about meeting Kara and Jenna and how they changed my life. I tell them how I even memorized poetry to impress them both. Mr. F snorts at this information. Livvy smiles.

"So you knew the Fox from the very beginning?" Carver asks.

"The Fox?"

"Sorry, I thought you would have known. That's what Jenna and her branch of the Network was called. The Fox connection. That is, back when she was active."

"Right," I say, like I did know. I guess now I'm part of that connection. "Yes, we knew each other from the very beginning."

"Please, continue."

I tell them how close we all were, the accident that stole away our lives, and the BioPerfect that gave it back.

Carver leans forward. "But you didn't get your life back right away, did you?"

If he knows this detail, I'm sure he knows a lot more. I have no doubt that Father Andre culled every bit of information from Jenna and Allys that he could.

"No," I answer. "I didn't get it back right away. Jenna's dad built a new body around what was left of her, but my mind and Kara's were scanned and uploaded into six-inch cubes and then forgotten on a storage shelf for a long time."

"A long time? Just how long would that be?" His lips are parted, feigned surprise, anticipation, timing, waiting.

Click. Now I know why he's probing these details. He wants to see how fragile I am. How sensitive. Am I really up for this task? *This is no ordinary Favor.* How much pushing can I take? Will I blow? A year ago, I might have.

I look directly into his eyes. "Two hundred sixty years," I say. I don't raise my voice. I don't blink, not even when Livvy muffles a groan.

"That's a very long time," he says. "That kind of wait could make almost anyone go insane."

And he knows about Kara too. *Nice job, Father Andre. You didn't overlook a single garish detail.* "Yes. Almost anyone," I answer. If he thinks that little push will rattle me, he's wrong. I don't miss a beat and go on point by point so he can see just how sane and in control I am. I tell them about the environments where our minds were uploaded, and the BioPerfect that Gatsbro developed. "He gave us a second chance and new bodies that were near exact replicas of our originals, but it came with a catch—we were prisoners on his estate. He used us as floor models to show off his illegal technology to potential customers. When we found out what he was keeping us there for, we ran."

So there you have it, Carver and illustrious Team. Deal with it. I have a body created in a lab. Eighty percent bioengineered human, twenty percent composites, one hundred percent illegal.

"You said 'near exact.' Tell us about the changes."

With a brief scan, I can see the anticipation in all their faces. *I'm a curiosity.* Something they've never seen before. "Gatsbro was a stickler for detail. He even managed to engineer our tissue with our saved DNA so we would retain our original identity. That's how I knew the changes weren't an accident. I'm four inches taller now. A lot stronger. Green flecks in my eyes. No cowlick. Straighter teeth. Gatsbro made improvements to help sell his product. But there were some things he didn't plan on. That's the wonder of experimental technology. The BioPerfect created some changes he didn't calculate." I lean forward, resting my arms on the table. "I can read lips—from very long distances. I never could do that before. That's how I nailed a cheat back in California."

Livvy and Jake exchange glances, probably making mental notes to guard their lips carefully.

"I'm also learning to read faces."

"Meaning?" Carver asks.

"When I concentrate, I can dissect a face into multiple planes. Emotions stand out the most, usually the ones we try to hide. Fear, anger, hatred." And also things like blatant lies and exaggerations. I glance at Xavier. "I don't always get it, but I know when I see something that isn't quite right."

"That might be useful," Livvy says.

Carver nods. "Are you concentrating now?"

I look at his face. *Hunger. Need. Hope.* I shake my head. "No."

"Any other changes?"

I think of my lapses. He said to share every detail, but I haven't had a lapse in several weeks. Maybe I'm over that. What about my sensitivity to pain? Is that really a wise thing to share?

Gatsbro used it to control me. Or that I heal quickly? In less than a quarter of the time it might usually take? Would knowing this allow them to take greater chances with me? If I'm going to risk life and limb, I don't want the odds stacked against me. I decide to stick to something that Xavier has already witnessed.

I sit back in my chair. "I can see in the dark—if I push myself. Not a lot, but dim outlines, enough to find my way. When we were coming down the stairs I could see Jake ready to bust in our brains long before Xavier did."

Carver raises his brows. This piece of information transforms his face.

"But I don't like the dark," I add. "I don't want to spend a lot of time in dark places."

"You're *afraid* of the dark?" Mr. F asks.

I make no apologies to anyone about my fear of the dark. When you've spent 260 years in a black hole with no sound, touch, or light, you have a whole new understanding of what darkness can mean. "Yeah, *Xavier*. You got a problem with that?"

"I got all kinds of problems, kid, and that's the least of them. Cool your heels." His eyes are locked on mine, neither of us ready to back down.

Carver stands and walks in the shadows like he's trying to divert our attention. "What about this woman named Miesha?" he asks. "I understand she helped you get away from Gatsbro. What do you know about her?"

"She's tough—at least that's the act she puts on. She's had a hard life. She spent some time in prison. Turns out she's my niece. Sort of. About eight generations removed. I guess technically, I'm not related to her any more than I am to anyone else, but it's all I've got."

"Trust her?"

"With my life."

"She was part of a Resistance movement, wasn't she?"

Knowing about me is one thing, but I'm surprised he knows so much about Miesha. *"Was,"* I answer cautiously. "Her husband and daughter died because of it and that's when she quit."

The others have fallen silent. Carver seems to be in control of where we're going. I watch him continue to pace in the shadows. "How did they die?" he asks.

"Burned. Their house was torched by Security while she was away at a market."

"Horrible. Did she identify the bodies?"

"No. She was arrested the minute she returned to the house. That's when she went to prison. She was in for eleven years."

There's a long silence. I wait for someone to speak, but they all seem to be weighing this information.

"Is that what this is about?" I finally ask. "Are you part of the Resistance?"

Carver keeps his face in the shadows, like he doesn't want to betray his expressions, but I note the hesitation in his step. "There's no Resistance movement anymore," he says.

"There's always resistance, whether you say it with a capital *R* or not. You may call yourselves the Network, but I don't see the difference. The Network exists to help the same people who are part of the Resistance."

"You're wrong," Carver says. "The Network is only a humble humanitarian effort, while the Resistance was proactive and political. Let's move along to—"

I push my chair back. "Can we just cut the semantics crap? You already know all about Miesha, Jenna, Kara's death, and probably the color of my underwear. Enough with the questions. *Why am I here?*"

"To help a Non-pact. We already told you," Mr. F grumbles.

"*Who?*" I'm not trying to hide my impatience anymore. I understand they aren't sure if they can trust me yet, are maybe even afraid of who or what I am, but I'm just as wary of them. Meeting shady figures in shady basements doesn't exactly inspire confidence. I've already sized up the room, figured out my fastest exit and the convenient obstacles to throw in their paths. I hope they can hear in my voice that I'm seconds from walking out the door. They either meet me halfway or they don't.

Carver returns to the table and sits. The four exchange glances. He opens his mouth to speak but Livvy cuts him off. "We aren't sure, Locke. There's been a rumor for the last year that the Secretary of Security is holding someone in a special detainment area somewhere in the city. Usually arrested Non-pacts are sent to Reformation and Reassignment Centers in the desert, but not this one."

"What did he do? Violate public space?"

Livvy shakes her head. "No, for that he would have been whisked to the desert years ago. We think he might be someone who stole some money sixteen years ago. A lot of money."

I let out a quick puff of dismissive air. "Why would you want to help someone like that? Stealing's a crime, in case you haven't heard."

"If it's who we think it is, he didn't do it for himself," Carver explains. "He did it for the Resistance."

Bingo. We're back to that after all. I raise my brows in victory, but they don't seem to notice, more entranced with this long lost thief.

"It was pure genius," Xavier continues. "He hit every government contractor who built security systems to keep Non-pacts from public spaces. Nine contractors, eighty billion duros all funneled instantly into a secret account. They went down like dominoes."

They have my attention. *"Eighty billion?"*

Mr. F smiles like he's reliving it all over again. "Besides the financial hit, the humiliation factor for the so-called security contractors was so high, the theft was never revealed to the public. He had done maneuvers like this before on a smaller scale, but this time he outdid himself. The day he did it he sent us a 'complete' message in the afternoon along with the account numbers, but by evening he was—"

Carver jumps in. "Gone. And access to the account for eighty billion was gone with him. We thought he had sent us all the numbers, but apparently for safety reasons he only delivered half via cyber-transmittal. We later learned that the other half was to be hand-delivered." He opens a note window, writes something on it, and flicks it toward me, a virtual memo floating across the air to me. I grab it and it becomes tangible material at my touch, almost like paper. "That was all we got," he explains, "twelve numbers that are virtually worthless without the rest. He said he'd make sure we got the missing numbers but he never had the chance. He disappeared without a trace. He was either missing or dead."

"Or he took off with the money. Isn't that what thieves do?"

"Not him." Xavier's ears redden and he looks like he's going to tear off my face.

I blink slowly so he knows I'm unaffected. *A lesson for you, Xavier: Never show the enemy your weakness.* "Okay. So missing or dead. But you don't know which?"

"His house was raided by Security Forces," Carver says. "Burned out. His body was never produced. His widow—"

It hits me.

I finally hear what they're trying to tell me. "Hold on. Are you saying that—?" My chair squeals back behind me and I walk away to the other side of the room then right back again. I lean on the table and shake my head. "No! No way! He's dead. Miesha's husband is dead. She told me so. I saw the scars on her arms where she—"

"There are rumors about Karden," Livvy says. "We have to know. If they're true, he's been holed up for sixteen years and no one's tried to help him. We owe him that much."

I backtrack, trying to remember every word Miesha told me about that night. She never saw them. All she saw was a burning house. *I was walking back from the market. . . . The front door was open and bursting with flames. . . . I ran, screaming, breaking a window with my bare arms. . . . I thrashed, desperate to get to them, and then I felt a tazegun at my neck. . . . When I woke, I was in prison, and they told me they were dead.*

She said it herself. She never saw them dead. She only knew what the prison officials had told her. *They wouldn't even let me make any kind of arrangements for their funerals. . . . As far as I know, their remains were shoveled up along with the burned rubble of the house.*

Unless Karden's body wasn't there to shovel up. And with eighty billion duros at stake, the Security Forces would have covered all their tracks. But why now, after all these years, are there finally rumors? And if he's been missing all this time, why the sudden urgency to find him? They all act like time is running out. I look at the four of them seated across from me waiting for me to respond. The table is turned—do I trust *them* enough to meet them halfway? Eighty billion duros gives them a lot of reasons to lie to me.

"Is it Karden or the money that you're really after?"

"Karden," Livvy and Xavier both say firmly and simultaneously. Jake nods his agreement.

Carver is slower to respond. He leans back in his chair and pinches the bridge of his nose like he's tired and then gets up and begins pacing in the shadows of the room again. A nervous habit? But he doesn't strike me as the nervous sort—more of the slow methodical type. "We all want to help Karden if he's alive, but I'm not going to deny that the money is a big consideration too. There's a small but growing movement in higher political circles that's mumbling about reunification. They want to have one united country again, but there's strong opposition from both of the fractured sides. That kind of money could give the Resistance a lot of mileage, and now there's a small contingent in power who would actually listen. It could mean an instant end to the subclass of people the division created. No more Non-pacts, and as you know, *Non-pacts* has become a catch-all phrase for anyone who doesn't meet certain standards."

Like me. I know he's playing to my sympathies, my lab-created body falling way short of meeting so-called legal standards.

Miesha's bitter words cut through me. *The human race has always found a group to marginalize—every culture, every time, every race.*

But that inequity still doesn't mean I'm going to risk what I do have without more answers. "The money has always been out there somewhere. Why the sudden urgency now?"

"Bank accounts with no activity for fifteen years are absorbed by the country where they're deposited. There's a one-year grace period to reclaim them," Livvy says. "We're in that grace period now. But more importantly, if Karden is alive, once the money is gone for good, there will be no reason for the Security Forces to keep him alive. He's living on borrowed time."

"*If* he's alive," I say. "It might be just that, you know? Only rumors."

"We're well aware of that," Carver answers.

They all stare at me, silent and waiting. The cards are laid out and it's my turn to play.

This is no ordinary Favor. With this one I could lose everything I've managed to gain in the last few months. My *freedom.* After all those years of being a prisoner, first in a hellish cube and then on Gatsbro's estate, I could end up in prison again. Big-time prison. Or worse, dead. In my old neighborhood, people could end up dead over a Benji in their wallet. With eighty billion duros at stake, plugging someone wouldn't even be an afterthought.

But we're talking about Miesha's *husband.* Leader of the Resistance. I'm still trying to get my head around that possibility. I remember the knife in my pack. His knife. It was the only thing of his that Miesha had left and she gave it to me. I remember using it to cut away the CabBot's fingers that clutched my wrist. And before that it slashed and disabled the iScroll on my palm that

Gatsbro was using to track me. His knife has saved my skin twice already. It's a long shot, but if it is him . . .

"I'm not here to join any Resistance," I tell them. "Just to return a Favor."

Carver and Livvy both nod.

I throw my pack onto the table and sit down. "Okay. How do I fit in?"

The Set

I walk around the apartment. Small but extravagant. Beautiful, even. Impressive. And that's the point. To impress. Louisburg Square means as much now as it did when I lived in Boston, but I never set foot in one of these houses back then.

"How can they afford this?"

Xavier opens the bedroom door and waves me in. "I told you. They've sunk everything they have into you and finding him. The funds are drained. I probably don't need to tell you the money didn't come easy either. A lot of skipped meals for a lot of Nonpacts who wanted to contribute."

I'm already feeling the weight of their hope on me.

"We only have the apartment until the end of next month. That's when the real owners move in."

End of next month? I don't plan on playing this role for a week. I need to get on with my life, my plans, all the things that have been put on hold for too long. I need to figure out who or what I am. I need to live the life that Jenna wants me to live. I need to *hurry* and live it. Catch up. Is that possible? Can I ever catch up to Jenna?

"It shouldn't take that long," I say.

"Says you who's never met the Secretary."

I ignore Xavier and open a closet. It's full of shirts and pants and shoes that are all equal to any of the expensive clothing that Gatsbro provided me. And it all looks like my size. They knew I would do this. I turn to Carver who has followed us into the bedroom. "Is all this really necessary? This expense?"

"We only get one shot at this. He has to believe that you are who you say you are. We have to get you in a position where he lets his guard down."

All they need is for me to get close enough to the Secretary of Security to find out where he's keeping Karden—that is, *if* he's keeping Karden. I'll be sneaking through files, reading lips, listening—any slip of information that will help us. They know Karden's not in the usual temporary detainment center in the city, but there's no record of any other facility. They've tried to find a way into the Security Headquarters to get information but it's an impassable fortress. Besides, they think the Secretary and his cohorts have their own secret stash of prisoners that would never be in the official records—prisoners they keep for their own purposes.

"I still don't see how having all this is going to get me into his house."

"You have to play the part. Xavier will explain later." Carver is distracted, shuffling through files at the table, one Vgram after another flipping up as he searches for the right one. "These files aren't indexed," he complains, shooting a glance at Xavier. "Ah. Here it is, File Twelve. Over here, Locke. I need to review this with you."

I join him at the table. "This is the layout of his house—at least the last known records of it. It's the Tudor Apartments. Don't let the name fool you. His is a double unit and takes up two floors and eleven thousand square feet. He may have made interior changes, but it's not likely, given the historical nature of the building. It's going to take you a while so start memorizing the layout. Every inch of it. You won't be able to bring this with you." He slides a disk toward me. "Here's your new ID."

"I already have a new ID."

He shakes his head. "That was just to get you here. There can't be any traces of where you just came from. We have a new history for you. Besides, we decided using your own name is best. There's no present-day record of a Locke Jenkins anywhere that we haven't recently created, and we can't afford slips. Your name is perfect. You'll answer to it without hesitation. That's what we need. You'll be believable as Locke Jenkins."

I listen as he methodically goes step by step through this new person I will become, even if he has the name Locke Jenkins. I'm the son of a Barrett Jenkins, a resource consultant currently on assignment in Bvlsavia. Livvy will play my mother as necessary. We've lived abroad for years but are returning home to complete my education and because of my mother's undisclosed health problem. He tells me I will be believable because unlike other Non-pacts, I'm physically fit and already have the advantage of an advanced education, not to mention my other special abilities, which will come into play later.

"He'll do a background check on you, and given enough time and enough digging, he'll figure out you're a fake, but before he digs too deep, you're going to find what we need. That's why we have to get you in and out as fast as we can."

We can hope.

He reaches for my pack resting on the edge of the desk. I put my hand out to stop him. I may be on his "team," but I still guard my own space.

"What's in it?"

"Just a few things. Personal things."

"We need to know."

I hesitate and then reluctantly dump it out. My dad always told me, *Save your battles for the big ones.* This isn't a big one. My few possessions tumble across the desk. Protein cakes. Water. The crumpled tissue and pit from the chocolate peach Allys gave me. The Swiss knife Miesha sent along with me. My phone tab. The green eye of Liberty. Kayla's one-eyed elephant that she had insisted I take along.

Xavier walks closer to take a look. "A stuffed elephant?"

"A farewell gift from a four-year-old."

He smirks and I think I'm going to smash his teeth in right there but then he catches sight of something else on the desk that interests him more. "Where'd you get that knife?"

"Miesha gave it to me. It used to belong to—"

"I know who it belonged to."

Carver picks up the knife and looks it over. "It's the one Karden left at my house the day before he disappeared. He came over while I was gone, and forgot it there. I gave it back to Miesha when she got out of prison." He runs his thumb over the red enameled casing. "It's a crude tool. An older model at that. I don't know why Karden was so attached to it."

"His father gave it to him," Xavier says.

"It's come in handy for me," I add, without going into details of amputated CabBot fingers.

Carver rolls his eyes. "You can keep it. Just say your dad gave it to you if someone sees it." He picks up the phone tab. "But this has to go."

I argue bitterly with him. This is a battle worth taking on. It's my only connection to Jenna and Miesha. I promised them I would stay in touch. He concedes one last phone call to them when I say they'll show up in Boston if they don't hear anything from me—but one call and that's it. He doesn't budge on the fact that it must go. "No past connections. I told you. We can't afford one slip. Besides, this will peg you as a Non-pact. Only the poor use phone tabs. We have an iScroll for you. Here, give me your hand."

I never thought I'd get another iScroll. My hand is healed where the last one was slashed away. This tattoo is a different color than the last, a swirl of blue and silver. They teach me the basics. One light swipe across the tattoo with a finger to bring up the Assistant. Two swipes and he's a three-dimensional hologram in my palm. Three swipes and he's life-sized. The Assistant can connect me with anyone of my choosing within the allowed directory. For communications, they've already disallowed anyone outside a two-hundred-kilometer radius. This is how they will contact me most of the time.

He allows me to keep the eye of Liberty. Of course, only because I tell him it's just a talisman, a bit of green sea glass I picked up in California, which it is, even if it means more to me than that. "Sea glass is pretty rare these days, but you can say you picked it up at an antique store. Go ahead, keep it." Like it's a favor.

When the grand inquisition is over, they allow me to go into the bedroom to make a last call to California before they confiscate my phone tab. I only get to talk to Miesha. Jenna is putting Kayla to bed.

"Everything okay?" Miesha asks.

"Yeah. Fine." My heart pounds knowing what I do about Karden, but I can't tell her. It would be too cruel to give her hope if it does turn out to be just a rumor. Or worse, what if he did just take off with the money and leave her to rot in prison? I can't get that possibility out of my mind. And even if he is alive, we may not be able to find him. She lost him once. I can't let her lose him twice.

"You don't sound fine. You want me to come out there?"

"*No!* I mean, no, that's what I need to tell you. This Favor requires that I lie low for a while. I won't be able to call. Maybe not for a month—"

"*What?*"

"Don't shout, Miesha!"

"I think I should come out there. I don't like the way—"

"Miesha, stop. I'm not a kid. I'm way older than you, remember?" I laugh, but it comes out forced.

I hear her grunt. She knows she's powerless right now and would do me no good here anyway. She's weak and still recovering from being hit with Gatsbro's tazegun.

"Tell Jenna," I say. Silence slips between us. Only with Miesha can it mean so much. "Is she all right?" I finally add, almost hoping the answer is no.

"Jenna's fine, Locke. Fine."

I've always hated that word.

More silence and a knock on my bedroom door.

"I have to go, Miesha."

She hates good-byes more than I do. "Remember Dot," she says. "If you get a chance, that is. And you're in a Cab. And—"

"Got it. Dot." She didn't need to remind me. I would never forget Dot. Our words dwindle away but the word *good-bye* never passes over our lips. We both need practice at that.

I walk to the door to go back out with the others but pause instead, leaning my head against the cool slick wood, looking at my feet, my hands against the door like I'm holding the world out. Maybe I am for just a few minutes. I see my mother, my father, my old bedroom, a quick flash. A letter fading on granite.

Locke. The sound of my name on their lips. *Good-bye.*

"Locke?"

"Coming," I call and step into the bathroom and turn on the water.

I splash water on my face and when I come out of the room, Carver is standing at the door ready to leave. "Xavier will wrap up a few more things with you. Stay put. We'll see you in—" He stops, spotting my coat lying on the back of a chair. He shakes his head. "Almost missed that." He snatches it up in his hand and leaves.

I don't say anything. I know. It might peg me as a Non-pact, but the coat is almost the hardest thing to give up. I remember Allys frowning the first time she saw me in it. *Some people wear them for protection, others with purpose. . . . You wear yours like you own the planet.* That's how it made me feel. It felt like armor, like I was through apologizing for being different from everyone else. Like I was claiming my rightful place in this world.

"Over here, kid."

Xavier shows me the code to lock the door if I leave. "But don't leave. Not yet. You can use your iScroll to enter the code too."

"From how far away?"

"The moon. Forget to feed the cat, you can let someone in wherever you are. But don't. Carver, Livvy, and I have the code. That's it. Not even your Assistant can save it. You have to keep it up here." He taps his finger on his temple. "If anyone else other than us tries to come through that door, you toast 'em."

Does he think I have special frying abilities? That I'm more Bot than I am human? I could argue the point with him, but I don't.

"What do you need in Manchester?" he asks.

His question catches me off guard. "Need?"

"Carver gave you his word. There are plenty of people who will do whatever you ask, just so you get this job done. We need all of your concentration *here.* So what do you need there?"

Assurance. And I'm not sure I want that task left to some Non-pacts who can barely read. A flash of guilt hits me. I remember the line of land pirates armed with rifles who showed up to drive off Gatsbro and his goons. They saved my neck. "There are labs in Manchester. I need to know what's stored there." I tell him about Gatsbro Technologies. "Kara and I sat on a storage shelf for 260 years because no one knew there were copies of us there. I need to know with certainty that there aren't more copies of us waiting for someone to come."

"And if there are?"

If there are. I haven't devised a plan beyond knowing. "If there are—"

What? What do I do then? I stare at his scar where it intersects the corner of his lip, the dip, the crease, where whole meets wreckage, staring at skin, pores, division. I feel myself slipping for the first time in weeks. *If there are.* Would that Kara be different? Would that Locke be different? Would I be a better or worse version of myself? I pull myself out of those dark endless hallways before I have gone too far, snapping my gaze from his scar to his eyes. "If there are . . . bring them to me."

"Done. Now get some rest. You do rest, don't you? We'll be back early. The pantry's stocked." He grabs his coat and heads for the door.

"Wait."

He turns to look at me, heaving his body so it's one big sigh like I'm keeping him from brain surgery.

"Yeah," I say. "I *rest.* I rest just like anyone else."

He shakes his head. The corner of his mouth pulls into a grin. "You're an easy mark, kid."

"My name's Locke."

"And my name's *Xavier.* You gotta problem with that?"

Touché. I could almost like this guy if he wasn't such a jerk.

"That it?" he asks.

"No. Carver said you'd explain how all this would get me into the Secretary's house."

"Oh, yeah. That." He smiles. "File Fifty-two." He points to the desk. "You better start crankin' up that charm. You've got a long ways to go."

He leaves without further explanation and I go straight to the desk and bring up File Fifty-two and read it. No wonder they both left before I could look at it.

The In

File 52
Raine Branson (pronounced: rayn)
Age: 17

I stare at the girl I'm supposed to abduct. When I agreed to a favor, I never agreed to this, but there's no turning back now. Of course kidnapping is Plan B. Only if the first plan fails. I guess I'll have to make sure it doesn't. I quickly flip through the holograms. One image is pretty much like the next. Her expression doesn't change. Grim. Bored. It's hard to tell what's going on in her head, but smiling isn't part of her repertoire. Every hair is smoothed into place and pulled back into a long ponytail tied at the base of her neck. Utilitarian. Jet black and severe. The Secretary's daughter.

There are ten images but nearly all are the same. Same hair, same range of expression. Zero. I go through them again, this time slower, examining her features more closely. I'm looking at the fourth image, a full frontal view, her lips slightly parted like she's about to speak, when I stop and turn my attention to my arms, a prickling sensation shooting through them. I watch one arm as the hairs on it literally rise before my eyes. This has never happened to me before. It's like the BioPerfect has suddenly found this long dormant animal response and is testing it. I'm almost fascinated by this beastly reaction but in the next second my stomach clenches and a flash of heat hits me. My heart pounds. I look back at her image. Sweat beads on my forehead. This is insane. Something isn't right.

Something isn't right about her.

I stand up and walk away from the desk, pacing the room, trying to shake off the alarms I don't understand. Is my body telling me something before my mind has put it together? The alarms subside. Was it just a random hiccup in my BioPerfect? I return to the desk and increase the image size. I look into her blank eyes, just inches from mine. Her irises are large and dark, such a deep dark brown I can barely see her pupils. But I do. They're pinpoints, tight and guarded, on alert, belying her bored expression. What's she hiding? But her face reveals nothing else. She's had practice at this. Is that what disturbed me?

I look back through the file. The information is sparse.

Mother: deceased

At least we have something in common.

Schooling: The Virtual Collective

Not a clue. I swipe my iScroll and the Assistant appears. "What's a virtual collective?"

"To activate, please give Assistant a user name."

A name? But then I remember having to give my boxing instructor a name with my last iScroll. "Percel," I say.

"Welcome to the Assistant, sir."

"Locke. My name is Locke."

"How can I be of service, Locke?"

I repeat my question for him.

"The Virtual Collective is a state-approved educational program."

"What does the program do?"

"It provides guidelines and requirements for students who are in independent study programs."

"So they don't go to an actual school?"

"An actual school, sir?"

"You know, walls, bells, lockers, detention, that sort of thing? Real people seeing one another face-to-face?"

"Anchored Educational Systems exist within walled units for students who prefer that structure. No matches for the bells, lockers, and detention portion of your inquiry."

"Thank you, Percel. That's all." He blinks and disappears back into my palm.

So, she doesn't go to school. She's isolated. Is that why she's bored? I read more of the file.

Interests: Fencing. Chess. Bonsai.

Bonsai? Seriously? Having an odd interest is one thing, but something doesn't ring true about having three. She's seventeen years old. Girls couldn't have changed that much in 260 years. Those all sound like old man hobbies.

Objective: Ingratiate yourself with Raine and her friends

They really have a way with words. And she has friends? That's a surprise. Or are they all virtual? What kind of life does she lead?

First Meeting: 09/19/21

I push away from the desk and walk to the window. So this is my in with Secretary Branson? Get in good with his daughter and her friends so I'm invited over? Carver and Xavier couldn't do better than that? And our first meeting is two weeks away? How's that going to happen if she doesn't even go to school?

I turn and look back at her image. I zoom in on her mouth, poised to speak, and I try to imagine what she's about to say. I follow the lines of her lips, the curves, looking for a clue, and my pulse begins to race again. There's something disturbingly familiar about her, but that's impossible. I'm certain I've never laid eyes on her before. Yeah, something isn't right.

Especially around her, I'll need to watch my back.

Training

The next day goes by in a regimented blur. Xavier, Carver, and Livvy arrive early. They take turns with my training. Carver tests me on my background, asking me detailed questions about my "father" and the places he's been assigned. Next, Xavier brings up Vgrams of each city where I've supposedly lived: Paris, Hamburg, Milan, Sydney, and half a dozen more. I'm apparently well-traveled. I walk virtual streets, climb stairs to apartments, memorize addresses, learn transportation routes, visit local bistros, and shop in the marketplaces. Every city is different, but by the eighth one, they all begin to look alike and we start over.

"Didn't I do anything for fun?"

"No."

After a second review of my newly created past life, Livvy takes over. She drills me on the staff who work for Secretary Branson, both at his office and at his residence. His right-hand man is a fellow named LeGru. She tells me to watch out for him. He's often seen at Branson's house. The home staff is minimal according to Livvy. Three full-time employees for one apartment hardly sound minimal to me. Dorian is the household manager and cook. Jory is the all-around maintenance person, and Hap is the personal assistant to Raine Branson. Her own full-time personal assistant? I roll my eyes at this piece of information. Even Jenna and Kara weren't that spoiled. Livvy reviews the layout of the house again, at least as they currently know it, and which rooms they suspect might be Secretary Branson's office. The apartment occupies the whole of the eighth and ninth floors. Most of the living quarters are on the ninth floor. Above that is a rooftop garden.

"Raine dabbles in bonsai and is sometimes seen up there."

They're watching her. Watching everything. I find it unsettling that this girl has become a target just by virtue of being the Secretary's daughter. As Livvy finishes up with a few last details about the guard who works the front desk of the Tudor Apartments, I hear Xavier and Carver speaking in strained hushed tones in the next room. I try to listen but Livvy speaks louder, like she's trying to mask their voices.

"Any questions, Locke?" she asks, demanding that I become engaged in our conversation.

"They're arguing," I say.

She shrugs and whisks some V-files back into their folders. "What else is new? It's nothing for you to be concerned with."

But I am. "Not a good sign for two guys on the same team."

"Their differences are smaller than their mutual goal. That's all that matters." She stands. "Come on. It's time for Mother and Son to go for a walk in the city. You need to be up to date on that too. We can't have you gawking at changes like you're an alien who's just landed."

As far as I know, no real alien life has landed, so I'll assume she means that figuratively, but I can't help but feel there's some hint of implication in her remark too. "What about your health? According to the files, you aren't well."

"According to the files, I'm also rich. I guess for now, we'll have to ignore the files because I guarantee neither one of us will be spending any money."

As we leave, Carver and Xavier are hunched over large sheets of yellowed paper, running their fingers along faint lines I can barely see from across the room. It looks like they're viewing maps or very old architectural drawings. They both shoot us dark glances while they bring their voices down to barely mumbled whispers. But I can still see their lips.

wait till he leaves

can't trust

not time

And then they both lean forward, their hands casually tucked just beneath their noses, guarding their mouths.

Livvy pushes me through the door and shuts it behind her. Who can't they trust? Me? Each other? Livvy?

She leads me down Charles Street toward the Boston Public Garden. "How did you get around town when you lived here?"

she asks.

"I walked or took the T."

"You were familiar with the T, then?"

"Sure. I had to take it to school. Pretty much everywhere. I lived off the green line. My school was on the red line, my grandparents the blue. Other family on the orange. I had a pass so I used them all. Are we taking the T where we need to go?"

"There is no T anymore. At least not usable trains. It was abandoned long ago. But the tunnels still run under the city."

"No T?" I shake my head. I can't imagine Boston without the T.

"It's been replaced by Personal Automated Transportation. You do have your new ID on you, right?"

I nod.

"Then let's take PAT for a spin."

We walk down steps at the corner of Charles and Beacon to a brightly lit cavern with a revolving platform. Like the T, the PAT is only steps beneath the city, but unlike the T, it doesn't go down several stories. It's a sleek network just below the surface, sometimes even passing through basements of buildings, not much more intrusive than a ventilation duct. The pod cars are small and streamlined, only meant to hold one to two passengers. I'm dubious when I see their size and don't see how Livvy and I will both fit into one pod. They circulate slowly on an oval track by the platform until a passenger steps in.

We approach a pod with its hatch open waiting for a passenger. "That one," Livvy says, and pushes me toward it. "Just get in and lie back. The pod does the rest." Livvy jumps in and I follow. The hatch closes and the seat molds around me, holding me securely around my head and hips. A voice asks us for our destination. "Quincy Market," Livvy says. We're spit out of the revolving track and into the PAT Network. I feel the thrill of speed, like I'm in a race car, lights flashing past me, a high-pitched hum peaking as the pod accelerates. My body is pressed back in the seat, my stomach fluttering with the velocity. It's like a ride at an amusement park, and the closest thing I've had to fun since I left California. I don't want the trip to end.

The pod voice begins a countdown. "Destination, forty seconds, thirty seconds . . ."

"Can we keep going?" I ask.

"New Destination PAT: Fenway," Livvy says.

The pod makes a series of turns and we are speeding in the opposite direction. When we are almost there, Livvy lets me try redirecting the pod. "New Destination PAT: Faneuil Hall." The pod spins and we head back in the other direction.

When we're almost there I try to make another request, but Livvy stops me. "Third strike and you're out. You can only redirect three times without exiting. They don't want kids tying up pods for joyrides." I forgot, kids aren't supposed to have fun here.

We exit and walk up the stairs to Congress Street and then over to Quincy Market, just behind Faneuil Hall. I'm excited when I first see it, feeling a familiar rush, remembering all the times Jenna, Kara, and I ate ourselves from one end to the other and then I sat in the food court with packages and my cell phone while Kara and Jenna continued to shop, but as soon as we near the front steps, I stop.

It's almost as though I've run into an invisible force field. I stare at the crowds, the carts, the kiosks, the entire world that has shifted from the one I knew. It's all slightly off, like I'm watching a slow-motion movie of a sister city, one that's trying to imitate the place where I used to live, like every person walking past is an actor on a set. Everything is a degree off, even the smell of the salty air. A chill crawls up my spine.

It's not that things have changed—I expected that—but even what I thought would be familiar is foreign now. The people walking in front of me aren't the ones who are actors. It's me. *I'm the actor.* A visitor. Worse, an alien. Is there anyplace left in this world now where I truly belong?

"Locke?"

I look at Livvy. She's turned, waiting for me to follow her. I do. I need to get this Favor over with. The sooner the better. We spend the next two hours walking through the market. She's friendly with shopkeepers, even those who are Bots, dropping our names, making sure they know I'm her "son." We walk from one end to the other, and then back down the other side again. We take the free offerings of samples, roasted squab on a stick, candied carrots, spiced curly protein strips, but we don't buy anything. I have a money card in my pocket that Miesha gave me, but it's clear that money is in short supply so I don't waste it on market trinkets or snacks.

After Quincy Market we walk back to the PAT. Livvy is quiet, occupied with other thoughts, perhaps wondering how she got stuck with the job of being my mother. She's a small, thin woman, her dark brown hair clipped short, a razor-straight line of bangs cutting across the top of her forehead. She's articulate, driven, and focused, and seems like she should be carrying a briefcase into a courtroom instead of hanging out in basements with the likes of Xavier.

"I know the answer's probably obvious, but I have to ask, are you a Non-pact?"

She stops walking and looks at me. It's apparent from her expression that she's insulted. "Obvious? There's no good way to take that question, Locke. It's obvious because I clearly look and act like a Non-pact? Or obvious that I'm not because I don't look or act like one? Just how do Non-pacts act and look to you?"

I sigh. "I was led by a Non-pact to a dark basement, where I met you, Livvy. You appear to be working for the Resistance. That's what I meant by obvious. Why are you all so knee-jerk defensive?" I shake my head and continue walking.

She keeps step with my long stride, like a frothing Jack Russell trying to sink its teeth into me. *"Knee-jerk?"* she says. "You've lived life as a citizen, Locke. Maybe it was another era, but you know what that freedom feels like. I'm a fifth-generation Non-pact. It's been 125 years since the Civil Division. My great-great-grandfather was an engineer. He built bridges and buildings that touched the sky. He had ancestors that reached back to the *Mayflower*. He chose not to become part of the Division. He didn't believe in it." She grabs at my arm. "Stop walking, dammit! I'm talking to you!"

I stop. Defensive doesn't even begin to describe what I've unleashed.

"You've been back for what, a year? Most of that time you were coddled on a luxurious estate. Wait until you taste thirty-eight years of being a Non-pact like I have. Wait until you have to tell your children that they can't play in a public park because you might all be arrested. Wait until you've known someone who has violated public space and they're sent off to the desert and you never see them again. Wait another thirty-eight years and then you can lecture me on being defensive."

I stare at her, her nostrils flared, her chest rising in heated breaths. Is she going to bite my leg?

"Why don't you tell me what you really think, Livvy?"

She looks at me, her brows pulling together like she's confused.

"It's a joke, Livvy. Trust me, you don't need to say another word. I get it. You do joke, don't you?"

She reluctantly pulls the corners of her mouth back in an embarrassed smile. "Okay, maybe I overreacted a bit." She tucks her chin to her chest.

I roll my eyes. "A bit."

"Knee-jerk. Is that a curse word from your time?"

I look sideways at her to see if she's playing with me. She isn't. "Yeah. One of the really bad ones. Sorry. Don't know what came over me."

Her reluctant smile and my stab at levity don't erase the tension between us. Words have been said that can't be taken back, and I learned a long time ago that words have longer lives than people.

We walk the rest of the way to the PAT station in silence. Thirty-eight years of being held back. Yeah, tough. But I had 260 years without a voice at all. You can't even compare the two. We're not even in the same stratosphere. Coddled? I'd trade places with her anytime. At least she still has family. I can never get mine back no matter how many laws are swept away. But what I'm mostly thinking is I'm not waiting around another thirty-eight years for the world to change. I've already done too much waiting.

When we finally return to the apartment, Carver is gone and Xavier is just leaving.

"Where are you going?" I ask.

"Home."

It seems an odd thing to say. Like he's clocking out from a typical day of work. It didn't occur to me that he even had a home, unless he calls that abandoned basement where we met home.

"Me too," Livvy chimes in. "I'm late." She grabs her coat and heads for the door.

Where do Non-pacts live in the middle of Boston? They're both in a hurry to get there. They leave, Xavier telling me the same thing as the night before. "Pantry's stocked. Don't leave."

Good night to you too.

I look around. An apartment all my own. It's something I would have bragged about in another lifetime. With everyone gone, the extravagant space that came at high cost to others is cold. It's only an in, just like me.

One more lesson: Don't be fooled by the fancy apartment, the expensive clothes, or even the promise of Favors. You're only a pawn to help them achieve their goal. Nothing more than you were for Gatsbro. First and foremost, watch your own back. Their backs come second.

Secrets

For the first time since I've been here, Boston is the Boston I want it to be. Almost the Boston I remember, and ironically enough, it's darkness that has brought me this gift.

This darkness is nothing. Barely dark at all. Only middle of the night darkness. Three A.M. darkness. Wind still on my face darkness. Sliver of moon darkness. I listen to the rustle of life. Probably rats in the bushes. Maybe a family of ducks. The sounds that darkness should hold.

I sit perched on the enormous gnarled root of a tree in the Commons. My fingers run along its knots and veins like I'm touching an old knobby knee. I've been here for two hours, almost forgetting why I came, taking it all in. The rest of the world is drugged. I watch while it sleeps. Calm. It gives me a sense of power.

I came to Boston, feeling tough, ready to take on a simple Favor. A loaf of bread for a Non-pact. Justice. Show off some of my newfound strength. Prove something. Be a man. Tough like my uncles who never let anyone walk all over them. But it's already getting complicated. It's grown from a simple ten-piece puzzle to a towering Jenga. Nothing is ever simple, or quick.

The wind picks up, blowing hair across my eyes. The bushes rustle. The nightlife is nervous with my presence. I stand, reluctant to leave, and look back at the Tudor Apartments directly across the street from me. It looks almost exactly the same as when I lived here, except that the building that it used to butt up to is gone, maybe a casualty of the Civil Division. Now a five-story office building built in Old Boston style replaces it. I came to watch the apartments, perhaps spot Secretary Branson coming or going, ready to lead me right to Karden, but not a single person has gone in or out of the building since I arrived. A few scattered windows glow dimly with golden light in the lower apartments, but the top two floors are completely black.

I turn to leave but then a flash of white on the roof catches my eye. It's gone again just as quickly. A bird? It reappears farther away. Someone is at the edge of the roof looking out over the Commons. I duck back in the shadows of the tree so I can't be seen. It's a person. A woman, or a girl, I think. Nine floors up and in the dark it's hard to see details. Raine? Maybe Dorian or Jory who work there? Someone else? I can see only the shoulders of her white nightgown and loose black hair tossing in the wind, and then she does the unexpected—she climbs up on the ledge and sits, her feet dangling over the edge, her gown whipping in the wind. Nine floors up.

Is she crazy? Is she going to jump? My mind races as I wonder what I should do. I take a step forward, but she just sits there, and then I notice she's doing something with her hands. A bright color flashes in the moonlight. *An orange.* She's peeling an orange and throwing the peels one by one to the sidewalk below. I stay in the shadows but slip closer, hiding behind a pillar at the entrance to the Commons so I can get a better look. I strain and my vision zooms closer. She pulls the hair from her face, preparing to eat the orange and I see.

It's Raine.

Not the Raine from the files, the one whose face was all but dead to the world. I see an exhilarated Raine. She's enjoying this. Her face is turned upward toward the moon. Not quite a smile on her face, but a happy defiance, like she's on top of the world and commands it. I watch as she eats the orange, breaking the sections apart, savoring each one as she bites it in half. Her bare feet swing below her. Her gown ripples in the wind.

She's beautiful. The thought comes to me whole and at once, like a surprise. *She's beautiful.*

Why didn't I see that when I looked at her file? Why did I only see a face that made the hair on my arms rise? Even now, I find that discrepancy disturbing. She's a girl with secrets. And hobbies too. Hobbies that are much more dangerous than chess. And secrets that I need to know.

Showtime

"What the—!"

I open my eyes. The knees of Xavier's rumpled pants are inches from my face.

"The code didn't work," I tell him. I spent what was left of the night in the nook at the top of the stairs leaning up against the apartment door, trying to sleep.

He opens the door and I fall backward. He steps over me, banging his way into the apartment, a string of rumbling curses trailing behind him.

I pull myself up and follow him inside.

"Morning to you too."

He turns around and angrily pokes his head with his finger. *"Here! Here!* I told you that you had to keep it up here! How hard is that? Alpha. Ampersand. Seven. Zero. One. One."

"You never said Alpha."

"There's always an Alpha at the beginning of an access code. Everyone knows that—"

He stops, noting his error.

"I'm getting coffee." I walk past him to the kitchen. I never used to like coffee, but Jenna did. Now the smell of it brewing reminds me of her and California and our mornings together. The taste is growing on me.

"What were you doing outside in the first place? You were told to stay in."

"Yeah, yeah. I know. Whatever," I answer, waving away his words. I tap on the brewer and the cup begins filling with hot coffee. Xavier follows me to the kitchen and stands there waiting for an answer. Technically I could be his grandfather ten times over, and he's pulling curfew on *me*?

"I was bored and wanted some fresh air. That's all."

"Bored?" He exhales a slow disgusted breath. "Did anyone see you?"

I remember the flash of white on the rooftop. Did she see me before I saw her? Before I ducked back into the cover of the tree? "No," I tell him. "It was the middle of the night. No one was out."

He seems relieved and then chuckles. "Stuck outside, huh? I guess I've had worse pillows than a door."

I take my coffee from the brewer. His sympathy is over-whelming. "Glad you find it amusing. Where's everyone else?"

"It's just you and me today, kid. We're going exploring—down in the T."

I learn that even though the T has been abandoned, its underground guts still exist—at least some of it near the old city center. He takes me to the red line first. The entrances were walled up long ago, but the Non-pacts have whittled their way back in, creating discreet new entrances that are nearly invisible. Virtual cities exist belowground but they're only clustered in the open areas of the underground stations. The Non-pacts don't venture down the dark tunnels that lie beyond. The ventilation is bad and there are many dead ends, blocked off by rubble, and those that aren't blocked are rumored to have half-dogs at the end of them.

"Half-dogs?"

"Wild things that resemble dogs. Lab creations gone wrong. A few got loose, bred, and now rumor is they live in the tunnels. I wouldn't worry though. I've never seen one. But then, I'm smart enough not to go down into the tunnels."

Their version of the bogeyman? We can hope so.

We visit parts of the blue and orange lines too. The underground stations are where Non-pacts shop for food, meet in the abandoned restrooms for medical care with doctors of questionable abilities and credentials, sell scavenged items like clothing for whatever they can get, and sometimes just mill around searching for conversation and company. It's a darker, drearier version of the Non-pact Bazaar I went to in California, this one reeking of sour air and the smoke of grilled meats.

I remember the days these stations were packed with people in a hurry to get somewhere. There was music, bright lights, vending machines, the whistle of trains. It was full and busy—so busy I never thought it could be any other way. There's no rush here anymore. These people have nowhere to go.

Why didn't they just choose one side or another long ago? The Democratic States of America or the American United Republic? They had the choice to be citizens once. Maybe they would have chosen if they'd known they would end up like this, but then again, I guess a lot of us would take a different path if we could see into the future.

Xavier acknowledges various acquaintances as we pass. They eye me suspiciously. I stick out like a cop in a pool hall. Xavier notices but doesn't say anything. "I don't think I'm going to bump into Raine and her friends down here. Or the Secretary. What's the point of the tour?"

"Let's go outside and talk." He motions to the Non-pact–created entrance and we climb the uneven steps, squinting at the sun as we emerge. He leads and we walk through overgrown bushes that hide the entrance from view and step out onto a path that leads to the street.

"You're familiar with the green line?" he finally asks.

"I already told Livvy. I lived close to it. The D branch in Brookline."

"Well, as near as we can figure, the green line was expanded with two more tunnels after you lived here, so it probably isn't quite how you remember it."

"Are we going there next?"

He shakes his head. "No Non-pact in his right mind would go down into the green line—stations or tunnels."

"What? Because of the bogeyman?"

He stops walking and stares at me, clearly not amused at my comment. "Bodies. At least parts of bodies. A headless torso. A leg. Sometimes the bowels." He looks away and resumes his pace. "But we think they could be ruses, placed there to keep others away. One well-placed body part has years of scaring power. Especially for Non-pacts, who are pretty much defenseless."

I would hardly describe Xavier as defenseless, but maybe for the typical Non-pacts scrabbling out a day-to-day existence in a city where they have no rights, defenseless sums it up. Especially when it comes to some unknown creature that leaves body parts scattered in their underground realm.

"Maybe there really are half-dogs."

He shrugs. "If there are, the Secretary's right-hand man isn't afraid of them. We saw him slip into a green line entry point at the public gardens and when he came out hours later he wasn't missing so much as a finger."

"Why would someone like him even go down there?"

"Because it's a helluva good place to hide something—and he has something big to hide."

He doesn't have to say what the something is. Karden and the Secretary's own secret detainment facility that's under the radar of officials.

"Can't you check it out? See what he's up to?"

"We did, but only for a short way. There's the matter of the half-dogs, plus it's dark down there. Very dark. And using any kind of light to see is not an option. A few tried that once and they barely got past the entrance. They were immediately arrested for trespassing. There must be some sort of light sensors down there. They want it to stay dark, which is a problem for us because there are hundreds of tunnels. During the Civil Division, half the city was fleeing underground and creating shelters. There are lots of unauthorized passageways that lead nowhere and aren't on any maps, and the old engineering plans that we have are incomplete at best. We don't know just what's down there, or which tunnel to follow. A person could get lost for years. But we think one of the green line tunnels leads straight to the Old Library Building and coincidentally, the Secretary seems to visit there often for no apparent business."

"You mean the Boston Public Library? Maybe he goes there to read."

"It's a food warehouse now, and he never leaves with any packages."

I weigh this bit of information. "Maybe it's another entry point to the tunnel?"

"Maybe, but we can't find it." He stops and looks cautiously behind us and then back at me. "When you first met me, I had a limp. Remember that?" he asks.

"I remember. I was wondering if it was an act."

He pulls up his pant leg. It wasn't an act.

I see a large round scar on the side of his calf where it looks like the flesh has been gouged away. "Two more like that in my thigh." He drops his pant leg. "When I first got whiff that Karden might be alive, I broke into the Old Library, no plan, just searching for a lead. It was impulsive and a miracle that I got away at all. Security shot me. The only thing that saved me was their bad aim, and me jumping into the river and nearly drowning in the process. I made the mistake of not following one of my own rules.

Some lessons you have to learn over, and over. As much as we're in a hurry, we're taking our time to get this done right."

I hear the frustration in his voice. He wants this badly. I grab his arm to stop him and he looks at me surprised. "Why are you doing this?" I ask. "You know Karden could be dead. He probably is. All this work might be for nothing."

His lips pull tight, like he's contemplating that possibility. "Could be," he finally says. "Or we might all fail miserably, but I have to try. Karden said to never stop believing that things could change. I haven't and right now this is our best shot at change."

And your best shot at eighty billion duros? But I keep that thought to myself.

We resume walking and he tells me they think they have it narrowed down to the stretch between the public gardens and the library. "A half mile at most," he says.

"A half mile of dark tunnels that go in all directions isn't exactly narrowed down."

"Out of an entire city it is. And if there's a detainment facility between the gardens and the library, it shouldn't be hard for you to find—"

"What do you mean, for *me* to find? I'm not going down into any dark—"

"Relax, pretty boy. I'm the one who's going down. You just have to charm Raine and her friends so you're invited into their little circle. The Secretary keeps close tabs on her. Where she is, he is. We just want you to find out what's down there and where. Do some discreet snooping. Keep your ears open. Pinpoint the location for us. That's all. You can handle *that* much, can't you?"

His last sentence drips with patronizing sarcasm like he's talking to a seven-year-old.

I straighten my fingers, trying to resist the urge to curl them into a fist. *A Favor.* That's what I'm giving back. For Karden. For Miesha. I have to remind myself of this fact over and over to keep from recentering his nose on his face. I work to hide my anger. I won't let him push my—

He sighs, shaking his head. "You're as soft as a baby's powdered butt."

I pounce, but he sidesteps with lightning speed, grabbing my arm and twisting it behind me, smashing me up against the wall. He wedges his body weight against me so I have no leverage, no room to move. It doesn't matter that I outweigh him, or that I'm stronger. He's got the moves and plenty of practice at them. *"Lesson two,"* he says. *"Restraint.* Never let the enemy push you to move before *you're* ready to move." He leans close and whispers in my ear, twisting my arm up just a little tighter so I wince. "And just as important—*lesson three*: you may never know precisely *who* the enemy is."

He lets go and I spin around, arching my shoulder where he wrenched it. He smiles, reminding me of my brother after the dozens of times he beat me in wrestling matches, never wanting to leave lasting marks that my parents would see, but inflicting enough pain to make sure I got his message. "We need to get back," he says. "We've had some unexpected good luck. We got you entry to a mixer at the Somerset Club tonight. Your meeting date with Raine has been bumped up. Showtime, pretty boy."

The Meeting

Livvy, Carver, and Xavier trying to dress me is far worse than
Miesha choosing clothes for me to wear. They fuss and cluck over
every detail. Buttoning my coat, unbuttoning my coat. Smoothing my hair until it looks like a bowl on my head. Changing
shirts three times because none of them can agree. It becomes a
nervous frenzy that rapidly spirals downward. This meeting has
come too soon. Xavier may have portrayed it as good luck because he's eager to get it under way, but they're not ready, or maybe
it's just that playing stylist is simply not in their repertoire.
Every grooming decision is blown out of proportion and spawns
squabbles among them. Black silk pants. No, the brown with
cuffs. No, the old-style tunic with billowing pants. Livvy takes a
comb to my hair again.

"Stop!" I stand, ducking out of her reach. "Out! All of you,
out! I'll dress myself! I don't need you!"

They stare at me like I'm a raving lunatic about to destroy
their plans.

Livvy steps forward. "We—"

"*Out!*"

We're all stuck in a silent showdown. Carver's eyes narrow
like he's weighing this new development. "Maybe he's right," he
finally says. "Let's step out for a moment and see what he comes
up with. He needs to feel real to be believable, not a complete
creation of ours."

At last. Someone who trusts me. But when I look at him to acknowledge this concession, the look in his eyes doesn't seem like trust. More like a gauntlet thrown at my feet. *Don't screw up.*

They leave and I immediately begin tearing off layers of clothes. I shove my head under the faucet to wash away whatever it was that Livvy put in my hair to make it as smooth as porcelain. I shake the drips away and run my fingers through it, leaving spiked clumps in their wake. I put on the pants I was wearing when I arrived, frayed at the hems and split at both knees. I slip on my scuffed black boots. The only thing I choose from their wardrobe is a plain, perfectly pressed white long-sleeved shirt that I roll up to my elbows.

I walk out, water still dripping from my hair. "Ready," I tell them.

"He's lost his mind," Livvy blurts out instantly.

"If he ever had one," Xavier adds and flops back in a chair like the whole mission has been aborted.

Livvy groans. "This is the Somerset Club we're talking about. They have dress codes. Especially this crowd. You're meeting Raine, for God's sake."

"Have *you* ever met her?" I ask, knowing none of them have, and no one replies.

"Have any of you ever been to the Somerset Club?"

More silence.

Carver hasn't expressed his opinion yet, examining me, starting at my shoes and stopping at my wet hair. He finally shrugs. "It might work. She'll notice him and that's what we want."

"That's if they even let him through the door."

The walk from Louisburg Square to the Somerset Club is short. Only a few blocks. It's on Beacon Street just half a block from the Secretary's home, both buildings facing the Commons. I'm sure Xavier, Livvy, and Carver are all following me in the shadows, but they don't accompany me. From here on out, I'm on my own. Except for Livvy on occasion as needed to play my mother, they won't even be coming to the apartment anymore. It's too risky. Once I meet the Secretary's daughter and her friends, I will be under the Secretary's scrutiny.

The sun is down, but twilight still illuminates the sky. I think of Jenna. It's her favorite time of day. *It's the time the world whispers,* she says. *Even the winds quiet, ready to change their course. Twilight is a gift, a brief quiet hour in the day to slow down and think, to be grateful for what the day has brought.* That's how we spent our twilights together, slowing down, enjoying the quiet and each other. I miss that time. What's she doing right now? Does she think of me at all during her twilights in California?

I turn the corner and see the bowed facade of the Somerset Club half a block away. Carver, through a series of mysterious "Favors," was able to get me a coveted spot in the Beacon Hill Virtual Collective. Apparently the state has face-to-face socialization requirements for the Virtual Collective, so members must meet for various occasions on a regular basis. Tonight's event is one of the required whole group meetings. Approximately 130 students ranging in age from sixteen to nineteen will be there. My job is to secure a spot in Raine's smaller group so I can participate in the more intimate meetings at the members' homes. Raine's home is used for most of her group's meetings, either because of its size or because the Secretary wants to watch Raine's every move. The catch is, you have to be invited into the smaller groups. Just as I left the apartment, Xavier reminded me, "Crank up the charm, kid. This is your one and only chance."

Nothing like a little pressure. I'm wondering which Raine I'll be meeting tonight—the bored, restrained one, or the risky one who sits on rooftop edges. Either way, I know I'll be meeting the Raine who has secrets. As I get closer, I see others arriving and walking up the front steps. Two of the guys wear tunics with loose, billowing trousers—reds, blues, purples, and brilliant greens—very showy and as colorful as strutting peacocks. Another guy has on a black suit resembling a skintight tuxedo. His shirt is black too. The only color is a bright red rose attached at his lapel. Do they always dress this way for these meetings or is this some special event—like prom? Livvy's words come back at me like a bad lunch. *If they even let him through the door.* I look down at my frayed pants and back at the last flash of color disappearing through the front door of the Somerset Club. Here goes.

I pull myself up another inch and walk up the steps. The door opens before I can ring, and a Bot greets me. He doesn't seem to be bothered by my clothes, only asking for my name. Apparently I've been added to his memory database and he welcomes me into the foyer. So far, so good. I haven't set off any alarms, real or imagined, which is always a cause of concern for me because of my BioPerfect. Gatsbro made it so I could pass through standard micro-scans without detection, but I always worry what kinds of other "nonstandard" scanners might be out there and how deeply they might see what's beneath my skin.

The Bot seems to know all the information Carver supplied in my application to the Collective. He's aware that this is my first visit to the Somerset Club, telling me where various rooms are that I might need, and also telling me some history on the Somerset Club itself including its many uses and renovations over the centuries. He reminds me of Dot in that respect, always part tour guide. I watch politely as he points out Venetian tapestries, carved rosewood balustrades, and elaborately framed oil paintings of old, long-dead members on nearby walls. The place smells of aged wood, polish, and plenty of money.

"The gathering is in the room at the top of the stairs to the left at the end of the hallway. If I can be of any further assistance, sir, please let me know."

"Thanks."

He makes a slight bow and steps back into an alcove to await the next arrival.

I walk up the stairs, already hearing murmurs and music and an occasional excited shout. Or were those screams? Halfway down the hallway, I stop, examining all possible exit routes—the way I came, another hallway that leads to unknown parts, and a third-floor stained-glass window—only a desperate exit option. I take a step toward the unknown hallway.

"Can I help you?"

I turn slowly, making an effort not to jump at the unexpected voice, and see a tall thin man with protruding cheekbones looking like he's more skeleton than skin. It's LeGru. I recognize him from the file photos. He's the Secretary's right-hand man who Livvy warned me about. He slithered up on me as quietly as a snake, seemingly out of nowhere. What's he doing here at a student gathering? Or maybe the club is used for other purposes as well? I mask my recognition with a confused smile. "Actually you can.

It's my first time here, and I just want to make sure I'm going to the right place—the Virtual Co—"

He cuts me off, pointing back to the end of the hallway with a long, bony finger. "Over there. You were headed in the right direction." He smiles, a pasty tight-lipped smile. "You should trust your first instincts."

I nod. "I usually do." I look at him, forcing a more genuine smile than he offered me. "Thank you." Livvy was right. This guy is trouble and I don't need to study his face to figure that out. He wears it like a badge of honor. I turn and walk to the end of the hall, feeling his gaze on my back. I resist the urge to turn around again to see if he's still watching as I walk through the doors.

The blast of noise masks my entry. I'm surprised to see that the room resembles a modern nightclub, a stark contrast to the revered antiquity of the rest. Music blares and the large dark cavern has colored accent lighting to highlight perimeter areas. Groups of students crowd the edges, either standing in tight circles or sitting together on tufted benches that bend in half circles. There's a large dance floor in the middle of the room with only four people on it doing something that doesn't appear to be dancing at all—rigid tight movements that look more like spasms than a dance. None of this is exactly what I expected for a student gathering. Steps lead to another level at one end of the room that overlooks the dance floor and has more students sitting at tables and drinking. Even though there are several groups standing at arm's length from me, none move to acknowledge my presence. If I ever felt like an outsider, it's now, but somehow I must find a way to fit in—and fast. I spot a refreshment table over against the far wall and head for it. I'm halfway across the room when a boy stumbles out of a group and into me. He falls to the floor, nearly taking me with him.

He rolls over and looks up. "Sorry, friend, I . . ." His eyes spin and he forgets what he was saying. I reach out a hand to help him up, deciding it will be wise to choose my refreshments carefully.

"No problem," I tell him. "It's dark in here and I probably got in your way." He laughs, apparently cognizant enough to find humor in the bending of facts in his favor. I pull him to his feet and turn him back in the direction he came from, but as I walk away I notice the music has stopped, the dance floor has cleared, and every face has turned my way, following me as I walk to the refreshment table. I try to pretend I don't notice. I'm not sure if they're staring because of the kid who stumbled into me or because I'm a stranger who doesn't look like the rest of them. Maybe I'm standing out too much.

Thankfully, when I reach the table the disturbance is forgotten and the music and rumble of conversations resume. I sniff a sweet white liquid that smells safe enough, but I don't take a chance and pour myself a glass of water instead. Who knows what kinds of banned substances these students have snuck in. I don't want to end up flat on the floor like the kid I just helped up. I lean against the wall, observing the crowd, and try to casually scour the room for Raine. At first I think she isn't here, but I finally look up and see her standing on the opposite end of the second level with a small group of friends—and she's looking straight down at me. It's the restrained Raine who's here tonight, her black hair pulled back in a tight ponytail, her clothing a dull gray from head to toe.

But as hard as she tries, she's not expressionless. I see the bare hint of a condescending gaze. Charm *her*? Good luck. I smile at her, giving it my best shot. She looks away.

Fine. Have it your way. But you aren't going to like Plan B.

I don't really like Plan B either. I grab a handful of nuts from the table and head for the steps to the second level. I slip through the crowd and walk straight toward her. I don't have time to waste. If I can't charm her, I'll work on her friends. I have to find a way in. I step up to their group of five. Raine, two other girls, and two boys.

"Hi. I'm Locke Jenkins. New to Boston—and all of this."

Raine doesn't respond. She just looks down at the torn knees of my pants and then away. The blond girl next to her smiles. "I heard there was a new guy in the Collective. We rarely get new blood. I'm Vina." She holds out her hand, the backside of it up, like I'm supposed to kiss it. I'm caught off guard. I missed this lesson on social graces, but since I don't know what else to do I take her hand in mine and lightly kiss it.

"A pleasure, Vina."

The group's eyes widen and I know I've missed the mark, but Vina giggles and seems pleased.

"And you are?" I say to Raine.

"Bored," she replies. She begins to look away again but I don't give her a chance to disengage.

"Not having fun?"

She's a piece of work. She blinks her eyes at glacial speed. "This is a requirement of the Collective. Do I look like I'm having fun?"

"Dance?" I grab her hand and pull. She doesn't budge, but

there's a brief moment of surprise on her face. It's a relief to see any expression there at all, but just as quickly she gives me a very firm and deadly, "No," and shakes my hand loose. From behind her shoulder I see a large Bot rapidly approaching us. He's taller than me and his skin is rigid metallic gold. Even his eyes are gold and he has no pupils at all. He looks like he's been extruded from one solid chunk of metal. He steps around her and grabs me by the throat, lifting me off the ground so we're eye to eye.

"Never lay a hand on the Secretary's daughter unless you would like your hand permanently removed. Do you comprehend?" I claw at his grip, unable to respond.

"Hap! I have it under control! Put him down!"

Hap drops me and I land on my feet coughing. I put my hands up indicating I'm backing off. "No problem, pal—she's all yours."

I turn to her friend, trying to rescue the situation. "Dance?"

Vina's shoulders rise in a happy gush. "I'd love to."

I shoot a disgusted glance at Raine as we leave and I'm happy to see what I think is irritation on her face. At least it's something.

When Vina and I reach the dance floor, I look at the upper level and see that Raine's watching us. Vina grabs my shoulders, her arms board stiff, and begins making the spastic dancing movements I had seen earlier. I'm in trouble. I don't know how to do these moves. With all the things Gatsbro taught us in our year at the Estate, modern dance was not part of our studies. I reach out and put my hands on Vina's waist and sway to the music instead, periodically glancing up to see if Raine is still watching.

She is. Just beyond her I see the gold muscle-head in the corner probably still ready to dismember me, but then something much more interesting catches my eye.

Sitting in the shadows at a table is the Secretary. He's chatting with LeGru, who must have entered another way. The Secretary finishes his drink with a quick backward movement and rises, whispering something to Hap. He's not an easy read, cautious with his lip movements, but I make out, *Leaving for the night*. He disappears through a door on the second level, followed by LeGru. I see other adults on the upper level so he wasn't the only parent here, but I suspect he's the most intimidating. As soon as he leaves the volume in the room rises and I notice more people coming out on the dance floor.

"Locke?"

I look back at Vina. "Sorry, what did you say?"

"Where'd you learn to dance this way?"

"Oh. This? I can't remember. I guess it's kind of old-fashioned."

"No, not at all," she says. "But it is strange. I like it! Show me!"

The music changes to a slower beat and I slide my hands around her back, pulling her a little closer. "Well, you just—"

"Excuse me. I need to speak with Mr. Jenkins. Do you mind, Vina?"

Raine cuts in. No one is more surprised than me. "I don't think so," I tell her. "I don't want to lose a hand."

"I've spoken to Hap." She stands there waiting like I'm a huge jackass for even mentioning it.

I look at Vina and shrug. "We'll dance more later?"

She nods and smiles but aims an annoyed roll of the eyes at Raine before she walks away.

I turn to Raine, leery of touching her first. "You sure?"

She grabs my shoulders, her arms stiff, keeping me at a distance. I don't put my hands on her waist. "So, what kind of clothes are *those?*" she asks.

"Regular ones."

"You don't think much of social codes?"

"Ones that matter."

"I see." She bites her lower lip, all orchestrated affectation, like she's really contemplating my words. "Does that include peeping at girls in the middle of the night?"

The charm is punched out of me. Busted. That's why she was staring at me. She saw me last night. Going on the offensive is my only save. "You own the park?"

"Yes, for the most part." Her fingers dig into my shoulders. "The truth's a bitter pill," she says. "Don't look so put out."

Put out? Hardly. I study her, trying to figure out what she wants. Her face is hard. Each plane a mask, hiding something beneath. She closes everyone out. I think my chances with Vina were better, but then, her father isn't the Secretary who has the information we need.

I shrug. "I couldn't sleep."

"So your mother lets you walk the streets of Boston in the middle of the night?"

"And your father lets you straddle rooftops?"

She glances over her shoulder to where the Secretary had been sitting.

"He's gone," I say.

She looks back at me. Her eyes are large worried pools of deep brown, soft and beautiful, but her pupils are the tight hard circles from the photos. Something inside of me catches. Is she frightened of her own father?

"I won't tell anyone," I whisper. Her hands relax on my shoulders and I reach out and try to pull her closer like I did with Vina so we can really dance.

She vacillates between stepping forward and pulling back, both of us acutely aware of my hands on her waist, a moment that seems to stretch on forever, and then she jerks away from me. "Never come to my park again. Capiche?"

She stands there waiting for a response to her ridiculous order with her hands on her hips and her brows raised like I'm her dense gold-headed Bot.

Capiche?

Lesson two: Restraint. Restraint, Locke. Don't blow it. Don't let her push you. But something else inside of me speaks up. I'm not a Bot or her lackey. I'm not anyone's lackey.

"I don't speak Italian," I finally answer, my tone thick with ice.

She hesitates for only a second before rage flashes across her face and she turns and walks away.

A Pig's Eye

I walk down the steps to the PAT station. I'm not ready to go back to the apartment.

Her park? Capiche?

I'm livid. At myself. At her. I want to break something. Maybe my own bonehead. I didn't let Carver push my buttons when he asked about my past. Why did I let her push them? Yes, something about her is dangerous. And incredibly annoying.

I hope Xavier doesn't try to call me tonight but I know he will. *Did you charm her? Are you in?* What will I tell him? Is there any way I can salvage this? Vina took an interest in me, but Vina won't open the doors I need. Even if she gets me into their small group, that isn't going to get me close to the Secretary.

The PAT pod opens and I step in. "Ashmont," I say.

"Not a valid destination."

How can Ashmont not be a valid destination? But I don't care where I go. Anywhere away from here is fine. "Jackson Square."

"Not a valid destination."

"You've got to be kidding me!"

"Not a valid destination."

"Copley Square!"

The hatch closes and the pod takes off. I try to focus on the speed, the lights, the thrill, but none of that feeling is with me now. I redirect three times and exit as I'm required, still feeling just as ready to blow as when I started. I've walked two blocks before I realize I'm not even sure where I've ended up.

The skin of my palm ripples. The iScroll is alerting me to a message. I don't answer. Whoever it is, Xavier, Carver, or Livvy, they'll have to wait. It ripples again a minute later. I swipe the iScroll, and yell, "Off!" The iScroll goes silent and disappears, the tattoo invisible in my palm. I imagine Percel cowering somewhere in my hand, wondering what set me off.

I look around for a street sign, trying to figure out where I am, but there are none. I sit down on the steps of a nearby stoop and lean forward, running my hands through my hair, staring at my scuffed boots. How could I let her rattle me so much? Something about her gets under my skin.

My park. Maybe that was it. Those two words exploded in my head when she said them. With all the change I've had to deal with, the Commons is the only thing that still seems the same in Boston. It's belonged to everyone here for hundreds of years, and in one dismissive sentence she bans me from it? In a—

I smile. Pig's eye. One of my dad's favorite phrases. I haven't thought of it in years. I almost forgot it. But it fits perfectly.

That's right. In a freaking pig's eye I'll stay out of her park.

The long walk to the Commons and the darkness of the park calm me. For 260 years, I hated the darkness. It terrified me. But now, for the second night in a row, I find this darkness freeing. It disguises the world I'm barely hanging on to. It blurs its edges. At least for a few hours, it makes it the world where I once belonged. No way will she ever ban me from the Commons. I plant myself on the same gnarled tree root as last night, looking up, just daring her to appear on the rooftop. I hear the rustling of the bushes. The nightlife better get used to me. I plan on coming here a lot.

"You don't follow orders well, do you?"

I leap to my feet and whirl around, my heart pounding so hard I think it's going to burst through my chest.

"Sorry. Didn't mean to startle you."

I catch my breath. "I think that's exactly what you meant to do."

Raine grins. "Maybe." She's shed her drab gray clothes and wears a simple sleeveless blue shirt and some dark blue pants that reach only to her knees. Her feet are bare.

"Going to sic your rabid Bot on me?"

"I've dismissed Hap for the evening. He knows the routine. My nights are my own."

"So it's you who's going to kick me out of your park?"

She shrugs. "I suppose you can stay. Tonight, anyway."

"Wow. Thanks."

We stand there, awkwardly. Or maybe it's just me who is awkward. She seems comfortable with the silence. She comes closer and touches the trunk of the tree where I had been sitting. There are only a few feet and the massive tree root between us. "This is one of my favorites too. It's a great tree, isn't it? I've always loved how the root's twisted and out of control." She runs her fingers over a large knot like she's familiar with it and then looks up at me. "What brought you here?" Her voice is soft and genuine, and I can't deny I'm taking in the transformation of her appearance as well. The hardness is gone there too.

I see the beautiful Raine I saw last night on the rooftop, her hair loose on her shoulders and her movements relaxed. But I remember her sweeping disdain earlier this evening and remember too that chess is one of her hobbies. Is this a calculated move? I can't forget that there was something about her picture in the file that disturbed me. LeGru's words come back to me. *Trust your first instincts.* But I'm not sure what those instincts were telling me. I rely on my own new motto instead: *Watch your back, Locke.*

I glance around me, wary of an ambush. The park is quiet, and even the bushes have stopped rustling. I look back at her. Is this sudden turnaround in her to make me let my guard down? I walk closer to her and she takes a step back. *"You,"* I say. "You're what brought me here. I don't like being told where I can or can't go, especially by people who are a little too full of themselves."

I'm waiting for her to come back at me with a snide remark, but she's silent, her chest rising in deep slow breaths. She never takes her eyes from me and she finally nods.

"I think it's time for me to go. Good night," she whispers. Without another word she walks away.

The air is squeezed out of me. She's already at the top of the steps that lead to the street but the memory of her eyes still pierces me. In her own clumsy way, I think she was trying to apologize. Have I become too much of a cynic? I want to call after her but she's already crossing the street to her apartment, and then I see the oddest thing I never expected to see. She climbs a narrow rope ladder hanging from the roof, almost hidden in the shadows. Nine stories.

What makes a girl risk her neck like that, just to go for a three A.M. walk? That's why she was barefoot. And why not just use the apartment elevator? She reaches the top and pulls the ladder up behind her and then briefly looks back toward the park before she disappears into the shadows.

I'm batting a thousand. Twice in one night. A double bonehead. I need to stop thinking so much and just listen. Maybe Xavier was right. Maybe for this Favor, they did choose the wrong person.

An Impression

"Good work. You're in." I finally turn my iScroll back on and Carver's image looms in front of me. "Livvy will be over this morning in case anyone decides to stop by."

"Wait a minute." I'm still trying to wake up, rummaging

through the pantry while my coffee brews. I pull the half-filled coffee cup from the brewer and pour in cream. "I'm in what?" I stuff half a protein cake into my mouth. "Who's stopping by?"

Xavier's image pops up too. He glares at me. "Were you out all night again?"

"No." I swallow the cake and try to pay more attention to them.

"The Collective called," Carver continues. "You have been invited into Raine's group. Good work. You made quite an impression."

Not as I remember. "Are you sure? When did they call?"

"Last night," Xavier says. "I tried to call you to let you know but you didn't answer."

His call came long before I met Raine in the park and ticked her off even more than I had earlier. It couldn't have been her who put in a good word for me. Maybe it was Vina? "Did the Collective say who recommended me?"

"You scored big. It was the Secretary himself. Apparently—"

"What? I never even met him. This doesn't sound—"

"Would you just pipe it and listen?" Xavier grumbles. I hate that he's echoing my thoughts from the night before.

"Like I was saying," Carver continues. "It seems he was there last night and saw you help a boy up off the floor who just happens to be LeGru's son. Smart move. The Collective quoted the Secretary as saying that he found you to be 'very gracious in an unpleasant situation.'"

Sheer luck and timing. But if he saw that, he must have seen me grab Raine's hand too. Is he the one who sent Hap over to choke me? Something about this doesn't feel right, but if the

Secretary is the type who keeps hidden prisoners in the city, choking his daughter's classmates might be par for the course. Or maybe he's already checked out my profile and my conveniently rich dad is what did the trick. "What now?"

"Their next meeting isn't for ten more days but then it really ramps up—you'll be on nearly every night. The meeting is at the Secretary's residence, as most of them are. We'll check in with you, but in the meantime stay put. The less you're out and about, the better. Study the files, and make sure you have them memorized."

I nod. Barely. I'm not thrilled about days filled with nothing but reading files in a quiet apartment.

Carver signs off but Xavier lingers, just looking at me.

"What?" I say. It's more of an accusation than a question.

"You'll come have dinner with me tonight."

"Carver said no more face-to-face contact."

"What Carver doesn't know won't hurt him."

Some team they are. And I'm in their hands. But I agree to go with him because I'm sick of the food in the pantry, sick of the apartment, and curious about what kind of life Xavier leads outside of a basement.

I sign off and go sit on the living room couch to finish my protein cake and coffee, but I know it's more than curiosity or being sick of the apartment that makes me want to get out. When I'm alone my mind wanders to places I never want to visit again. I think about where I am and how I got here. I think of all the people I'll never see again. My parents, my brother, my sister. I think about how building a new life is too much work and how much I still want my old one. I think about all the wasted years trapped in a cube and not a single soul on the planet knew I was there but Kara. And Kara opens another whole new dark corridor of guilt for me to get lost in. I think about her and how I made it and she didn't, and I still wish I could trade places with her. I hear her voice over and over again, *for you Locke . . . always there.* But I wasn't there for her when she needed me to be. I still miss her even though she wasn't the Kara I knew anymore. The Kara I loved was gone long ago. That's the Kara I miss. And Jenna. I miss her too. I think about her even though I know I shouldn't. She wants me to live life. Move on. Grow up. Can I ever do that fast enough for her?

The Favor at least gives me some relief, something else to think about, an area of my life where I'm making things happen instead of remembering what happened to me.

But if I'm honest with myself, I can't deny there's one more reason I want to go to Xavier's. I can't get the image of Raine out of my mind. I pictured her over and over again last night as I walked home, and then again first thing when I woke this morning. I see her climbing up the side of her apartment building, and then I hear Dot whispering, *Escapee.* Is this another odd hobby of Raine's, or does she have something she's trying to escape from too?

I shake my head and down the rest of my coffee. *Thank God for Xavier's invite.* I can't spend the whole day and night thinking about the complications of Raine's privileged life when I have plenty of my own.

A Bot Named Dot

I take a cab for part of the way there. Not because I need to. According to Xavier's directions it's only about three miles away—in just about the same deserted section where the Network hid me and Kara in the basement when we escaped from Gatsbro. I'd rather walk the whole way there after being stuck in the apartment all day, but I've been in Boston for five days now and haven't done one of the most important things I came here to do.

I didn't need Miesha's reminder. I remember Dot. She's with me every day. It's hard to forget someone who gave their— What do you call it? A life? She was a Bot. A half Bot at that. But she had hopes, dreams, she wanted to become more. I guess she didn't realize she already had.

It's risky for me to hail a CabBot. I know that. I could get an *infiltrator* as Dot called them, but her story has to be told so it can be passed on just the way she wanted, the way she *hoped* it would be. I owe her that much.

"Where to?" the CabBot asks.

"Just head toward South Boston. I'll tell you when I want off."

"Yes, sir."

I immediately see he's not chatty the way Dot was. I hope I made the right choice and he's not a CabBot in search of a bounty and legs.

"What's your name?" I ask.

"BobBot#124, sir."

"Mind if I just call you Bob?"

"That would be fine." He glances at me suspiciously in his rear viewing glass.

"Did you ever meet a CabBot named Dot Jefferson, Bob?"

His brows rise and he hesitates. "No," he finally answers. He knew her. But it could be he's afraid to admit it—or he's planning on turning me in for points, but there's no going back now.

"There's a story I heard about Dot. You might like to hear it?"

"If it pleases you. But we're quickly nearing your destination."

He's right. Traffic has thinned. Cars headed toward this part of Boston are few. "The story won't take long," I tell him and I jump right in. "Dot used to drive for Star Transportation just like you. She was DotBot#88 but said she hated that name so she named herself Dot Jefferson. The way I heard it, one day she got a customer who needed to Escape. She decided to help him even though it meant she might be released or even recycled. You ever hear of *Escape*, Bob?"

"No, sir."

"Really? That surprises me." He doesn't respond. "Well, Dot had and she risked everything to help this customer she didn't even know because she understood what it was like to have no future. She retooled her cab and drove him and his friend halfway across the country but Star Security found the cab signal anyway and disabled the vehicle."

"They got her?"

At least I know he's listening. "Almost, but the guy she was helping couldn't just leave her in the disabled cab after all she had done for him so he yanked her out and gave her some temporary wheels to get around. She continued on the journey with him and then went off in another direction to act as a decoy. She saw more of the world, more than she said she ever hoped to see—Texas, Mexico, California. When she met up with this guy again, she told him about seeing the mystic orange sunsets of Santa Fe, and the jewel blue sea of the Gulf. Jewel blue. That's just how she described it. Can you believe that?

"She told him a lot of other things too. She told him she had hopes and dreams. She said as a CabBot she had always imagined where her customers went and what they did. She imagined their secret worlds and dreamed that those worlds would one day be hers too. She told him that Escape was not about moving from one place to another but about becoming more. She said she would do anything to help an Escapee—that it was her chance to be somebody too—the most she could ever hope to be. She said she would be able to share the story of Escape with others like her, and if for some reason she didn't make it, then stories would be told about her because it might help other Escapees. That's what I'm doing now, Bob, telling stories about her just like she wanted."

"She didn't make it?"

I shake my head. "Her last act was to save this guy and her last words were, 'Mission accomplished.' She was buried beneath a tree and given a marker with the full name she chose, including her title. Officer Dot Jefferson, Liberator."

"A marker for a Bot. That's quite a story," he says.

"Yes. It is."

"Have you told this story to anyone else?"

"No. You're the first, Bob."

He stops the car and swivels in his seat to look at me. "We're at your destination."

"That's it? That's all you have to say?"

"That's all."

I reach into my pocket for my money card. I'm not sure anything I said sunk in or if the story will be passed on, but there are other CabBots. There have to be others like Dot. I'll find them.

I lean forward to wave the card over the scanner and he grabs my wrist. I freeze. The last time a CabBot grabbed my wrist, I tore off his arm. *Restraint, Locke,* but I keep thinking of Karden's knife in my pack on the seat beside me and how fast I can get to it. Our eyes are locked on each other. I'm not sure what I'm seeing. "Are you going to let go of my wrist?"

"I suppose I'd be a fool not to, wouldn't I?"

He knows. Somehow, he knows. Whichever side of the Network he works on, the news of the severed arm has traveled fast. He slowly loosens his grip and pushes my card away.

"What do I owe you?"

"No charge. I like a good story."

Xavier was clear. Don't walk in a straight shot. Double back. Watch. And make sure it's dark. No one's following me. I'm good at memorizing faces and crowds now. I looked over my shoulder all the way from California to make sure that what was left of Gatsbro's goons weren't on my trail. I spotted Xavier a mile off when he followed me to the cemetery. No one is following me tonight. It's nearly dark when I arrive at the street Xavier told me about. The neighborhood appears to be deserted. It's an area of run-down row homes and apartments that I think date back to my time. Most look like they're ready to fall down with a good wind, but I'm guessing the real estate around here is free for the taking and that's probably the right price for Non-pacts. Some of the lots contain nothing but mounds of rubble and weeds, like the earth is swallowing up the decaying neighborhood in gradual bites. I walk down the middle of the street to avoid the dark shadows on either side. This is where Xavier lives?

He said to turn right down an alley when I reached the four-story brick building. I see it ahead, like a looming black monster. This is a long way to go to share a can of beans with someone who's lousy at conversation. I stop at the end of the alley before I walk down. It looks like a dead end ahead. I hate dead ends. I might be strong but I can't jump four-story walls in a single bound. I walk, slowly and deliberately, tall like I own the planet, like thinking it will make it so. This has to be the blackest, most depressing place anyone could live.

Halfway down the alley I hear murmurs and music and when I reach the brick wall at the end of the alley, I turn left and find myself looking into a huge open area bordered on all sides by more tall brick buildings making it a private courtyard. Dozens of people occupy it. At least sixty. Scavenged chairs, sofas, and crates form a circle around a bonfire in the middle. Children run on the perimeters, laughing and playing tag. I take a few steps closer. Slabs of meat cook on an open grill in one corner, and in another three men and a woman play a violin, a guitar, a flute, and something that looks like a small harp. A little farther over, three old women laugh, trying to persuade some young children to dance with them. A younger woman stands near the fire in the middle, telling a story to a few who are sitting close by, her hands expressive, chopping the air with punctuation and passion. The sounds of all the activity bounce off the surrounding walls and blend together in a pleasant rumble.

I scan the group, looking for Xavier, and finally spot him on the far side of the fire ring. He's sitting in a low chair, patting an infant on his shoulder, and talking to a small child standing next to him. I watch his lips, *Go get your mother,* and the child races to an open doorway.

I can't move. I can hardly think. I just watch until Xavier spots me and waves me over. Heads turn. A young girl with long braids squeals and runs and grabs my hand like she knows who I am and she drags me over to Xavier.

"Locke's here!" she says over and over until we reach him. A woman approaches and takes the baby from Xavier and he stands. In an instant, he looks different to me. Stronger? Younger? More formidable? He hides things well. Especially all of this. He hesitates for a moment like he's trying to gauge my reaction and finally says, "Welcome." He turns to the small group that has gathered. "Everyone, this is Locke."

I feel a hand on my shoulder. Someone grabbing my hand to shake it. Shy faces, smiles, whispered welcomes, a cadre slipping close to take a first-hand look. They say a word, two words, then more, spilling of eagerness.

Thanks, thank you, thanks for inviting me, nice to meet you too, yes, it smells good. Hello.

I'm Em. I'm Jane. Leon. Caran. Fretta. Jacob. Erina. Lou. A dozen more names I can't remember.

I'm led to a chair and another pair of hands push on my shoulders until I'm seated. *This is the best seat, especially for someone your size.* The small crowd slips away as quickly as it came upon me, and they go back to their preparations, conversations, and music.

Xavier and I sit beside each other in chairs, both of us silent.

"You have children," I finally say.

"Two."

"I didn't expect this."

"You thought I lived in that basement? And only ate stale nuts? Non-pacts have lives too." He motions to our surroundings. "Such as it is."

"Is Livvy here somewhere?"

"She lives in a different neighborhood a few blocks south of here."

"And Carver?"

"Same as Livvy."

I watch him survey the courtyard, like he's trying to see what I see. *Such as it is.* We mumble an occasional word to each other, usually me asking a question about one person or another, but mostly I take it all in. The squalor is impossible to ignore, but there's still something compelling about it all. Some sort of energy that's impossible to extinguish. It swirls in the aroma of a meal about to be served, the frenzy of last-minute preparations, the clanking of pots and platters, the calling of this child or that to fetch something, and then unexpectedly, grace. They say grace. One by one a hand is outstretched to the next, one by one, until a circle of hands that include mine is connected. I bow my head. My chest aches. It's been so long.

Food is spread out on a long table and everyone helps themselves. It's simple but good. Roasted vegetables, hot bread, fresh greens with sliced red onions, grilled meat, smoked fish, pickled eggs, an amalgam of foods brought from different households to share. It reminds me of the potlucks my relatives used to have, only this one is bigger. No one takes more than their share. Maybe less. I'm careful with my portions.

We eat from plates in our laps and older men tell stories with full mouths and children finish their meals first and return to their play. Each of my forkfuls is watched as it enters my mouth and when I nod in approval at the taste I see a smile on the person who provided it. I acknowledge every morsel. My mother would be proud.

When meals are done and dishes cleared, the music resumes. It's not just the three old ladies dancing now. Couples, women with women, men with men, children, everyone dancing together. The woman who took the baby from Xavier at the beginning of the evening comes and grabs his hand now and drags him into the circle of dancers. I see a ring on her finger. His wife. He doesn't protest. He's a different Xavier, soft putty in her small hands.

It's not long before a thin old woman grabs my hand. I can't dance. Especially not this dance, but I go along. I don't think I really have a choice. I do my best and my missteps provide laughter for everyone—plus a couple of bruised toes. A few of the girls are closer to my age, maybe fourteen, and seem embarrassed when we occasionally end up as partners. I really make an effort not to step on their toes. Occasionally everyone steps back and claps as a few of the more accomplished dancers step forward and entertain everyone with steps that amaze me. I'm surprised to find myself laughing and hooting along with everyone else.

It's way better than sitting alone in my quiet apartment studying files, and right now nothing is required of me except to enjoy myself. It's a feeling I haven't had since some of my nights looking up at the stars with Jenna. That already seems so long ago. My thoughts jump to Raine, who seems to transform under a night sky and stars. I wonder if she's on her roof now?

A new dancer enters the center of the circle, but both Xavier and I turn our attention somewhere else at the same time. Bright lights illuminate the walls of the alley where I entered. Xavier steps forward and holds both of his hands up and the music stops and everyone's quiet. It's a signal they recognize. We hear a vehicle coming down the alley just seconds before it appears—a long white van. Xavier looks at me with some desperation, glances to the surrounding buildings and back to me again. "Too late to hide you," he whispers. "Sit in that chair, don't talk, keep your head down." I follow his instructions, moving to the closest chair around the fire ring. A few others follow suit. An older woman throws a shawl over my head and stands in front of me.

The van pulls into the courtyard and two men wearing uniforms get out. I recognize the badges on their sleeves. Security.

"We need some workers," one of them says. He's tall and broad-shouldered and looks like he could handle any kind of work by himself.

Xavier steps forward. "It's late, friend. We've already put in long days. We're about to retire for—"

"Looks like you're just getting started to us," the shorter one says. "You can't spare a few strong backs for some unloading at the docks?"

Non-pacts must be cheaper labor than Bots. No one responds.

"Maybe these Nops are so rich they don't need work anymore."

I grip the arms of my chair trying to remain seated. Last time I heard that term for a Non-pact I almost flew across a plaza at the man who said it. These two guys are clearly outnumbered and yet no one moves. The one guy is big—as big as me—but I could take him. At least I'd like to try, but the tension in the air tells me there's more at stake here than insults. His words drip with authority and threat. *Do this or you'll never get work again.* Or maybe worse.

"Wait." An elderly man steps forward. "I'll go."

The tall thug brushes past him nearly knocking him over. "We said strong, old man." He motions at the fellow who had been playing the violin. "We'll take this one." He walks around the group looking them over. They are no more than cattle to him and he's shopping for the strongest. "And this one." He looks around at some of the others like he's disgusted. Non-pacts tend to be smaller and thinner than most people.

He spots me. The shawl shadows my face and disguises my shoulders, but he can still see that I'm sizable. "And him."

Xavier rushes over and steps between us. "You don't want him. Can't follow instructions." He taps his head like I have jelly for brains. "He's simple."

Come on. Push it. I'd love to work for you.

The thug shakes his head in disgust. "Which of you aren't?" He points out two other men near him and says, "Let's go. We don't have all night."

The men load into the van and they're gone. That fast. The party is over. Of those who remain, most return to their homes in the surrounding buildings. A few return to the chairs by the dying embers of the fire, perhaps not wanting the further desolation of empty dark apartments. Xavier sits in the chair beside me. A vein that crawls across his temple is raised like hot lava is flowing through it.

"We could have crushed them," I say.

"We will," he answers. "When we have Karden."

Turning Out the Lights

I spend the rest of that night and the next three days studying the files back at the apartment. Suddenly it's not a chore. I know the entire hierarchy of Secretary Branson's staff, from LeGru all the way down to his driver, who is a Bot named Gor. I know the days of the week he visits the Old Library Building and how long he spends there. I know who delivers groceries to his apartment and how many bags they carry. I know how many times the Collective has met at the Branson apartment in the last three months and who attended. What I don't know is how the Network observed all this without detection, but I do know I've underestimated them.

Each night I turn out the lights and close the window coverings to block out all light. The first night I can only manage the complete blackness for a few seconds before I turn the light back on. The room is still there. I breathe deeply and try again. I know I'm not trapped in that small cube again, but my body still reacts. Sweat beads on my forehead. My lungs flatten like there's no air in them. I repeat Jenna's words to myself. *Change doesn't happen overnight. It's molded by people who don't give up.* I try again and again and each time I picture the Security thug shopping for Non-pacts like they were tools in a hardware store. That image fuels me to withstand what I hate.

I work up to a minute of complete darkness, then two minutes, then five, and I practice maneuvering through the apartment. I concentrate and learn I can push my BioPerfect to hone skills I've barely tapped into. My night vision improves. By the end of the second night I can see more than dim edges of objects. Seeing those objects gives me more courage. I develop depth perception and can move through the rooms without bumping into a single table or wall.

Walking home the other night from Xavier's neighborhood, I made a decision. When it comes time to go down into those tunnels searching for Karden, it won't be Xavier who's doing the searching. He has family who will miss him if he doesn't make it. I don't.

I search through the files, looking for an image of Karden. If I'm going down for him, I need to know what he looks like. Curiously, even though the whole Favor is about him, there isn't a single image of him. I make a note to ask Carver for a picture. If I ask Xavier he may catch on to what I'm planning.

I tap into my Assistant's skills too. I may be strong, but I need to be quick and anticipate moves. I learned that twice the hard way when Xavier outmaneuvered me. I practice Strategic Combat with Percel. It's hard to move in the apartment, and the sound of me falling—which I do a lot—might alert neighbors so we practice in the small fenced park across the street.

I study the layout of the Secretary's apartment so that I know every turn, hallway, and room by heart. Of course, no one has been inside so we don't know for sure which room is for what purpose or which is the Secretary's office. I suspect the southwest corner bedroom belongs to Raine. It's the closest to the rooftop garden. As detailed as all the files are about all the other players, including LeGru, the files for Raine seem incomplete. Only the basic information, which seems odd since she's the one I have to get close to. There's nothing about her friends, early life, or her dead mother, but as tight a rein as the Secretary keeps on her, maybe there's no more information available.

On the third night I pin Percel in three moves and decide I've earned some time off for a while. I know where I'm going. I've been thinking about it for days, trying to stay away, but I need to know more. More than the files are telling me.

I silently turn over a waste can in the recessed doorway and sit on it. It's a good place to wait and it's plenty dark. I don't have to wait long. It's all too easy and perfect and I almost feel guilty. The ladder is lowered and I spot her climbing down. She'll land just a few feet away but I know I'm hidden in the shadows and she can't see me. A small overhang casts me in complete darkness.

She's graceful and confident as she comes down the ladder, but it occurs to me that I shouldn't startle her until her feet are firmly on the ground. But I do want to surprise her—the same way she did me. Somehow I think she'll appreciate the effort. I can't wait to repeat her words verbatim back to her. *Sorry. Didn't mean to startle you.*

The ladder ends about four feet from the ground, so she'll have to jump the last few feet. That's when I'll make myself known.

I watch as she descends and wonder if she likes the thrill of coming down this way, or is it the only way she can leave without her gold thug Bot in tow? Is he more of a guard than a Personal Assistant? She only has a dozen more rungs to go and I hold my breath. She's as silent as a shadow, the rope only occasionally rasping against the bricks. She reaches the last rung and jumps the remaining few feet to the ground.

I continue to hold my breath, my plans suddenly gone out of me, watching her as she rubs her hands where the rope has dug in, watching her as she brushes the hair from her face and some dust from her eye. *Surprise her, Locke. Startle her before she walks away.* But I don't. I just watch and wonder. She pauses and turns her head like she senses a presence. I remain silent, using the moment to examine her, stare at her face, every angle, every line. There's something about her. She's pleasant to look at. Is that it? Am I just admiring the stark contrast to the face she wears for everyone else? Or is it something else?

"Raine," I whisper.

She stiffens, and looks into the shadows where I'm hiding. I can see the fear on her face.

"Who's there?" she asks.

The trash can grates against the pavement as I stand. "It's me. Locke." I step from the shadows so she can see me.

She doesn't move or respond.

"I'm sorry if I startled you."

She lets out a slow uneven breath. "Touché, Mr. Jenkins. Game point to you."

I step closer. "Really, I am sorry. I guess I was trying to get back at you, but then I changed my mind, and then it was too late to—"

"Shh," she says. "I believe you. Maybe." She walks over to where I'm standing. "Why are you here? You couldn't sleep again?"

"Something like that. You?"

"Nothing like that."

We stand there for only a few seconds but it seems like an eternity before one of us speaks again. She glances at the windows above us. "Can we go somewhere else before someone hears us whispering?"

"Hap?"

"Anyone."

"Let's go."

She pulls some thin slippers from her waistband and slides them onto her feet. We head down Beacon Street, at this hour mostly deserted, only a few passing cars breaking the silence.

"I looked for you the next night after our last meeting," she says. "You strike me as the type who likes to make a point. When you didn't come I thought you were over it."

"I've been busy."

"And now you're not?"

"I've been wanting to come. I knew my last words to you were a little rough. I shouldn't have said them." She doesn't reply, like she's still hurt by what I said. "I'm sorry. I don't really think you're too full of yourself," I add.

She sighs. "Of course you do, because I am." She stops walking and looks at me. "But not always. Most of the time I feel like the tiniest speck on the surface of the planet."

I wasn't expecting this confession. It stops me like cold water. *Swagger, Locke. Swagger like you own the planet.* I know that feeling, the fear you can't reveal, the show you have to put on to survive. This is genuine. Not a game play. Not a strategy. I see it in her eyes.

She looks away, lowering her lashes like she's embarrassed, and resumes walking. We reach Arlington and she points across the street. "Let's walk back through the park."

We cross the street and enter through the park gate, stopping for a moment on the bridge just inside the entrance. The water below is like glass. "How long before Hap notices you're missing?"

"Hap?" she says. "He knows I'm gone. We have an understanding. I have my secrets and he has his."

I can't imagine that gold nugget-head even understanding the concept. "He has secrets?"

"Hap has an odd weakness for talking to other Bots. Father forbids it. So a few times a week I take Hap to a public Netlog to chat with other Bots."

"Even if it's odd, it seems like a pretty harmless activity. Why does your father forbid it? That sounds a little stern."

"My father's an important man. When you're in a position of power like he is, you have spies and enemies. He's warned me about them from the time I was a child. He's told me I must be careful. He has to be careful as well. And that sometimes means being stern." She climbs onto the lower rail of the bridge and leans over, looking at her reflection below.

"Is that why you straddle rooftops in the middle of the night? Is he stern with you?"

Her foot slips and she tumbles forward. I grab her by her waist just before she goes over.

"Don't. Move." I grunt. It's an awkward position and I'm afraid I still might lose her or that we both might somersault into the water. I tighten my grip around her waist and hoist her in one quick lift. We both tumble backward and fall onto the bridge.

She sits up, rubbing her wrist. "It wouldn't have been the end of the world if I fell in. I can swim. I've fallen in before."

I lie there on my back and shake my head. "You're welcome."

She gets my point and smiles, the first real smile I've seen on her. "Thank you," she says. She stands and offers me a hand up. I take it and we continue across the bridge and through the gardens. There's a long period where we say nothing. I'm conscious of the silence and the space between us as we walk. I try to think of something to say. I came to get information, but everything seems too much like prying and I think asking her just one thing about her father is what made her lose her footing on the bridge.

I finally ask her about the Collective, a safe topic that might provide some insights, and she tells me who the members of the A are. That's what they call their small group. The A Group. According to her the A stands for Agony. She says the people in it are tolerable enough, but the very controlled socialization is a complete bore.

"But Vina's thrilled that you'll be joining our group."

I note that she doesn't say that she's thrilled.

"Well, Vina may find I'm not so thrilling once she gets to know me."

Raine looks sideways at me. "Where did you say you were from?"

I hear suspicion in her voice. "I didn't say. But for the record, I'm Boston born and bred. Only I've been away for a long time." A very long time and I wonder if it's showing.

"Are you here to stay now?"

"I don't know. I hope so. For a while at least."

She crosses her arms in front of her like she's cold. "There's something very different about you."

I slow my pace. What difference has she noticed? Something minor? Or has she sensed something else? Something deeper beneath my skin? I'm always on guard about what my BioPerfect might reveal. It's blue for God's sake, and I know there's a lot Gatsbro didn't tell me about it. What if one day I start oozing the damn stuff? I reach up and wipe away the moisture on my upper lip, checking the palm of my hand as I return it to my side.

"How so?" I ask.

"You're not like other boys."

I attempt to redirect her thinking. "I've traveled a lot. Maybe that's what makes me different. You travel much?"

"No, it's not that. It's something else. Maybe it's the way you watch the world. You're always thinking, aren't you? Thinking about big things. You're intense."

A little side effect of not having a body for 260 years. "Sorry. I don't mean to be intense."

"I didn't say it was a bad thing." She kicks a pebble in the pathway and runs ahead to kick it back to me. "Tell me about your family, Locke. Are you close with them?"

I hesitate, caught off guard at the mention of my family, surprised at the instant tightness of my throat. I stare at the pebble at my feet. *I want to tell her about my family.* With a wild passion that makes no sense, I want to tell her everything. I want to tell her how my mother had beautiful wavy hair and saved feathers that fell from the sky because she said they were gifts from loved ones in heaven. I want to tell her how my dad was the strongest man I ever knew and he wasn't afraid to cry in front of me. I want to tell her about my grandparents who took us in when my parents were trying to save money for a new house in a better neighborhood. I want to share how my uncles helped gut and fix up that house and my aunts would bring casseroles and we'd eat on tables made of plywood and sawhorses. I want to share about my real family and how much I miss them, and how I let them down and how more than anything in the world I wish I could have just one more minute with them all, so I could at least say good-bye. I want her to know who they were and how they once walked this street, this sidewalk, this park, and breathed this air. Just like us.

I look down at the pebble still at my feet.

Kick it back, Locke.

Kick it.

I kick the pebble back to her and I stick to the story the Network has created for me—the family who doesn't really exist. The lies are sour in my mouth.

We end up back at the Commons and the tree with the giant twisted root. We look at the tree, the sky, the lawn. We listen to rustling in the bushes. Finally there's nowhere else to look but at each other.

"I need to go," she finally says.

"Sure."

"Will you have a hard time sleeping tomorrow night?" she asks.

"I think I might."

She nods and leaves but when she's only a few yards away she turns and says, "You answered my question. It's only fair that I answer yours. Yes. Sometimes my father is stern with me too."

A Sudden Dip

I sleep through early afternoon. My habit of "sleeplessness" is catching up with me. For the last four nights I've met Raine in the park.

Each night our visits grow longer, mostly walking through the Commons and public gardens, and each night I get a piece of information from her, probably small and useless, maybe not. I don't push. These are small slips in passing. She offers these freely. The A Group has been together for three years. No new additions in that time. She's surprised I was invited to join. I don't tell her that I'm surprised as well. When I mentioned meeting LeGru at the Somerset Club, she told me she hates her father's assistant. She thinks he has soulless eyes. When he comes to their apartment, which is often, she stays in her room or goes to the roof to feed the pigeons.

I noted her spontaneous smile when she told me about feeding the birds even though it's against the rules of the apartment association. It seems the rooftop is her domain and she does as she pleases there. A fat white pigeon that she's named Rufus is her favorite. There's still tension between us, distance that she's clearly maintaining—and yet she still comes. And every night as we part she asks again if I might have a hard time sleeping the next night. And every night my answer is the same. Yes.

I throw on some clothes and grab my pack. I've stayed put in the apartment during the daytime for as long as I can. I need to get out and I head for Quincy Market, walking at a brisk pace like something inside of me is stuck in high gear. I wonder how Raine fills her days? Will I ever see her in the light of day?

I walk through the shops taking samples that are offered, mindful of not using my money card. It's Miesha's money and I'd like to give it back to her if I can. Free samples are scarce today so I finally splurge and buy a sandwich, an old-fashioned Italian sub. It tastes almost like the ones my mom used to bring home from the deli at her market, loaded with peperoncini.

With the first bite, a wave of homesickness hits me, even though technically, I am home, and in practically the same moment, I think about the disposable phone tabs I saw at the checkout. Three on a card, each good for twenty minutes. Carver may have said no phone contact, but what harm would a disposable phone tab do? No one would know and I would throw it away right after I used it. I eat my sandwich, thinking about Jenna, Miesha, Allys, and Kayla, the closest people I have to family now, and after my last bite, I walk back to the counter and buy the phone tabs. I walk outside looking for a private place to talk and spot a dark, quiet service entrance for a gelato shop.

"Hello? Jenna?"

"Locke?" In one word, I can tell she's surprised to hear from me. "Miesha said you wouldn't be able to contact us."

Hearing her voice makes the knot in my throat twist tighter. "Yeah, so I need to keep this short, but I had to call."

"Are you all right?"

I lean against the brick wall staring down at my boots. It's only been a short time since I saw her, since she kissed my cheek at the train station, but it already seems like a lifetime ago. "I'm fine."

"Locke, what is it? Something isn't right. I can hear it in—"

"No. I promise you everything's okay."

"But?" She won't let it go. I should have known I couldn't hide anything from Jenna.

"But the Favor turned out to be a little more complicated than I expected. It's going to take a lot longer than I thought."

"Things that matter usually do."

"I know, I know, you told me, change doesn't happen overnight," I parrot back to her, "but . . . there's more to it than that."

She's silent waiting for me to continue. There's no video on these cheap phone tabs, but I can imagine her biting her lip, holding her breath.

"You have to promise you won't tell Miesha."

"You know I won't."

I tell her the rumors about Karden, the Secretary who is possibly holding him, the eighty billion duros, and the Secretary's daughter who is my in to get me closer to him and his hidden information—if there really is any to be had.

"The Network doesn't jump on things like this without reason," she answers. "Karden was a good man, one of the bravest, most determined people I ever knew. If after all this time, he's alive—"

"But he might not be. That's why you can't whisper a word of this to Miesha."

"Of course. What about Miesha's baby? Do they know what happened to her?"

The baby? We never talked about her and I never asked. "There was no mention of a baby. I assume she died in the fire."

Jenna sighs. I know she's become very fond of Miesha. And having her own daughter—and almost losing her—probably makes her understand Miesha's pain in ways that I can never begin to. A flash of shame hits me that I never even asked about something that would be so important to Miesha. It's times like this that I hate the divide that time has created between us. Jenna's a mother. A woman. Our last conversations echo in my head. *I may look like the Jenna you knew so long ago, but I'm lifetimes from that girl. . . . Tell me, Locke! What are you? A boy? A man? Something else? . . . You need to find out.*

My fingers curl into my palm. A fist. I want to erase the years and events with one quick blow.

Jenna gives me quick updates on Miesha's progress—still walking with a cane but much more stable. The daily exercises to strengthen her damaged muscles are helping. The herb garden I built is flourishing, and Kayla misses me. And finally she asks if there's something she can do to help.

"Not without getting me into deep trouble with Carver. I wasn't supposed to call you. He's afraid the Secretary might track my calls once I'm on his radar."

"How could he do that? It's quite illegal and he's—"

"Keeping secret prisoners is illegal. If he's doing one, the other isn't much of a reach. That's why I'm talking to you on a disposable."

We hear the one-minute warning beep on the phone tab and our words become hurried overlapping last reminders.

Say hi to Miesha and Allys. Bone too.

Try to call me again.

And Kayla, give her a hug for me.

As soon as you can.

I miss you, Jenna.

We know you're where you need to be.

And tell Allys the chocolate peach was gone in the first five minutes.

Be careful, Locke.

Always.

And one more thing, this girl Raine. Be careful about collateral damage, even for a noble cause. She's only a girl.

I wi—

The phone goes dead. Our time has run out. Like it always seems to.

I close my eyes, crumpling the phone tab in my fist.

"Hey. You gotta move. We bring supplies in this way."

A kid looking around a stack of boxes in his arms waits for me to move. I leave, squeezing past him, and throw the tab into a trash can I pass out on the market mall.

Collateral damage. What does Jenna think I'm doing? And talk about collateral damage? What does she think I was for 260 years? Kara and I were the price of progress. And I'm still paying that price.

I would never hurt Raine, not the way I've been hurt, but nothing is going to stop me from getting this Favor done, one way or another. I'm not going to carry illegal ID forever and this is one step to get me where I want to be.

I pass a basket of the government issue charity coats near a recycle chute. The small cylinders that contain each coat look dusty and old, which isn't surprising. Most citizens won't touch them and a Non-pact could never pick one up here because it's restricted public space. I remember the first time I put one on and saw my reflection in the train station window. I saw someone I didn't recognize. Someone I needed to be. Someone dark and dangerous.

I reach down and grab one of the coat cylinders from the basket and throw it into my pack. I know I can't wear it, but I want it just the same, maybe as a talisman like the green glass of Liberty, a reminder of why I'm here in the first place.

Carver calls twice about nothing in particular, just checking on me. It's clear he's on edge when he sees I'm not at the apartment, but he doesn't lose his cool. He never seems to. Everything about him seems neatly tucked and squared away. Still, I see the hunger in his face again. The eagerness. That he can't hide. I guess the things you want the most aren't so easy to disguise. I need to remember that.

I ask him about Karden and the lack of images in the file.

"We don't have any," he says, and cuts off suddenly. I don't know if the cutting out was deliberate or if modern communications still suffer from dropped calls. He seemed agitated so I will assume the former. It's hard to believe there are no images of Karden, considering his notoriety and role in the Resistance. On the other hand, he did keep an extremely low profile in order to avoid detection. He would have avoided recorded images at all cost. I can always get a physical description from someone, maybe from Jenna. I don't want Xavier to know that I plan to take over his role in getting Karden.

In the afternoon I take what appears to be a slow leisurely walk along where I think the green line used to run. A lot of the buildings have changed and that skews my point of reference, but I remember walking the streets and knowing where the tunnels ran beneath the city. I walk the distance between the Old Library

Building and the public gardens looking for anything that hints of a detainment complex under the streets but see nothing suspicious so I go to the public gardens where Xavier said there was a hidden entry point to the tunnels. It's not that hidden, only a few overgrown bushes cover a makeshift stairway made of rocks and rubble, but I guess with sightings of body parts, no one would venture down there even if there were flashing neon signs pointing to the entrance.

I take a few steps down. In the light of day, I can see the pathway ahead easily. I assume the body parts were a ruse but I'm not foolish either and I listen for any kind of sound. It's quiet, not even the rush of a fleeing rat. I proceed down a few more steps until I can see into the cavern. It's dark but there's still enough daytime light filtering down the stairway for me to see that it's the old Arlington station. A few of the turnstiles are still there and some of the white tiles that used to cover the walls are there too, but most of it's a grim decaying mess smelling of waste and neglect. I can't imagine the very fastidious LeGru walking five steps into this rathole, much less all the way down one of the tunnels.

My eyes adjust to the dim light, and I take a few more steps in until I'm on the edge of where the real blackness begins, the original green line tunnel, and miles of other tunnels that could go anywhere.

I hear movement, a faint skitter, something small, maybe a mouse or a rat. I take another step and a loud screech blasts the air around me seeming to come from all directions, bouncing off walls so it sounds like a hundred screeches. I bolt for the entrance and scramble up the steps as fast as I can, stones tumbling down behind me. In seconds I'm back in the gardens and I breathe deeply, telling myself I was just spooked with all of Xavier's talk of body parts and half-dogs. It was probably just an owl. Lots of normal creatures could live down there. They probably do. Their noises may be what started the rumors of half-dogs in the first place. Still, next time before I go down, I think I'll have Karden's knife out of my pack and ready in my hand—with the largest blade extended.

When I'm almost back to the apartment, Xavier calls. He wants to make sure I'm staying in tonight. I tell him I plan to do some reviewing. "There's always more to learn."

"Good idea," he says.

Last but not least, Livvy checks in with me. She offers to come over and cook something hot for dinner. "Thanks, Livvy, but no. I think I'm going to turn in early tonight. I didn't sleep well last night. I'll fix myself something simple."

She tells me to rest up.

"I will."

"Locke," she adds, and then hesitates. "Be careful."

The moon is barely a sliver, peeking from behind clouds that drift past so slowly they look like they're painted across the sky. There is no startling tonight. Everything is slow. I'm in plain sight sitting on the tree root. She's in plain sight as she approaches.

Locke, be careful. Livvy knew I was leaving. Did she see it on my face? The lie? Or maybe it was in my voice? What was I not able to disguise?

Raine's not in a hurry as she walks toward me. She must be confident that no one is watching her from above, or maybe she just doesn't care.

No. She cares.

I've seen it in her eyes over and over again, quick furtive glances, but she knows her moves well—when it's safe to sit on a rooftop, or climb down a rope, or talk to me. Maybe that's where her study of chess comes in handy. I think about what she said that first night, about feeling like the smallest speck on the face of the planet. Was it a slip? Or did she just feel safe with me? I guess that's my job. To make her feel safe. To get information. I don't like this part of the Favor.

She stops a few feet away from me. "Couldn't sleep again?" she asks.

I look at her, taking in every aspect, her voice, her hair, the way her hands hang loose and relaxed at her sides, the color of her skin under a sliver of moonlight. I've been studying her files day after day. So much is missing, so much the files don't tell. The disturbed feeling I had when I first saw her has grown into something else. An intense curiosity. She's more than just the Secretary's daughter. More than my in, but what the *more* is, I'm not sure. "No. Still can't sleep."

She steps closer, her knees nearly touching mine, and she stares at me. I try to adjust my position on the tree root to escape her close scrutiny, but she doesn't waver.

I swallow. "Something on your mind?"

"Volumes. There's always a lot on my mind, but right now it's you and wondering why you really come. I don't know if I can trust you."

"Only a week ago I saved your life, remember? Doesn't that give me some sort of Level Ten trust status?"

She smiles. "You saved me from falling off a low bridge and getting wet. That's all. Level Two status only."

I watch the smile fade from her lips, but not entirely from her eyes. There's definitely still a glimmer and it empowers me to know I put it there. "Only Level Two." I sigh. "Looks like I have a long way to go."

"Let's walk."

We walk toward the far end of the Commons near the burial grounds. She says she likes the fact that she can talk to everyone there and they don't talk back, they just listen.

"Are you sure they're listening?"

"I like to think so."

"I'll listen. Why don't you tell me what you tell them?"

"Those are very private things," she says. She looks at me sideways. "I think you're probably the type that's good at keeping secrets—but not as good as dead people."

"You'd be surprised. I haven't told anyone about your rooftop walks or our nightly visits."

"Not even your mother?"

"Especially not her. That should elevate me to Level Three trust status."

"Two and a half."

"That's something. I'll take what I can get."

I ask her about the Collective meeting in two days. She tells me two of the members won't be there because they're traveling out of the country. "Only six of us. Besides you and me, Vina, Shane LeGru, Cece Carrington, and Ian Dvorak will be there."

"It's at your house this time, right?" I already know this but I don't want to let on that I have every detail of her life memorized—at least the details the Network has been able to gather.

"Nearly all the meetings are at my house. That's the way Father prefers it."

"And the others don't mind?"

"If they do, they keep it to themselves."

"Because he's important?"

She reaches out and plucks an elm leaf from an overhead branch as we pass and twirls the stem in her fingers. "That's right."

"So tell me about him. What makes him so important?"

"I'm surprised you don't know already. Everyone else seems to. My father's Secretary of Security for the DSA, fourth in line to the president. It's his job to keep us all safe."

All? Hardly. I don't think she has a clue about his dirty dealings or secret detainment centers. "Really? That does sound like an important job."

She looks at me sharply. "Are you mocking him?"

I thought I said it sincerely, but maybe some of my cynicism seeped out. I note, however, that she's defensive of him, loyal even. I make a mental note that it's a subject to broach very carefully with her. "I don't even know him. How could I mock him? I told you about my parents last night. Tell me about yours."

She tosses the leaf in her fingers aside. "It's only me and my father. My mother died when I was twelve. She was . . ." She shakes her head and I see the hardening of her face, like she's blocking out the memory.

"Sorry. I didn't mean to—"

"I was adopted. My mother and I were very close. She was the best mother anyone could hope for."

"You were adopted?"

"Yes. I didn't find out about it until I was eight years old. I started asking questions, wondering why I didn't look like either of my parents. My mother overruled my father's dictum and told me. She had always wanted to be honest with me and never understood why he wanted to keep it a secret. My father was furious with her."

"Do you get along with him?"

"He's my father—and I'm his daughter. We deal with it. What else is there to say?" And then in a softer voice, "It's been hard for him since my mother died. He was very close to her too, and he depended on her for a lot of things. I don't think he quite knows what to do with me now." She shakes her head and her eyes narrow as she looks into the distance. "Actually, he probably never did know what to do with me. I don't think fatherhood was a role he was comfortable with. Now that he has to play both mother and father, he tends to go a bit overboard."

I know I'm walking on shaky ground but I ask anyway. "Overboard?"

She's careful with her reply. "Because of his position, he has certain . . . expectations for how his daughter should conduct herself in public—and private too for that matter. But I suppose I'm better off than most."

Than most what? Non-pacts? But I don't say it. I hear the strain in her voice. This sharing is pushing her limits.

I change the subject with more than enough new information to chew on. Like how the Network didn't know she was adopted. "How did you ever find a rope ladder long enough to reach down nine stories?"

"Hap made it. From twine no less. He's quite resourceful." I remember his grip around my neck. Resourceful isn't quite how I would describe him. Shrewd maybe. Is this part of the way he pays for Raine's silence about his Netlog activity?

We enter the cemetery. She seems to know where she's going. She heads for the center, gracefully hopping over graves and markers and tiptoeing between others. She should be a dancer, not scaling walls at two in the morning. My dislike for the Secretary grows. She stops at a large memorial and presses her palms against it, her fingers sliding into the recessed letters. She stands there stone still for the longest time. "Tell me, Locke, what did you think of the gathering at the Somerset Club?" she finally says.

I'm surprised she would bring it up, considering it didn't go well between us, but I try to put a positive spin on it. "I didn't think it was as boring as you did."

She turns to face me. "It wasn't completely dull. I was especially curious about that dance you did with Vina."

"I would have shown you but . . . someone cut me off."

She raises her eyebrows. "Which I regret."

Is she asking me to dance with her now? "It's really pretty simple. I can show you."

"I suppose that would be all right."

It seems wrong to dance on someone's grave, so I suggest we step over to a small clearing between graves. She stands in front of me waiting for instructions. "First of all, you keep your arms loose and relaxed, not stiff and straight. And you place them, well, really anywhere that feels comfortable. There aren't rules."

"It's odd for a dance not to have rules."

"Maybe, but that's what keeps it interesting."

I reach out, wishing that maybe there were rules so placing my hands would be less awkward. I place one hand on each side of her waist. "Now you put your hands where they feel comfortable."

She lifts her hands, holding them up in the air, uncertain where to put them. Finally she brings them down so they're resting on each of my arms. "There. That feels comfortable. Is this right?"

"There's no right or wrong."

"Now what?"

"Relax. Pretend there's music. Soft music. And sway to it. Like this."

She steps on my foot and grimaces. She may be graceful most of the time, but not when there isn't a game plan to follow. "Our feet are so close," she complains. "How can you dance so close to another person with no rules?"

"You're trying too hard." I slide my hands around her back and pull her closer. Her hands are forced to slide farther up my arms, until they're resting on my shoulders. "Now, don't lift your feet so high. Just let them glide along the ground. Like mine."

She looks to the side trying to see our feet like she's memorizing each step. "Relax," I repeat. "Just go with it."

We fall into step and I feel her arms grow softer, the angles disappearing, molding to me like she's finally getting the hang of moving without a plan. Not her specialty, but she's a quick learner.

She looks up at me. "I'm not sure what to think of a dance without rules."

I look at her, caught off guard at how close her face is. I can't study it, can't examine planes and lines and what expressions she may be hiding. I can't see anything but her chin, her nose, her mouth, her eyes. I can't see anything but Raine. I swallow. I quickly swing her away from me and throw her back in a dip. "And you have to watch out." I bring her back to her feet. "Because you never know what might happen in a dance without rules."

She laughs. "Like you said, that's what keeps it interesting." I let go of her and step back, bumping into a gravestone. "Thanks for the lesson," she says. "I guess Vina has nothing up on me now. She can be rather annoying that way."

"Right."

We talk for another minute or so, but none of her words really sink in until she says good-bye and leaves.

Good-bye. Was it only a petty competition with Vina that made her want to dance? She's right. Vina has nothing up on her. I watch her walk away and decide that this will be my last time visiting her in the middle of the night. I've probably learned enough. And I think I'm "in" as far as I should be.

Slipping

She doesn't show and she doesn't show, and just when I think she's not coming at all, I see a glimmer of white at the rooftop edge. She's wearing a nightgown, which means she doesn't plan on coming down, but then she lowers the rope ladder anyway and begins her descent, her nightgown flapping in the breeze against her bare legs.

It's both a frightening and strangely beautiful thing to watch, an eerie marriage of freedom, desperation, and insane risk. I hate that she's coming down, and yet that's what I was waiting for. Why am I here? I spent all day telling myself I wasn't going to come tonight, but then I did. Maybe I really am developing a sleeping problem.

I maintain my position on the tree root until she's walking across the lawn, and then I stand, wondering if it was her father who prevented her from coming earlier.

"I can't stay long," she says.

"You didn't have to come because of me. I already told you I just like hanging out in the Commons at night."

She looks at me, her chest rising in a long, slow breath. "Really? Is that all it is?"

The Commons is big. There's a million places I could perch myself besides right across the street from her building. She's not stupid. But I can't really answer why I'm here. Only more information? It's not just that.

"It's not safe to climb down the side of a building in a night-gown," I tell her.

"It's not safe to climb down at all. That won't keep me from doing it if it pleases me." She walks past me and sits on the root, her legs jutting out in front of her like she's ready to trip me.

I watch the hard Raine return. The closed one who pushes people away. But it affects me differently now than it did the first time I saw her. She's afraid. She covers her soft underside with prickly armor.

I make a deliberate show of stepping around her outstretched legs and I sit down beside her. "So tell me what pleases you, Raine.

When I'm not here how do you spend your nights? Where do you go? What do you do?"

She slides her feet up on the root, hugs her shins, and looks at me. Her eyes grow warmer, like the question has unleashed a part of her that she lives for. Her pupils widen in the deep brown pools and I watch the play behind them, almost like a feral animal . . . like a fox who enjoys the cleverness of her game, and I realize she's probably the most complex, contradictory person I've ever met. Her eyes narrow. "If my father's anything, he's a man of order and routine. That's both his strength and his weakness. I know I have four and a half hours of guaranteed freedom each night. He doesn't sleep much but when he does, he sleeps as deeply as a corpse. The only time I've ever had a close call was once when he became ill and woke during the night. Hap covered for me."

At least I know with certainty where Hap's loyalties lie.

She stares unfocused into the shadows of the trees surrounding us, a glimmer in her eyes. "I use that time to breathe. To do the things he would never allow. The first time I went out, I was looking for my mother."

"I thought your mother was dead."

"She is. This was after she died. I was looking for my birth mother. Not because I wanted to talk to her or know her. I just wanted to see the kind of woman who would abandon a baby. She threw me in a trash bin."

I wince, unable to fathom Raine being thrown away like trash.

"Maybe that's why Father didn't want me to know my origins in the first place. He's the one who found me crying in a heap of garbage. He fished me out and took me home as a temporary measure, but as soon as my mother laid eyes on me, she wouldn't let me go. Of course they made it all legal, but I wasn't exactly a planned acquisition."

"Did you find your birth mother?"

"I may have seen her. I don't know. I went to the parts of town Father would never let me enter—the places where Non-pacts live—and I looked at women there, wondering if one of them was the woman who threw me away, wondering what kind of animal she was. Wondering why she did it. Not many Non-pacts are out in the middle of the night, but a few times in the late hours I found gatherings hidden away in other parts of the city, and I watched them from dark alcoves, looking for a woman who looked like me."

"How do you know your birth mother was a Non-pact?"

She shrugs. "The location where I was found. The clothes they found me in. Besides, Father said they're the only ones who would throw a baby away. He reminds me every day of the life he saved me from. He had me scanned regularly for years, looking for any lasting damage. He still has me scanned occasionally."

I can't imagine anyone throwing her away, especially not a Non-pact. I saw how the children were well cared for at Xavier's dinner, and the way he tenderly looked after his own children. I know that sort of thing happens—I've heard news reports like that before—but no one in his neighborhood would do such a thing. Why would Raine's father tell her this, even if it's true? It seems too cruel. Maybe some lies are for the best.

"I'm sorry, Raine."

She shakes her head. "Nothing to be sorry for. Ancient history. A mere curiosity," she says, like she doesn't care. "After those excursions, I went to other places Father wouldn't allow, like the cathedral on Washington Street."

"Holy Cross?"

"You've been there?"

Every Sunday at 11:30 A.M. At least until I was twelve. I was an altar boy when I was just ten years old. I can still see my parents and grandparents beaming as I walked in the processional with my hands folded in front of me in prayer. When I was getting ready in front of my sister, I pretended I hated the cassock and crisp white tunic I had to wear, but I remember secretly thinking that maybe God would see me wearing those fancy holy clothes and mistake me for a priest. That, I was sure, would give me a direct line to God, because my regular connection to him seemed pretty shaky. Even though my house, my neighborhood, and my family are gone now, it's comforting to know the church we went to has survived the ages. Still, I answer cautiously, not knowing what kind of shape it's in now or if it's even used as a church anymore— especially since the library is now a food warehouse.

"I only drove by. I don't remember much about it."

"That's a shame. It's beautiful. Spires of open emptiness, jeweled shadows, musical echos, and best of all, I listen to whispers from the stained-glass saints surrounding me. I always sit in the center pews all alone and pretend . . . *I pretend I'm somewhere in heaven.*"

I hear the desperate hush of her last few words, as if she's embarrassed. I swallow at the sudden stab in my throat. I should leave, but I can't. *Somewhere in heaven.* She has to run away in the middle of the night to get a small piece of heaven? To a lonely dark church? She's telling me more than I have a right to know. I don't need this kind of information. Or maybe I'm just afraid I might start sharing information with her about myself, the *real* me. It feels like it would be so easy to do, so natural to share with her, but I banish any thoughts of truth. I have to keep up the charade of who I am. The Favor is more important than anything I might be feeling at the moment.

I look up and see her studying my face like she was watching the battle going on inside of me, like she saw me hiding away the truth.

There's a loud rustle in the bushes and she stands. "I need to go," she says.

"It's only squirrels, or rats."

"It's not that. I just need to go."

"All right." I stand too. "See you tomorrow night at the meeting."

"Right. You know where it is. My place." Her voice is flat, all the warmth of just a few minutes ago, gone, like she's already bracing herself for tomorrow night when she'll have to resume being the cool, guarded Raine. "Good night," she adds, and begins to turn away.

"Raine—"

"Just leave it, Locke!" she snaps. "I have to go!"

"Hey." I put my hands up like I'm backing off. "Did I suddenly drop a notch on the trust meter?"

Instead of taking it as a remark to lighten the mood, I see her face darken even more. A furrow deepens between her brows and she bites her lip. She turns her back to me so I can't see her. The air is punched out of me and I race back through my words wondering what I said that sent her into a tailspin. Or was it the look on my face as she studied it? Does she know I'm hiding something? Or maybe she went one step too far in opening up with me—a slippery place for someone who always walks a very private tightrope.

I take a step closer to her, staring at her back. "I didn't mean to—"

She vigorously shakes her head, her hair rippling across her back. "You scare me, Locke! From the moment I first saw you, you scared me."

I'm unable to speak. *I frighten her.* That was the last thing I expected or wanted. I reach out and lightly touch her shoulder. "Raine . . ."

She turns to face me and her words run out in a breathless avalanche. "I've never done this before. *Ever.* I want you to know. I've never shared my nights with *anyone*, or told them about the cathedral, or my mother, or being found in the garbage. I'm not any good at this. Worse than not good. I'm a failure at people. But that first night, I saw you long before you saw me and you fascinated me. You looked like you were in the park waiting for someone, someone who never came, you looked so alone and lonely, and for a moment, I thought maybe I should be that someone who comes so you wouldn't feel all alone. And I thought about that all the next day. I couldn't get it out of my mind, and that scared me even more. And now everything that I was afraid would happen is happening. And that's why I told you that first night never to come here again." She shrugs a slightly hysterical shrug, her eyes glistening, and she adds, "I don't know Italian either. Only 'capiche.'"

And then, before I know what I'm doing, my head is lowering to hers, my lips to hers, my breaths becoming hers, and I forget about everything but the taste of her mouth, the scent of her hair, and the knots of her spine as my hands pull her closer.

The Rules of the Game

I'm in trouble. Big trouble. I'm exhausted. Not at the top of my game by a long shot. And worried.

It didn't stop with one kiss. Or two.

And then when I got home, I relived every moment. Her hands sliding along my back. Her tongue tracing my lips. Her hair brushing across my face when we fell to the ground. Her leaning over me, staring, and then lowering her face to mine again. Everything about her was sweet, and perfect, and dangerous. But I couldn't stop and neither could she. Our mutual trust status made an instant leap to ten.

And I said things. Things I never should have said. *You fascinate me too. I couldn't get you out of my thoughts. That's why I came. You're beautiful, Raine.* I don't know where it all came from. The words rushed out. For a few minutes every bit of restraint I had vanished. She made it vanish. And right now, the one thing I need more than ever is restraint.

I can't lose sight of the goal. I'm going to find Karden, no matter what—dead or alive—for Miesha and for everyone else too. Five years from now, if Security shows up in Xavier's neighborhood, they'll be begging on their knees for help, not demanding it, and I won't be hiding in the shadows with a shawl thrown over my head.

Xavier is on his way over, ignoring Carver's rule of no contact. He found out I was out again last night. He's not happy. When he arrives, he rings the bell and is wearing a delivery uniform, a cap pulled down over his eyes. He walks in with two bags of groceries.

"Nice disguise," I say, trying to lighten his mood. I even add the little lighthearted smirk that always defused Gatsbro's concerns. It doesn't work with Xavier. He slams the door and dumps the grocery bags on the living room floor.

"What were you doing in the Commons last night? Someone on the way home from the docks saw you across the street from Raine's apartment. We have a *plan* in case you forgot! Who do—"

"The plan was for me to get in with Raine and her friends, in case *you* forgot," I snap back at him, and then in a lower voice, I add, "I've gotten to know her."

"You what?"

"She likes to go out at night."

He stares at me, his jaw tight, his scar white against his reddening face. "How many nights has this happened?"

I pick the bags up from the floor. "Almost every night, if it's any of your business." A stupid thing to say. Of course it's his business. Everything to do with the Favor is his business.

He looks at me for the longest time. His jaw goes lax. "No. No." He shakes his head and turns. *"Noooo."* He groans. "I can't believe it." He spins around to face me. "My God, you've fallen for her."

I nearly drop the bags again. "That's the jump of an insane man."

"Look at you. It's all over your face."

"So now you read faces?" I turn and walk to the kitchen with the bags. "The only thing on my face is lack of sleep because I'm doing what you told me to do. I can't just walk into this thing without—"

"Have you kissed her?"

I stop and turn back to face him. *"What?"* But I can tell I've already given it away. All I can do now is damage control. I force my shoulders to relax and I shrug. "So what if I have? It doesn't mean anything."

"Nothing? You sure?"

Am I? I haven't been able to stop thinking about her for days. Not just the kiss, but even before that. Every time I try to focus on other things, I still circle back to her. But how could I fall for Raine when I still love Jenna? I've always loved Jenna. Thoughts of her are what got me through centuries of being trapped in a six-inch cube.

Locke, it just isn't right. . . . I may look like the Jenna you knew so long ago, but I'm lifetimes from that girl. I'm two hundred and seventy-seven years old now. . . . You deserve the chance to live a life. . . .

Xavier waits for a reply. I turn away and unload the groceries on the counter. "There's someone else in my life," I answer.

"Good. It wouldn't be smart for you to get mixed up with Raine that way. She can't be trusted. She *is* the Secretary's daughter."

I whip around at the remark, ready to defend her. "She's not like the Secretary. She's adopted. Did you know that?"

"But he raised her. That's enough to make her dangerous."

He doesn't miss a beat with his reply, which is more than a little odd. He's not surprised with this new information about her adoption. Maybe because it's not new to him. Why didn't he include it in Raine's files? If telling me that she likes fencing is important, it seems like this little fact might be important too.

"You look like hell," he says. "You better get some sleep, Romeo. You have the performance of a lifetime tonight, and the Secretary's going to be a much tougher audience than Raine to fool."

I note how smoothly he changes the subject. He's covering, trying to erase the ground he just gave me. I grab an orange from the groceries he brought and score the peel with the blade of my Swiss knife the way my dad used to. I sit at the kitchen table and plop my feet on top of it, lean back in the chair, and pull the neatly scored peel from the orange. Sometimes more can be said with silence than with words. I learned that from Miesha. Raine's incomplete files weren't just sloppiness. I wipe the oily orange residue from the blade with my fingers and fold it back into its red hilt, pulling out the scissors next, and then the tweezers.

"Why the sudden interest in the knife?" Xavier asks.

"Just paying attention to details."

"Did you hear anything I said about getting some sleep?"

I look at his face, staring at every angle, every plane. He knows exactly what I'm doing. He wants to turn away, but he doesn't. I have to give him that. I see anger. I see fear. But mostly I see a mountain of guilt.

And that's when I know.

All the clues that didn't add up before click into place. More than click—they explode. I drop my orange on the kitchen floor and run to the living room, swiping papers and maps aside as I bring up the file I need.

File 52

Raine Branson (pronounced: rayn)

Age: 17

Xavier follows me, talking, shouting, buzzing around me like an angry bee, but I block it all out, flipping through the virtual pages until I find the one I want. The image looms in front me, frozen on the virtual screen. Raine staring at me, her lips parted, the lips that made my hair stand on end. Raine's features are dark, her hair, her eyes, her thick line of black lashes, all of these new and unfamiliar to me, features that threw me off, but her mouth, the distinct V of her upper lip, the wide pout of her lower lip, lips I had seen countless times trying to hold back information from me until they no longer could. Miesha's lips.

I fall back in my seat, air trapped in my chest. That's why they didn't tell me she was adopted. That's why there were no images of Karden. *Dark and dangerous.* That's how Miesha described him, and exactly how you could describe Raine.

I shake my head in disgust. "You're trying to save Karden, but not her?"

"From what? The only life she's ever known?" Xavier doesn't apologize for the lie he has perpetuated. His tone is accusatory. "Save her from her life of privilege and leisure? Believe me, I thought about it. No one hates the Secretary more than I do. How do you think I got this?" He touches the scar that slashes the entire length of his face. "He personally dragged a blade across my cheek while his security forces held me down. A little message he called it, to all Non-pacts who ever considered Resistance again. So when I found out who Raine was a few months ago, my first impulse was to expose the Secretary's dirty secret." He looks away, the sneer on his upper lip fading. His voice becomes softer. "But she *is* Karden's and Miesha's daughter. What would I be condemning her to? She'd be caught between two worlds, not fitting in anywhere anymore, not to mention what the Secretary might do with her." He looks up at me. "But really, the bottom line is, after all this time she's part of their world now. She has a *life* in that world. That's where her loyalties are. Not with us. She can't be trusted."

I spring to my feet, jumping him, throwing him to the ground, moving so fast he doesn't have time to react, moving faster than anything he's ever had to react to. I wedge my hand against his throat. "It doesn't matter!" I yell. "She's a human being! Not merchandise! Not a pawn in this stupid game of yours!"

My hand tightens on his throat. He doesn't struggle. I let go, pushing away from him, and walk to the other side of the room, trying to keep from putting my fist through the wall, trying to process what all this means. I know what it's like to have other people playing with your life like you're nothing more than a game piece.

Xavier gets to his feet, rubbing his neck where I'd held it. "It's not a stupid game," he says. "It's a desperate one. One I've been playing for years. One I'm tired of playing too. But one I have no choice but to keep playing until the rules of the game are changed."

He takes a step toward me. "We're close, Locke. I can feel it. The climate's right. Everything Carver told you is true. There are rumblings about reunification. We can only bring those rumblings to the next level with two things—serious money, and a serious leader."

"And Karden can give you both those things."

"The Resistance lost its heart after he disappeared, and the Secretary's harsh crackdown afterward all but killed it."

I study him. He's only a man, the one I saw a few nights ago, the one who held an infant on his shoulder, the man quick on his feet when Security arrived, the man dancing with his wife. Not a calculating member of the Resistance, only one man doing what he can. But is it enough? Can all this ever be enough? And at what cost? I remember what Jenna said about the world always changing. *Just when we have one problem solved, a new one is created.* Xavier is one of those problems. So am I.

He sits down on the sofa. "I'm sorry we didn't tell you. We were going to, but after our first interview with you, we saw how close you were to Miesha. We thought knowing Raine was her daughter might just complicate matters for you."

"And make me slip."

"Yes, and we can't afford slips. It could cost people their lives. Since she was raised as the Secretary's daughter, we don't know a lot about Raine, but she does have a life and identity as a citizen. That means a whole different way of thinking. She has loyalties to that world now."

I nod, remembering how she defended the Secretary when we first met, maybe even showed some pride about his prominent position. And of course, she proclaimed her adoptive mother as the best mother in the world. Yes, she has some loyalties, but how strong, I don't know.

Xavier leans forward, tired lines creasing his eyes. "At the very least, if she were told the truth she might confront him and blow the whole thing."

Knowing Raine, I don't have any doubt about that. She would more than confront him. She would be an out-of-control force of nature, likely to sweep us all away in the process. But she doesn't live a life of privilege and leisure as Xavier implied. She's more like a prisoner in a tower.

Yes, knowing complicates everything.

The Meeting

The guard has rung the ninth floor. He whispers quietly through a privacy shield to someone on the other end. I examine a bowlful of green apples pretending I'm more interested in them than in what the guard is whispering. He eyes me suspiciously and nods, and then whispers again. A final affirmative dip of his chin and he signs off, turning his full attention back to me, suddenly all smiles.

"You may go up, sir." He points to a hallway behind him. "North lift."

I set the apple in my hand back in the bowl. The guard scrutinizes me as I step in the direction he pointed. I carefully control my movements and expressions. It feels like every single twitch is being watched, and not just by the guard. I saw the discreet surveillance eyes hovering near the crown molding the minute I entered the lobby, but I pretended not to notice. I need to look like a kid on his way to meet schoolmates and that's all.

The moment of truth has arrived at last.

The elevator door is already open as I approach, making me uneasy, like I'm not just being watched. I'm being anticipated. I step inside but there are no buttons to push. The door closes and the elevator begins to rise. The surveillance eyes hover in the corners of the elevator as well. No wonder Raine never exits this way in the middle of the night. I want to wipe my palms on my pants but resist the urge. I don't want to show nerves even though I have plenty right now. Everything has changed now that there's actually someone up there on that top floor whom I care about—and someone Miesha cares about too. Bravado has taken a back seat to precision.

The elevator stops but the door doesn't open. I wait, and then look around wondering if there's a bell I'm supposed to ring, like I'm standing on a stoop. I run my hands along the back wall and suddenly I hear the whoosh of the door. I spin around and am greeted by Dorian, the household manager.

"Welcome, Locke. Is that right—Locke?"

"Yes," I say. "Locke Jenkins."

She leads me through a marble foyer into a large living room, very old-world style, with mahogany paneling, tapestries, and lots of lavish brocade furniture. Not at all what I expected.

"You're the first to arrive. Please make yourself comfortable. May I get you a refreshment?"

"Just water would be great, thank you."

"Yes, sir. Of course."

I walk around the room when Dorian leaves, examining the

decor. The first thing I notice is books. Lots of books. The old-fashioned leather-bound kind. Gatsbro kept his collection behind glass. The Secretary obviously flaunts his. Does he read them, or are they only for show? Something like Raine, the model daughter who jumps through all his hoops?

"Welcome, Locke."

I spin around. It's the Secretary. But I'm not supposed to know that, since we've never been introduced. I step forward and reach out to shake his hand. "Hello, sir. Are you Raine's father? Mr. Branson?"

"Yes, Secretary Branson. Nice to have you join the group."

"I understand you recommended me. Thank you."

"Shane LeGru can make poor choices but he's a young man with potential. He comes from good lines. Possibly a good match for Raine—when the time comes. There are so few. And I was pleased to see your generous display with him. You might be a good influence on him and the others." His brows rise. "Tell me, Locke. *Will you* be a good influence?"

It's more of a threat than a question. I swallow. I hate this guy already. I hate everything about him. His patronizing attitude. His disingenuous smile. His weak handshake. His condescending voice. His ego. He owns the world, or thinks he does. But mostly I hate that he stole away Raine and told her she was trash.

I smile. I learned from the best, Dr. Gatsbro and Kara. I smile and I make it genuine, because I'm going to crush this guy. Crush him with everything I've got.

"I hope I might be able to share a few things with the others, sir, but I'm sure I'll learn far more from them."

"Good attitude, boy. Observe and learn. It's gotten me far." He glances at the time on an antique clock on the mantel and frowns—exactly seven o'clock—the appointed time of the meeting. I knew from the files that he was a stickler for punctuality and I made sure I wasn't a minute late. "I apologize for Raine's tardiness," he says. "It's unacceptable. She should be here to greet her guests. Hap tells me she's having a clothing issue, which is still no excuse. I assure you it won't happen again."

As we're speaking, more guests arrive, Vina, Ian, Shane LeGru along with his father, whom I expected to come, and finally Cece. Introductions are made, and we make small talk as Dorian serves refreshments. The Secretary is clearly becoming more impatient with Raine's absence. Just as he's whispering something to Dorian, Raine rushes into the room, stopping conversation.

"Sorry for being late." She briefly glances at the Secretary but then avoids his gaze—for good reason. He's not taking this well. I watch his hand tighten around the glass he's holding, wondering if he'll break it.

Her hair is loose and pleasantly unkempt like she's been out in a breeze. She wears a thin lavender-flowered shift that barely covers the top of her thighs. One sleeve dips off her shoulder. Her lavender sandals are light-years from the sturdy black loafers she usually wears in public.

She's radiant. And now that I know who she really is, it's as if I'm seeing her for the first time all over again. *Rebecca,* I want to say. *Your real name is Rebecca.* I stare at her lips, so much like Miesha's. That means the rest is Karden. Every time the Secretary looks at her he must see Karden too. I wonder how that makes him feel? If Karden is alive, does he throw that up in his face? That he's raising Karden's daughter? What kind of torture has he put Karden through? Something much worse than my centuries of silence?

"Pardon us, please," he says and he grabs Raine by the elbow and briskly pulls her into the foyer. The others instantly resume conversation, almost on cue, like they know not to interfere with the Secretary and his daughter.

I only have a side view of both of them, but I can still read every word.

Would you mind explaining?

I'm sorry, Father. I had my clothes laid out for the evening but—

But what?

I spilled tea all over them. And my others are—

Then you'll wear the wet ones. Go change. You look like a whore.

But, Father—

Are you speaking back to me?

She lowers her eyes. *No, sir.*

He yanks her back by her elbow as she turns to walk away. *There will be consequences for this, Raine. And pull your hair back before I cut it off myself.*

I force my clenched fist to open and relax as he returns to the group and smiles. "The teen years. So trying. You understand, don't you, LeGru?"

LeGru's lips pull back in a skeletal smile that makes my skin crawl and he agrees heartily with the Secretary. Big surprise.

"Continue on," the Secretary says to the rest of us. "Mr. LeGru and I have business to discuss in my study. Dorian will get you anything else you need and Raine will return shortly."

Everyone in the group responds with thank-yous and the

groveling replies that the Secretary expects as the two of them walk away and disappear down a long hallway.

I feel sick. I know why Raine did it. She did it for me. She didn't want me to see her in the drab institutional getup that the Secretary insists she wear, especially now that I've seen the other side of her.

"Excuse me," I say to the others. "I need to use the facilities."

"I'll show you where—"

"I know where it is," I say, cutting Shane off.

I walk down a hallway I've memorized a dozen times over. So far, the layout is true to form. If I get "lost" it will be by design. I figure I can use the lost oaf premise at least once if I get caught.

I know where I need to go. Downstairs. That's where the Secretary and LeGru went. I might at least be able to pinpoint his office. But where I really want to go is straight to Raine. I know where her room is—at least I think I do—and I still ache remembering her stricken face as the Secretary pulled her away. I more than ache. I want to hold her and never let go.

Fallen for her? I'm not sure what that even means. But I know something visceral vibrated through me when I could see but not touch her, an urgent need that rattled through whatever fabricated bones Gatsbro gave me when I wanted to run to her but couldn't. But I look for the stairway that leads down, because now the Favor is just as important to Raine as it is to anyone, even if she doesn't know it.

The hallways are narrow and dark. One point two meters across, exactly as the plans indicated, but at my very first turn, another hallway exists where there was none on the plans. I stop and listen, straining to hear any sound, any voices that might lead me to the Secretary and LeGru. Now I have to rely on my instincts more than antiquated plans. As much as my BioPerfect can instill dread in me, wondering what sort of unpleasant surprises it may hold, I'm counting on it right now. I feel the rush in my head, the buzz, and then the silence as my hearing divides the static from the distinct—the distant sound of Vina's laughter, the click of heels on the marble floor upstairs, and then the lowest of murmurs. Hushed voices that could be the Secretary and LeGru. I head down the unknown hallway, walking close to the wall to avoid creaks. The murmurs grow louder, and at the end of the hall a narrow shaft of yellow light streams through where a door has been left ajar. I edge closer trying to keep my breaths shallow, the sound of my heart pounding so loudly in my ears, I'm afraid they may hear it too. I take another step and the floor creaks. I freeze.

Damn these old houses.

I hold my breath listening for movement but I hear only the steady murmur of their voices. I say a prayer for the floor, the first prayer I've said outside of grace in years, and step closer. The floor cooperates and I ease myself into position until I can see through the eight-inch gap in the door. It's a very large room and at the far end I see LeGru's back. He faces the Secretary, who sits at a desk. LeGru paces like he's agitated. I hear a few words but mostly they keep their voices so low, I can't follow what they're saying, and with LeGru's pacing, I can't read their lips either, but at least I know: This is the Secretary's office. A critical piece of information for when I have the opportunity to return and look for information.

I'm just about to ease away when I hear movement behind me. I spin. Raine has snuck up on me.

"What are you doing?"

I step closer to her, trying to keep my voice low. "I was looking for the restroom. I must have taken a wrong turn."

Suspicion flashes across her face. "Down here?"

I shake my head and backtrack. "I was looking for you."

I hate lying to her but it works. She nods like she understands and holds her hand out to me. "Let's go back up."

The office door swings open wide and light floods into the hallway. "What's going on?" the Secretary asks.

"Locke got lost," Raine says. "He was looking for the restroom."

"Really?" LeGru steps past the Secretary. His beady eyes narrow, making him look even more ghoulish. "That's quite a wrong turn you took, boy," he says. "Upper floor. Perhaps you should ask directions in the future before you begin wandering."

"Of course, sir." I make my apologies, mumbling about my bad sense of direction, and Raine and I depart down the hallway. I feel their steady stares drilling into my back. We turn a corner and I stop to look at Raine, her hair pulled back in a severe braid at the base of her neck, not a hair out of place. I reach up, gently stroking her cheek with my thumb, and only briefly brush my lips to hers, not knowing how long we have before LeGru or the Secretary might follow after us. "Are you okay?" I whisper.

She clears her throat and swallows. "He embarrasses me terribly. I should be used to it by now." Her lower lids brim with tears and she blinks, willing them away, a skill she has perfected. She shakes her head. "It doesn't matter. Let's go back up."

I grab her arm as she pulls away, holding her so she has to return my gaze. There's so much I want to say but can't. She needs to escape and doesn't even know why and I can't tell her. That's the worst part. All the lines of my goal—the Network's goal—are blurring.

She waits for me to say something and I force words out of my mouth that have nothing to do with my thoughts. "Your clothes aren't wet," I say. "We need to take care of that before he notices."

"He's noticed. He notices everything."

Not everything. I'm still under the radar. At least for now. For the first time I'm grateful for *all* the possibilities of my BioPerfect and I'm going to mine them for all they're worth. "I think I should still pour some water down the front of you when we get upstairs."

She manages a smile. "You would." We start up the stairs and at the last step she stops me and kisses my neck, whispering in my ear, "Locke Jenkins, trust meter—a solid ten."

We join the others and the rest of the evening results in the forced socialization that the Collective requires. Shane LeGru is more than a boy who makes poor choices. He's a narcissistic bore. I also have to spend most of the evening trying to avoid Vina's advances. I notice Raine's expression darken every time Vina lays a hand on my shoulder, or my thigh, or my chest. She's not shy about where her hands land. I finally wedge myself into a small armchair across from her, a safe distance from her reach, and Raine gives me a faint knowing grin. It's more than just a new level on the trust meter between us. It's something else. I've never met anyone like her. Her eyes turn to watch me again, like she knew I was thinking about her. She seems to read my mind. How long can I keep the truth from her?

Ian Dvorak seems to be the most focused of the group, steering the conversation back to the project every time Shane steers it away, so concentrated he seems to be oblivious to Cece's constant gaze on him. It's an interesting ensemble. It might be an exclusive group, but aside from the virtual notes they talk into place on virtual screens, in many ways it's not that different from the assigned study groups I had when I was in school—an awkward mix of personalities trying to make the best of a few hours of enforced confinement. Probably the only thing they all have in common is money and pedigrees. I guess my supposed father's wealth is what opened the door for me.

Since it's the beginning of a new term, they must collectively agree on a community socialization project to engage in over the coming year. As a group their project will be researched, outlined, and then proposed to the Virtual Collective for approval. I try to follow and contribute to the conversation as they discuss possibilities but being the newcomer I can fake like I'm pondering it all, when what I'm really thinking is *How soon can I get into the Secretary's office and search it? How long do I have to keep up this charade for Raine? Forever?*

I stare at her, following the line of her profile, looking at the lips that eagerly kissed mine last night. She turns to look at me, again somehow sensing my eyes on her. My stomach twists. How can I feel this way about her? It's the last thing I ever expected to happen, but then again, my whole life has been one unexpected turn after another. Now Raine has become one of them.

Shane catches sight of the two of us looking at each other and I look away but it's too late. I know I've made a grave error. I make a point not to look Raine's way after that and try to join the conversation. Cece suggests three different projects including fund-raising for removing the ugly river abatement walls that are no longer in use. Vina wants a project to support the arts, especially dance. She winks at me as she says it. If she knew about Raine and me dancing together, that might dampen her enthusiasm. Shane suggests funding an additional Tour Bot to boost tourism at the shore. "Bring more revenue to the city and be done with it. I don't want to turn this into a time-sucking ordeal."

Ian shakes his head at every proposed project, wishing to do something that will make a more crucial impact. "Something more basic, like feeding the hungry."

"Right. Who's hungry in Boston?" Shane says, and pops one of Dorian's cookies into his mouth.

"Non-pacts for starters," Ian answers.

There's a brief hush, like Ian's treading on dangerous ground. We're in the Secretary of Security's house, after all, whose job it is to contain and restrict them.

Shane shakes his head. "Don't start in on that again, Ian. We're talking about projects for real citizens. No way I'm going to flea-infested dumps to help a bunch of lawbreakers."

"It's not a bad idea," Cece says, eager to show that she's on Ian's side. "It might get some of us out of our comfort zone, Shane."

"I don't need to get out of *my* comfort zone, Miss Cece Carrington, who arrived here with her own entourage, who are still waiting downstairs for her, including her own personal driver, assistant, and bodyguard."

Cece's cheeks tinge pink and she looks down at her lap.

I chance a quick glance at Raine to see her response to Ian's idea, but she remains silent, nearly frozen, like the idea terrifies her.

Is that because she's afraid she'll run into the woman who threw her away, or because she thinks that all Non-pacts are animals?

They continue to argue and toss out more ideas until they have it down to four, including Ian's. They agree to go on a group expedition on Friday to various sites for further research. I'll be able to see Raine in the light of day at last. Ian suggests meeting at the PAT but Cece blushes again, saying her parents won't allow it. We will have to take her car. For the first time Ian seems aware of Cece and her discomfort and nods. Raine says she cannot go before eleven o'clock because of her fencing practice. The others agree that eleven works best for them too.

"What about you, Locke? Is eleven all right?" Vina asks.

I resist the urge to look at Raine and keep my eyes focused on Vina instead. "I think I can move my other studies around it," I answer. Vina flashes me a seductive smile and I wonder how I'll avoid her clutches in Cece's car.

In spite of Shane's obviously watchful eye on me for the rest of the evening, I still manage to catch a moment alone with Raine in the foyer before we all leave.

"I'll see you tonight," she whispers.

"No, don't take a chance," I tell her. "Your father—"

"I'll be there," she says.

Her eyes are desperate and determined. There isn't time to talk her out of it and I'm not sure I could anyway. All I know for sure is that I want to hold her, kiss her, to relive last night right this minute, but I don't dare. Someone could walk into the foyer any second, and someone does. Shane. I offer a few cool parting comments to Raine for Shane's benefit and step into the elevator, which has just opened.

Shane follows right behind me and voices the command for the door to close before anyone else can enter. "You did me a favor at the club the other night," he says. "I always return my favors, so here's a tip for you."

I raise my eyebrows, waiting.

"Steer clear. Raine's spoken for."

"Really? I didn't know that."

"And now you do."

I look at him. And look. I look at him so long his entitled weasel face twitches.

"Thanks for the tip," I finally say. The elevator door opens and I leave. Like Father, like Son. I'm not surprised.

I stop halfway through the lobby and grab an apple from the bowl I saw as I entered and turn back to throw it to him.

"Shane. Catch. This one's yours." I volley it across the lobby, and as I expected, he misses. He misses a lot. It's the twenty-fourth century. Women aren't spoken for, especially not Raine.

Out of the Comfort Zone

I stand in the shadows of the underground lot of the Tudor Apartments waiting for Cece's car to arrive. I'm early, eager to see Raine again, even though we parted only a few hours ago. The last few nights . . . I'm not sure how I'll make it through today without touching her. And then last night—

I swallow. *Get it out of your mind, Locke. Focus.* But my mind jumps right back to her, the shadows of the parking garage becoming the shadows of the cathedral, the muted stained glass of midnight, the echoes, the pews we lay on, the sweet scent of candles, the sweet scent of her neck, our whispers. As dawn neared it was harder than ever for either of us to leave, to go back to our other way of living. To the pretending.

For those few hours I forgot about her being the daughter of the Secretary. Forgot about the threats, the Network. Forgot about who I was, who I had become. I was just Locke. She was just Raine. Rebecca. Someone who was sharing her most sacred place with me. A place of believing. I believed with her.

I feel a pinch at my waist and I whirl. Raine smiles. I swear she must have hidden wings she can move so silently. I glance around, looking for the nugget-head, but for the moment we're alone and I quickly take a chance and kiss her, knowing it will likely be my last opportunity of the day.

My timing has become impeccable. Two seconds later, Hap appears at the garage stairway with Shane at his side. They walk toward us. Raine and I casually step apart like we aren't even aware of each other's presence.

Shane inserts himself between us. "Cece's late as usual, I see."

"Why didn't you just have her pick you up at your own place?" I ask.

"Why didn't you?" he returns.

"I was already in the area."

He smiles. "As was I."

It's going to be a long day.

Cece arrives with Vina and Ian already in the car, a long black job with four rows of seats, a modern-day stretch limo that I imagine still sucks up fuel like a thirsty dragon—even if it is algae-based energy. Her family has to be loaded to get away with transportation like that. Maybe this is what the Secretary aspires to. Government pay, even when you're raking in untold kick-backs from government contractors, still has to be limiting for someone of his ambitions. Hap doesn't come with us. Apparently Cece's bodyguard was deemed sufficient protection for all of us. I manage to get a seat opposite Vina, though she stretches out her foot to keep connecting with mine.

Our first stop is the riverfront. The abatement walls are indeed ugly. I almost want to suggest graffiti as a way to improve them, but I doubt that spray cans exist anymore and don't want to even try to explain what that kind of art is. The walls were placed at the high-water mark before water levels began to recede slightly due to decades of global regulations. I look beyond these walls to the ones below that hem in the river now. Still large and still ugly, I wonder if they'll ever be able to get rid of those too. Cece performs measurements and density tests to help analyze the cost of removal. Ian shows only cursory interest in the walls, which I have to admit are crumbling and being taken back by the earth anyway. Based on my estimates, they'll be gone in another few hundred years, though unlike me, most people don't have that kind of time to burn.

I try to feign interest. Notes are talked onto virtual tablets and added to measurements and videos and we all climb back into the car.

Next we stop at an experimental dance academy, then an improv studio, and finally, due to Shane's continuing insistence, the waterfront public tour kiosks. We get out of the car and walk past three, finally stopping at the wharf. No one speaks. Vina shields her eyes from the sun, looking at gulls overhead. Cece leans over the rail, looking at the water lapping below. Raine sits on a bench in the shade, her bored mask firmly in place. Disinterest is worn like a badge by everyone. Shane walks over and sits close to Raine, draping his arm behind her on the bench. I suddenly feel like Hap, wanting to cross over to him in three steps and lift him by the throat. He shoots me a smile, almost a dare, like he can read my mind.

Don't touch her, pig.

"Well, I think that we have a winner," he says, breaking the silence. He goes on to proclaim his suggestion as the clear project choice and estimates that the ratio of tourists to Tour Bots is a hundred to one.

"How'd you come up with that number?" Ian asks.

"I eyed it."

"Who cares anyway?" Cece asks.

"The Collective will, for one. It would benefit the most Citizens. We want this thing approved don't we?"

"We aren't finished yet," I say. "We still have another stop."

"No we don't," Shane says. "The Non-pact suggestion was stricken as an option."

Ian steps forward. "By who?"

"If you must know, the Secretary himself. He said it was an inappropriate proposal. And of course, he's right."

Raine swallows. Her expression has gone from bored to alert.

Ian glares at Shane. "And just how did he find out about it?"

Shane shrugs.

I take a deep breath. And then another, my eyes drilling into Shane. *Don't let the enemy push you before you're ready.*

I'm ready.

"So, that's not stopping us, right?" I say, pasting on a cheerful smile. "All projects don't have to be on Collective time. I'm still in."

There's a brief moment of shocked silence before Vina chimes in, "Me too!"

"But—"

"You're right," Ian says. "We can do it on our own. I'm in."

"Wait a—"

"Me three!" Cece says.

Shane is still sputtering half-finished objections, but Raine has remained noticeably silent.

"What about you, Raine? In or out?" I ask.

She looks down at her lap and shakes her head and finally whispers, "I can't."

I feel a brief flash of anger. She's always so strong. Why can't she be strong for this? But watching her face slowly harden and disconnect brings a wave of guilt too. She has moved into her default survival mode. I know I pushed her further than I should have. She has more to lose than any of us. We don't have to live with the Secretary, and thanks to me, she already pushed her limits with him a few nights ago. It wasn't fair for me to push her again.

"No problem," I say. "We'll drop you and Shane off before we go to the shelter."

"Shelter?" Ian says. "There are no shelters for Non-pacts. They aren't allowed. We need to go straight to the source—their neighborhoods."

I try not to act overly surprised, but my mind is racing. *Flea-infested dumps.* That's what Shane called them. A shelter was never mentioned. Why had I assumed something like a soup kitchen or a local Y for the indigent? All Non-pacts are indigent and they're meant to stay that way—indigent and invisible, kept far from the respectable citizens in their own run-down neighborhoods. Neighborhoods like Xavier's where they know me, and probably the closest Non-pact neighborhood to where we are right now. I've made a strategic error.

"Let's go," Vina says. She turns to Raine. "Can't you two take the PAT home so we don't have to drop you off?"

Raine glances at me, a hint of shame and hurt on her face, but she quickly sweeps it away and with her trademark indifference looks back at Vina. "Of course. See you all tomorrow." She turns and walks away without any more good-byes. Shane follows after her.

Vina grabs my arm. "Come on, Locke."

But I keep my eyes on Raine, hoping and wishing as she begins to get lost in the crowds. Vina pulls on my arm again and I'm just about to turn away when I see Raine stop. She simply stops, looking down at the sidewalk. Shane is babbling something to her, but she shakes her head like she's blocking him out. And then she turns. She looks in our direction and begins walking back, and stops in front of me. Her pupils are pinpoints, panic filling them, and her breaths are uneven, but still her chin juts out like she's in control. "I'll go along. This once."

We step out of the car. "This way," Ian says. We walk down the alley in the direction he points. Shane is nervous. Good. This is definitely not in his comfort zone. I hope he shakes himself into oblivion. He doubled back and followed Raine when she changed her mind. He had an unexpected change of heart too. Only morbid curiosity, he clarified.

Raine didn't speak the whole way. She just stared through the window like everything out there was suddenly so interesting. But I watched her eyes. She didn't see a thing—at least nothing the rest of us could see. Now she walks between Cece and Vina, still not speaking, in spite of Vina asking a hundred questions. What will we say if we run into someone? Do we interview them? Find out what their income is? Ask if they're hungry?

"Let's just start with hello," Ian suggests.

Before we piled into the car, I pretended I had a call from my mother and stepped away from the others. I tried to reach Xavier but he didn't answer, so I left a message warning him that I might be showing up in his neighborhood with the A Group and that no one should recognize me. I'm hoping he got the message because that's exactly where we are now—walking down the alley to Xavier's courtyard. Ian had already scouted out neighborhoods, not knowing the Secretary had nixed this project. Population and distance made this the best choice in his opinion, in spite of me trying to sway him elsewhere.

Cece's bodyguard walks with us—seven feet of black metal and menace. She tried to persuade him to stay behind when she saw Ian frown, but unlike Raine with Hap, she couldn't override his orders. We turn at the dead end of the alley and I hold my breath, but the courtyard is empty.

Everyone takes in the grim surroundings, the boarded-up windows, the couches and chairs scavenged from Citizens' trash, piles of broken shutters, doors, and other wood foraged from crumbling buildings for fuel, the cold embers of the fire ring at the center of it all used for light and warmth in the night. It's dismal and bleak. Even with my memories of a few nights ago, a bright crackling fire, music, laughter, I'm overwhelmed by what I see. Now there are no dancing evening shadows to disguise the stark truth. This is the day-to-day harsh reality for Xavier and people like him. People like me.

We pause on the perimeter, only the occasional scuff of grit beneath our feet making any noise at all in the deserted courtyard. I look at Raine. Her eyes have focused on a child's toy, a soiled baby doll lying on the ground, perhaps left in haste.

"Are you sure that we're in the right place?" Cece asks. "This does not look like a neighborhood to me. Just some old abandoned buildings."

I'm wondering myself where everyone is. Hiding? Looking out at us from behind dark windows? And then the silence is broken. A child runs out, oblivious to our presence, and grabs the baby doll from the ground.

Vina gasps.

The Menace steps forward.

I put my arm out to stop him. "It's just a kid."

"Thieves, same as the rest," Shane says.

A young woman runs out the door after the child. "Alessa! Come back!" She spots us across the courtyard and stops.

"Hello," Ian calls.

The little girl looks up and smiles. "Mommy, they're here!"

The woman glances nervously at me and then back to her daughter. I hold my breath hoping the entire exchange goes unnoticed. It seems to, only because this whole environment is so foreign to everyone else that it's all strange. It's a lot to take in at once. Ian approaches the woman and we follow and soon others come outside to see these odd strangers who have entered their neighborhood. By now, they can see we're not part of the Security Force. Several mothers with small children on their hips and clinging to their clothing talk with us. One of them is Xavier's wife. She must have gotten my message and spread the word. Until the child ran out, they probably planned to avoid us entirely. She purposely dodges my gaze. But the conversations are easy, smoother than expected and lasting five, ten, fifteen minutes, both sides appearing to be intrigued by the other.

Raine hangs back, avoiding any conversation at all. She only watches as more people emerge from the dilapidated buildings. She watches Vina and Cece from a distance as they talk with two women and an older man, watches as the children play games around their feet. She's silent, examining their faces, and then seems to breathe again when no one looks anything like her. She stares at one thin woman who chats with Ian, tired lines fanning out from the corners of the woman's eyes and her hair graying prematurely. A sleepy toddler rests on her shoulder, patting her mother's back with tiny dimpled fingers.

I step closer to Raine, away from the others. "Not what you expected, is it?" I whisper.

"We should go," she says.

"What are you afraid of, Raine?"

She shakes her head, refusing to answer. I know what she's afraid of and right now it isn't her father. "They aren't animals, Raine. They never were."

We hear Ian thanking them for their time and the others saying their good-byes and they all turn to leave. A small girl runs a few steps toward us and waves at Raine. The girl stands there waiting with a shy expectant smile. Raine hesitantly lifts her hand

and waves back. The girl giggles and then looks straight at me saying, "Bye, Locke!" before she runs away.

Raine turns to me, confused. "I didn't hear you tell her your name."

"Yes, I did," I answer, with a reply that comes a beat too fast. "When we first got here."

"Oh."

I hear the doubt in her voice. Even now, I know she's retracing our steps through the courtyard, knowing she was distracted, but always aware of where I was and who I spoke to. Raine doesn't miss much. I'm wondering if I should try to explain further, but too much explanation can backfire, and right now I'm a ten on the trust meter. I decide to ride that and let her chalk it up to distraction.

Shane sees us whispering and marches over from his safe encampment with the Menace. "We've seen enough. Let's get out of here, Raine." He reaches for her hand, but I step in his way.

"We'll catch up with you," I tell him.

He tries to step around me. "I don't think—"

I block him again. "That's your problem, Shane. You don't think. *Back off.*"

He steps back, his shocked expression quickly changing to a glare. He looks at Raine, who gives him no ground, and then looks back at me. "So . . . that's how it is. Let me warn you, you're making a big, *big* mistake."

"Probably so," I answer.

He stomps off, heading toward the alley.

Raine shakes her head and sighs. "Oh, Locke, I could have handled him on my own. I have for three years now."

"I don't doubt that. But there's safety in numbers too. Sometimes it doesn't hurt to have someone who cares about you covering your back."

"He's hardly a threat. Just an annoyance."

"Maybe," I say, but I'm not so sure. Especially since the Secretary seems to think he's a good match for Raine, and the Secretary is used to getting what he wants.

When we reach the alley she pauses and gazes back over her shoulder into the courtyard, looking at what I don't know. The Non-pacts have all gone back inside. I watch the breeze lift loose tendrils of hair at her neck, her lashes casting a shadow beneath her eyes; I watch the tenderness of Raine, trampled beneath years of obsessive control, all the wasted years that even eighty billion duros can never buy back, and I think about how much Miesha would have loved Raine the way she deserved to be loved. If only she had had the chance.

Tossed

"And this?"

Raine and I lie on the grass looking up at the stars. It's a sweltering night in Boston. Probably one of the last before the season changes, before leaves begin sprinkling the sidewalks and winds bring on weather that my mother said made for hearty stock like us. Hearty. If she only knew.

"That's the pit of a chocolate peach."

Raine's nose wrinkles in disgust. "Why are you saving *that*?"

"Just a reminder. A friend gave it to me, telling me to savor it. Savor everything." I roll over and kiss her shoulder, her neck, and finally her mouth. "See? It works."

"Hmm," she says, licking her lips. "I guess I need to get myself one of these." She wraps her hands behind my neck and pulls my face down to meet hers again, our lips barely touching, our breaths mingling, smiling, then laughing, so close our noses bump. "Okay, enough of that." She playfully pushes me away. "Next!"

She reaches into my pack, and blindly rummages through it with her fingers to pull out the next surprise. When she first asked me what I carried in my pack, I shrugged, trying to avoid the question, but she pressed, and then I found I wanted to share with her. There's so little I can tell her about the real me.

She pulls out the Swiss knife. Her father's knife. "Something of substance—at last! Tell me about this."

"It's a Swiss knife. You've never seen one?"

"No."

"You need to get out more. They've been around for a million years at least. They're more than knives really. They're emergency tools."

She pulls out a few of the tools and blades and examines them. "Even a toothpick? Really? Have you ever used it?"

"No, as a matter of fact, I haven't. The only thing I've used so far is the large blade."

"That seems like a waste."

"I'll get around to them all eventually. I haven't had it very long."

"Where'd you get it?"

I roll back over and look up at the sky. *From your mother. She gave it to me. Your mother who doesn't even know you're alive.* But I stick to the Network story. "My dad."

She reaches into the pack again, pulling out protein cakes, energy water, phone tabs that I explain away as freebies, the black government-issue coat still in its small cylinder that I explain as a mere practicality, and the small stuffed blue elephant that I tell her was a gift from a little girl I used to know named Kayla, probably the truest thing I've said that night.

She leans up on one elbow, looking into my eyes. "Who are you, Locke Jenkins? You're not like anyone I've ever known. You are—" Her eyes glisten and she smiles like she's trying to erase the emotion behind them. "Don't you dare make me cry. But, I think—" She swallows. "I—" She leans down and lays her cheek against mine. I feel the deep breaths of her chest and the shuddering of air as she lets it out. She pushes away and grins, the potential flood of tears gone. "Next."

She rummages into the deepest corners of my pack and pulls out the last item. "And what in the world is this?" she asks, holding up the frosted green glass.

"That's the best piece of all. It's the eye of Liberty." I tell her the story that Lily told me, that the Statue of Liberty once had beautiful green eyes but they were lost at sea and after all these years of being tossed on the sands, this small piece of green glass is all that's left. But there's another eye of Liberty out there somewhere waiting to be found on a sandy beach.

She rolls to her back, a dreamy smile on her face. "That's probably the wildest history lesson I've ever heard."

"True. Promise."

She reaches over and threads her fingers through mine. "Then let's find the other eye of Liberty together. Promise me."

I squeeze her hand. "It could take a lifetime of combing beaches to find it."

"I don't have a problem with that."

Match Point

"Good evening, Locke. Again, I admire your punctuality." The Secretary glances at the time. "Early even."

I step out of the elevator. "Hello, Secretary Branson. Nice to see you again." I look around. Dorian, who greeted me last time, is nowhere in sight, and no one else is either. Not Raine, Hap, none of the A Group, not even LeGru. It's oddly silent, like the entire house has been cleared out. I don't have a good feeling about this, but there's nothing about the Secretary that makes me feel good.

"I was wondering if I might talk with you in my office before the others arrive." He waves his hand toward the hallway. "And of course, you remember where it is. I'll let you lead."

Our gazes lock. It's an abrupt and interesting greeting—one clearly orchestrated and meant to intimidate. I glance around again. There's nothing I can do but walk down the hallway—and watch my back like I never have before. The stairway down seems narrower, longer, and darker than before. We reach his office door and he pushes it open, waving me to a chair opposite his desk.

"Drink?" he asks.

"I don't drink, sir."

"Of course you don't. At least not in front of me, right?" I smile at his thin joke as I'm obliged to. He pours himself a small glass of something from a crystal decanter on a narrow table just inside the door. I take in the room. If nothing else, this unexpected meeting gives me a chance to gather more information that might be useful. I'm able to see things I couldn't see through the small crack in the door the last time I was here. There are four windows. The plans only showed two for the room on this side of the building. The office must have been expanded and reconfigured, which explains the new hallway leading to it. It's now long enough to encompass the recessed window that's on the west side of the building.

"An interesting day you had last Friday with Raine and the others down at the wharf," he says. He holds his glass up to the light like he's judging the quality of its color. "Time is short so I'll get right to the point. I think it's quite understandable that you would be attracted to Raine."

I open my mouth to object but he holds his hand up to stop me. He smiles. "Let me finish."

I lean back in my chair and wait.

"Raine *is* beautiful. Even as a father I can see that. And quite accomplished."

"I'm aware of that."

His smile fades. "Are you?"

He doesn't want an answer so I don't give him one. I know this is all as orchestrated as his greeting at the elevator. I let it play out. He walks over to a silver sword with an elaborate filigreed handle that's displayed on the wall behind his desk. He runs his finger along the length of the blade.

"A beautiful sword," I say.

"A smallsword to be exact, circa eighteenth-century France. Less than a pound, swift and precise. The perfect thrusting weapon, especially for wealthy noblemen of the day."

He turns to look at me. "Are you familiar with fencing, Locke?"

"No, sir."

"I didn't think so. It's a beautiful sport with a long and elegant history. More of an art really, much like watching a ballet, and it takes just as many years to master. It's the most refined form of deadly combat." He takes a sip of his drink and then pauses, taking a good long look at me. "Raine's been fencing since she was five. She's breathtaking to watch. Did you know she's taken first place in the Foil event at the National Fencing Championships two years in a row now?"

"No, sir."

He raises his brows in mock surprise. "I'm sure there's a lot you don't know about Raine." He walks over to my side of the desk so he's towering over me, and casually leans against it. "Just as there is so much I don't know about you."

"My life's an open book," I tell him. "Anything you want to know, it's out there."

"And yet, the Virtual Collective's records on you are so incomplete. Curious, isn't it?"

Curious my ass. He's been digging. "That's a surprise," I answer. "I thought they had everything. But most of my records are from foreign countries—that's where I grew up. Maybe some are delayed or lost."

"Yes, I suppose that's a possibility. I'm sure it will be corrected soon enough though. As Secretary of Security I can speed these things along."

"That's good to know."

"But in the meantime, I do know about Shane, and I think he's a wiser choice for Raine. Your wake-up call to him at the wharf last week is appreciated—he needed it—but no more will be necessary, not if you want to remain in the A Group. Do I make myself clear, Locke?"

I know all the things I want to say, as opposed to all the things I should say.

"Locke?"

Shane didn't tell him where the wake-up call actually took place—probably to keep his own image untarnished. I stand so now I'm the one towering over the Secretary. I look at him, forcing the anger out of my eyes, forcing the hatred from my face, forcing the disgust from my voice, especially forcing away how much I want to wipe the smugness from his face. I focus on the goal and not my immediate satisfaction. I mold every blink, pause, pore, and facet of my expression to be that of a seventeen-year-old boy who is appropriately intimidated and eager to please. "Yes, sir. Very clear."

He nods his approval and dismisses me to go upstairs because surely the others have arrived by now and I must be eager to begin our meeting. When I reach his office door, he calls out to me one more time. *"Merci de prendre le temps de venir me voir, Locke. Je sais combien le temps est précieux."*

I turn and look at him, waiting an extra beat or two, just long enough to make him sit forward in anticipation, before I answer. *"Personne ne sait mieux que moi combien le temps est précieux, monsieur."*

And then I add in German for good measure, *"Sie ist etwas, was nie verschwendet werden sollte."*

He smiles but I can see the defeat on his face. "A good lesson learned in any language," he replies. "I'm glad to see you used your time abroad wisely."

I just bought myself a little more credibility—and time.

But not much.

I emerge from the hallway with the nugget-head by my side. Apparently on my return trip the Secretary wanted to make sure I didn't take any detours. Raine spots us, and smiles, but the worried questions are obvious in her eyes. She'll have to save those for later. I give her the barest nod trying to reassure her.

The entire A Group has arrived, including two members, Brita and Carlo, who were absent at the other meetings because they were traveling. Introductions are made and we move to the living area where the newcomers are caught up on the proposed Virtual Collective projects.

Shane makes a point of sitting by Raine, hurrying to the empty spot on the sofa next to her before anyone else can take it. He smiles and stretches his arm out behind her, baiting me, obviously quite aware of my talk with the Secretary. I try not to let his antics bother me. I know Raine can handle him. One touch and she'll humiliate him in front of the others—or worse. I'm almost wishing his arm would slip to her shoulder. But what I'm really wishing is that I could pop his head off and put it in the fruit bowl.

A better match? I suppose for a girl he'd be easy enough on the eyes—maybe someone even Vina and Cece would be all over if they didn't know he already had his sights on Raine. And he and Raine do have similar backgrounds, similar educations . . . *similar anatomies*. Maybe even she would think they were a better match if she knew what was really inside of me. I'm not the flesh-and-blood person she thinks I am.

Ian doesn't bother to keep the meeting on task. It's clear he has lost interest in the official project, which will be decided at the meeting tomorrow night at Cece's house once Brita and Carlo have time to read over the notes and weigh in. The unofficial project is never mentioned. The meeting devolves into chatter as Brita and Carlo share stories from their respective trips.

The Secretary makes an appearance, obviously checking on me to see if I properly absorbed his directive. I never glance in Raine's direction and instead turn my attentions to Vina, who is more than appreciative. I hear the elevator door open and LeGru appears in the foyer. He silently shakes his head at the Secretary, whose face instantly reddens. He retreats back down the hallway, agitated, with LeGru following close on his heels. Something is brewing between the two of them and I don't want to miss it. I excuse myself to make a call while Raine is occupied with serving the dessert that Dorian has brought in on a tray, and thankfully Hap has disappeared back into the kitchen with Dorian.

As Secretary of Security I can speed these things along. Which means I need to speed things along too.

Knowing the layout of the apartment is paying off, especially now that I know how far his office extends. Instead of following them downstairs, I turn left at the end of the hallway and find the stairway that leads to Raine's domain—the roof. I walk up the stairs and exit quietly, gently easing the door shut   147 behind me. Even in the dark, I can see that the roof is a paradise. Greenery that I couldn't see from street level creates pathways, alcoves, and sanctuaries. Raine's exquisite pieces of bonsai, miniaturized windswept trees, sit on rocky pedestals in nooks. Twinkling lights as small as fireflies hover in arbors. Whatever Raine does, whether fencing, bonsai, or scaling down ropes, she does it expertly and fully. I cross to the side of the roof where she lowers her rope ladder and search for it. It's easily found in a burlap sack stuffed in a pot, which must mean she isn't fearful of the Secretary invading this part of her world. I pull it out and take it to another corner of the roof. It holds Raine's weight. I hope it holds mine too.

My plan plays out almost too easily, except of course that I'm dangling eight stories above the ground. I'm hidden in the shadows and have a made-to-order view into the office—and seeing the Secretary's cool blown to hell completes the perfect perspective. He and LeGru are looking at something on his desk and I have a clear shot of their mouths. It's only his anger and the occasional flailing of hands that makes me miss any words at all.

Tonight, dammit . . . running out of time.

We've done this a hundred times. We can't get anything. He doesn't know it himself.

He knows. He knows something. . . . Only eight days left. . . . I'm not letting this slip through my fingers now. Do you understand, LeGru?

What about his wife?

She's been underground for years. We can't find her.

. . . never should have let her go.

It wasn't really our choice, was it?

LeGru walks to a leather armchair at one end of the Secretary's desk and sits. *There is some hopeful news. In five days we should have some promising new technology in place. I'm going down tonight myself to check on the details.*

The Secretary raises his brows, waiting.

It can activate sleepers.

Dormant biochips?

Exactly.

I watch the angry red hue drain from the Secretary's temples. He's pleased with this news.

LeGru hesitates, like he's uncertain. *These scans are considerably more painful, possibly risky.*

As long as he survives, use it. The more painful the better after what he's put us through.

And the girl?

The Secretary pauses, randomly shuffling V-files on his desk. His cheek twitches. He finally leans back in his chair, his expression grim. *Try it on him first. I'll use the standard scan on her again. At least for now.*

LeGru stands and walks in front of the Secretary so I can't see either of their mouths anymore. I need to go anyway before someone comes looking for me. It would be hard to explain why I'm hanging down here on the end of a rope. I scale back up the wall, put the ladder where I found it, then slip quietly down the stairs. It goes so smoothly, I feel like now I'm the one who has orchestrated everything flawlessly. When I return, Hap is just starting down the hallway looking for me. He's a Bot of few words. Scowls are more his specialty.

I hold my hand up. "No need to thank me. I took care of him," I say. "Biggest cockroach I ever saw. We won't say anything to the others. No need to spoil their dessert."

Hap remains silent. Just as I thought. Some things are so timeless even a nugget-head can grasp it.

Yeah, flawless.

I join the others, hardly missing a beat, taking the raspberry tart that Raine offers to me on a delicate china plate, letting my fingers linger on hers a few seconds longer than I should, maybe bolstered by my success on the roof. I laugh at Carlo's joke like I was never out of the room, and compliment Dorian on the tart when she returns for dishes. Carlo tells another story about his family being detained while on safari in Namibia. I sit back like I'm listening but my thoughts return to the dark shadows where I dangled from the rooftop. *Tonight.* LeGru is going down *tonight.* To the tunnels? Could he possibly lead me straight to Karden? Could I forgo searching the Secretary's office for the exact location and let LeGru do my work for me? It would save time and time is running out. This might be a certain pathway to Karden and his freedom—if that's who they were talking about.

I'm also hearing LeGru's words over and over again. *And the girl?* Could the Secretary be so coldhearted that he'd hurt Raine to get information? He did hesitate. What was that I saw on his face? Concern? Earlier when he talked about her proficiency at fencing I was surprised that there was even genuine pride in his voice. Maybe on some twisted level he does care about her, but even considering hurting his own daughter for money makes him a ruthless bastard. He's only holding off *for now.* He drilled into Raine that Non-pacts were animals. If only she knew who the real animal was.

Vina's shrill laugh at one of Brita's stories jerks me back to the conversation and I laugh too like I heard the whole story. I grab one of the tea napkins from the table and step away from the others for a moment, pretending I'm looking out at the sweeping view of the Commons and beyond. When Raine comes over a minute later to look out with me, she maintains her distance, knowing that Shane and Vina watch our backs. I drop the napkin on the table in front of us—the code for my iScroll quickly scrawled on the corner. "Just in case," I whisper. Her fingers curl around it and she slides it into her pocket.

She loudly points out a few sights in the distance and then whispers, "Tonight?"

I don't know how long following LeGru will take. "I'll try," I whisper. "But I might be late."

Seeing Red

I wait outside the Tudor Apartments for almost an hour before LeGru appears. Xavier calls me twice, but I don't answer. Let him think our meeting is running late. I don't want him to catch on to my plans or he might try to stop me. Sure, they want me to find where Karden is being kept, but I think a personal vendetta that Xavier has nursed makes him think he's the one who needs to actually go get him, no matter the cost to himself. But I'm more than a pair of eyes that can see in the dark, more than someone who can read lips and find out secrets, more than an "in" to get information for them. I have plenty of stakes of my own now. The clock is ticking—not just for Karden, but maybe for Raine too.

As I follow LeGru down Beacon, hiding in the shadows of the Commons, my iScroll alerts me to another call. This time Percel makes a worried appearance.

"It's an emergency, sir. I am told to alert you at all costs."

I duck behind a tree. If I lose LeGru now, I may not get any other chance.

"Who is it?" I say, my first thought rushing to Miesha. Has she taken a turn for the worse? Emergency calls are never good.

It's Carver, Percel informs me, and connects us.

"What's wrong?" I ask him.

"Nothing," Carver says. "I just need news. What happened tonight?"

"You have to call *now*?" I ask. "I told you that when I—"

"Listen to me, you—" He stops, recomposing himself into his usual cool. He even manages a smile. "I'm sorry if this is an inconvenient time for you, but this is a team operation. And for now at least, I'm the head of that team. If I say I need news, I need news. Did you find anything?"

"No. Not yet. I found the Secretary's office. Tomorrow night I go back. I'll try to find something then. I have to go." I sign off before he can answer and I tell Percel no more emergency calls. *My lesson for Carver: If you want things done just your way, do it yourself. Like me.* Any other time I might feel guilty for dismissing him—he's been the most pleasant and level-headed member of the so-called team—but right now I don't have time to worry about it.

I take off, running through the Commons and then the public gardens, trying to catch up with LeGru, and then I think I spot him, or at least a bony silhouette that could be him slipping down the tunnel entrance at Arlington. A shorter route for sure than going all the way to the Old Library. Is he in that much of a hurry? I remember the Secretary's furious eyes. Yes, I guess shortcuts are in order and LeGru is giving me one of my own.

I continue running, trying to catch up, and then slow as I near the entrance. The tunnels are dark in the daytime. How much darker will they be at night? How can LeGru see anything at all? I make my way down the rough stone steps, trying to keep every part of me silent, including my breaths. When I reach the station area I see a small red light glowing in the distance and hear a faint high-pitched hum and then they both disappear altogether. I listen. There isn't a single sound. Not a hum. Not a footstep. Not a breath.

I let my eyes adjust. My practice in the apartment helps me accelerate the process. I concentrate, forcing my eyes to search for scattered light. In seconds, the dim walls of the station come into view, and then, the still dimmer walls of the tunnels that lay beyond. Dead silence. Not even the skittering of small animals. Something has frightened them away.

I step forward. There's only one place to go. Toward the red light that disappeared so suddenly. That has to be where he went. The air is dank, smelling of rot. I watch my steps, avoiding large pieces of rubble, but I can't avoid the grit that covers every-thing and it crunches through the silence. I fight the urge to call out. I know it would be suicide to make myself known, and yet, the last time I was in such a dark place, that was all I could do, call out to Kara and Jenna over and over again, hoping one of them would come. I fight the instinct that ruled me for 260 years.

Did the red light lead to a doorway? I reach the entrance of the main tunnel for the green line. I walk farther in and run my hands along the wall where I thought I saw the light. I can't find it. Was it an illusion? Light reflected from somewhere else? I make a decision. I'm down here. I may as well go for broke. I start down the tunnel. Karden's here, somewhere. I can feel it. I don't know how I know, but *I do.* Is this what my mother defended as intuition? If so, I've got it. Or maybe I'm still learning new things that my BioPerfect can do. Unfortunately it doesn't keep my chest from feeling like every breath is trapped inside. I'm swimming against the current of survival mode.

The old broken track still runs down the middle of the tunnel so I stay to the left side, which has a wider, more intact walkway. The farther I go, the darker it gets, the danker the air, the tighter my chest squeezes, the faster my pace. *Get in, get out, Locke. Do it now. Find him. Do it for Miesha. Do it for you. Do it for Raine.* It's a new kind of survival.

I come to a place where the tunnel forks. The path to the left is smaller and cruder, maybe a tunnel that was forged in haste during the Division. No trains ever went down this way, but what has? My gut tells me to follow it, so I do. Another ten yards and another fork. This dungeon is riddled with haphazard tunnels. Someone could get lost down here forever if they weren't careful and I make a special effort to note my steps and turns. I follow my gut again, this time to the right. I can barely see at all now. Even these BioPerfect eyes need the smallest bit of reflected light to work with and here there's none. My breaths are shallow in my chest, like the air has vanished along with the light. I remind myself: *I'm not there. There's ground beneath my feet, a real world that's only steps away.* I fight the temptation to turn on the light that's in my iScroll, knowing it would set off alarms and bring Security Forces swarming down on me. Damn Carver for calling. I move forward more carefully now, listening for sounds. The only ones are my footsteps, but the sense is even stronger now. Something is nearby. Something important. Something like Karden. He's alive. I'm close. I'm sure of it.

And then.

I sense something else.

I stop.

Cock my head to the side trying to understand what it is.

A breath.

A presence.

A closing in.

And then shadows.

Flashes of air.

A thousand screeches surround me and I'm knocked to the ground. Pounced on. Razors cutting into my flesh. Screeches ringing in my ears from all sides. I fight them off, whatever they are, tossing, punching, trying to stand and being pulled down again. There are dozens of them coming at me. I feel bites, gouges, claws, the snapping of jaws as they miss me. I roll and deflect them, gaining a moment of freedom and then losing it again. Teeth sink into my hip, tear into my arm. I kick one off and another takes its place. I finally grab what seems to be a small one around the neck, and I hear an agonized screech, and for a moment the onslaught pauses. I pull the creature closer, holding it by the throat until it whimpers louder. The rest hold back and even though I'm sure they can't understand, I yell, "I'll kill it.

Stay back or I'll snap its head off." And I could. Right now, I could do it in a heartbeat.

There's screeching and snapping, but they stay at bay, seeming to sense my desperation. I walk backward, holding the creature by the neck as it claws at my arms. With each step back I take, the shadowy pack follows, just waiting for me to trip or let go. When I sense they're getting too close, I squeeze tighter so the creature in my arms screams and chokes. I step carefully, knowing one stumble and they will be on top of me again. Blood drips down my face, into my eyes, my mouth. I feel every gash, the pain, the gouges where their teeth have riddled my flesh, but I keep moving. If I stop, I know I'm dead. The creature twists and slithers, razorlike claws shredding my shirt and digging deeper into my arms trying to escape, but I keep my hold.

I make it to the end of one tunnel, and then another, and I'm finally moving into the larger station area where scattered distant light once again gives the walls form. At last I can make out the features of the creatures. Even darkness can't disguise their gruesome distorted bodies. Maybe half-dogs. Maybe not. But it's the other half that sickens me, so much so that my arms nearly drop the creature in my grasp. The other half is unmistakable. Thin, gaunt, they stand upright. I stare at the largest ones, just feet away from me ready to pounce. Their lips are missing and the exposed sharp teeth give them a grotesque perpetual grin. Their eyes are frozen open, forever startled, because they have no lids. Their bodies are covered with slime, scabs, and filth. And long sharp claws protrude from their fingers.

Fingers that are distinctly human.

I look down at the creature in my arms. Even through the squalor and horror, I can tell—it's a child. A small one, not much bigger than Kayla. I look back at the pack, and single out a creature at the front, the one most eager to tear my head off—man or woman I don't know, but without a doubt, the parent. Our eyes meet and I see the panic. *Human* panic. I shove the child toward it and run. I get only a two-second lead, before the rest are after me again, slashing at my back with their claws, but I manage to get to the stairs and they fall back. They won't venture into the world aboveground and that's all that saves me. As soon as I'm in the open air of the public gardens, I fall to the ground, gasping for breath, my body shaking, convulsing, finally giving in to the damage.

I remember the gash on my side from when Gatsbro's goons beat me. I know this damage is far worse. It's everywhere. My back, my arms, my legs, my scalp. Is it blood running into my eyes, or BioPerfect? I reach down and feel the deep wound at my hip, the fabric ripped away by their sharp teeth. I bring my fingers to my face. Blood covers them, but worse, bright blue gel. I close my eyes and my hand falls to my side. The wounds are so deep, my BioPerfect is oozing out everywhere. I'm leaving telltale signs all over the ground. I have to get home before someone sees me. I drag myself to my feet and the world spins. I'm still programmed for pain and Gatsbro made sure it was my default. I concentrate, trying to force it away, knowing I can, but I can't get past the wall. Miesha's words vibrate through me. *You can do it. Figure out a way.* It's too much and I fall to the ground again. I crawl to a nearby tree and use that to lean against as I try again to get to my feet. I look down at my shirt, covered in red and blue, and then I hear a honk. A cab sits at the curb and the window is down. "Need a ride?" the CabBot calls. "On the house."

It's the CabBot from the other night. Bob. The passenger door is open. Has he been following me? At this point, I don't care. I have no choice but to rely on his help. I stumble across the lawn to the cab and fall in.

"Home?"

"Yeah," I gasp. "It's at—"

"I know where it is."

As we turn the corner the last thing I see is a stream of Security Force vans descending on the gardens.

I don't remember getting back to my apartment. I don't know how I got up the stairs, but when I come to on the floor of the living room, I know I'm in deep trouble and there's only one person who can help me. With my last bit of strength, I call her.

Panic

"Jenna."

"Who is this?"

"Jenna," I try again, but even words leave me winded.

"Locke?"

I swallow and take as deep a breath as I can manage. "I'm hurt, Jenna. I need a doctor. Someone good."

"Locke, my God, what happened?"

"There's blood and blue gel everywhere. I need someone who can really stitch, like you. Not like the one I had last time."

Even through my pained haze I can hear the panic in her voice. "How did you—"

"He's there, Jenna. I'm sure he's alive. I was so close, but then—"

"I'm on my way, Locke. I'll be there by—",

"No, Jenna. Not you. Someone here. Not you."

"I can be there in a few hours. There is no one else. No one good enough who understands about the Bio Gel."

"Jenna."

The phone tab slips from my hand, and then the world slips away too.

Hazy voices call to me. I call back.

I try to find them. Reach them.

> *Jenna, no . . .*
>> *not you . . .*
>>> *Dark . . . miles of darkness . . .*
>>> *Where are we?*
>>>> *I'm here for you . . . always here . . .*
>>>>> *Are you an Escapee?*
>>>> *Something more?*
> *not you, Jenna . . .*
>>> *the tunnels . . . endless black tunnels . . .*
>>>> *lipless grins . . . lidless eyes . . .*
>>>>> *prisoners . . .*
>>>> *There. Again.*
>> *Miles and miles of . . .*

I force my lids back and gasp for breath. Light. Blessed light.

But hovering in front of me is the last thing I want to see. Xavier's sputtering face looms in and out of focus. When he sees my eyes open he walks away, yelling, "He's awake!"

Jenna's scowling face comes into view next. "You are not immortal, you know?"

I look around, orienting myself. The apartment. Thank God I'm back at the apartment. I try to pull myself up in the bed and groan in agony. Every inch throbs. I look at my chest and arms, a zigzag of cuts, repairs, and bandages. It looks like I've wrestled with a lion. Maybe five of them. Like the last time she patched me up, I'm naked from the waist up. I can guess that the lower half is the same, and even though I know Jenna has seen me before, I try to pull the sheet closer to my sides.

She isn't done with me. She walks to the other side of the bed and pours me a glass of water, almost simultaneously waving her arms in the air, which is a feat in itself. "Honestly, Locke, you have your limits just like anyone else! You're only a boy with a few enhancements."

"And drawbacks," I add, noting how much I hurt.

"Oh yeah, you have plenty of those!"

I see the worry on her face.

"My God, it was like I was putting something back together that had been through a meat grinder!" She turns to Xavier. "And *you* have some explaining to do!"

"Stop!" A wave of pain slams me as I pull myself up in the bed. I lean back against the headboard, catching my breath.

Jenna turns to look at me and waits, fury painted all over her face.

I slowly draw air into my lungs, trying to minimize move-ment. "What I did last night was my decision. *My* choice."

"Well, it was a poor choice, wasn't it?" she snaps, and snatches up a pile of bandages on the table next to me.

I try to get up to prove her wrong, refusing to grimace even though my skull feels like it's cracking in two, but Xavier easily pushes me back into my pillow. "I'm not picking you up off the floor again. Stay put."

"I'm alive, so it wasn't that bad of a decision, and I discovered something if anyone's interested. He's—"

"Shhh!" Jenna says, glancing at the doorway.

I hear arguing in the next room. I groan. "Don't tell me Carver and Livvy are here too. One mishap and everyone's break-ing the rules and showing up?"

"Carver and Livvy are the least of your problems," Jenna whispers.

"By a long shot," Xavier adds.

I don't even have time to worry about what they mean when the door swings open and I'm facing my worst nightmare.

Miesha.

I look at Jenna. "What's she doing here?"

Miesha stomps closer. "What are you asking her for? I'm stand-ing right here." And she starts in on one of her tirades. I don't even try to argue. I let her get it out of her system. She repeats what Jenna said already. I know, I know. I'm not immortal. I have my limits. When she's done with me she moves on to Xavier, and then Carver and Livvy, telling them all the reasons they shouldn't have put me in this kind of position and who did they think they were anyway? And then she comes back to me, wondering what

I was doing down in the tunnels in the first place, "and what the hell is down there?"

I can't tell her the why or the what. The others know it and hold their breath waiting for my reply. I turn it back on her. "I'm doing something important, Miesha. A Favor, remember? Something that I think matters."

"But—"

"How old were you when you ran off with Karden?"

She doesn't answer. She doesn't need to tell me. She was eighteen. Technically only a few months older than I am now.

"And how old were you when you were carted off to prison?"

She walks to the window without answering and looks out, squinting her eyes like she's looking for something.

"You were there for *eleven* years, Miesha. I'm sure that was no tea party." I pause to take a breath, feeling winded by just a few sentences. "I'm alive, all right? It's not the end of the world."

Her gaze jumps from the window to me. "Just because I made stupid mistakes doesn't mean you need to."

"Are you saying what Karden did, what he believed in, was a mistake?"

She blinks. Again and again, like she's blinking away a question that she can't answer. She takes a deep breath and walks over to my water glass, takes a sip, and then turns to Jenna. "And what do you say? Is he going to be *okay?*"

It's my turn to be caught off guard. It's the way she says "okay," a familiar slow inflection I've heard before—my brother asking doctors if I'd be okay and their answer was no. *No, he's not going to be okay*, words spoken centuries ago and yet they ring as fresh as yesterday.

"I think the BioPerfect he lost will regenerate itself. His vital organs appear to be functioning for now," Jenna answers.

It's a better prognosis, but not by much. She's reaching. Doubt is thick in her voice.

"I'm going to be fine. I'm feeling better already," I say, adding a touch of convincing annoyance. I roll my eyes for added effect. Even that small movement makes fingers of pain claw across my scalp. But it works. I watch Miesha's shoulders lower two inches.

"We all need to get out of here while it's still early," Carver says. "Before someone sees us." He looks at Miesha. "It has to do with the Favor and we can't explain. Too much is invested. We can't blow our cover. But before we leave we need to talk to Locke. *In private.*"

Miesha stands her ground and I notice Jenna's back stiffen. It's clear they don't like taking orders in regard to me, but when Xavier steps in and asks them again, Jenna relents and says they'll wait in the next room.

As soon as the door shuts behind them, Carver lays into me. He's livid. Security is crawling all over that park today, he rants, not to mention the whole city, checking IDs on everyone. It's not safe for Non-pacts to be on any street. And even more important, now how am I supposed to go to the Secretary's house tonight? Xavier and Livvy join in, keeping their voices low, but it's still all hushed shouting. Why did I risk it? Why did I go down into the tunnels without telling them? What did I see?

I open my mouth to answer and then stop. Our goals don't exactly coincide anymore. Their goal is strictly Karden and the money. Mine includes Raine.

"I thought I saw LeGru go down there—"

"We already told you LeGru goes down there. That's not news. You—"

"I was curious. I wanted to explore and see what was down there. I won't make that mistake again."

"You're damn right you won't," Carver says, but Xavier just looks at me. He knows I'm lying, knows how I hate the darkness. He knows curiosity had nothing to do with it, but he says nothing, at least for now.

I move on, trying to get all their minds spinning in a different direction. "Raine's group is meeting all week. I'll be fine by tomorrow. I'll only miss one day. Notify the Collective and tell them my mother is sick and I'm playing the devoted son. You can manage a flare-up, can't you Livvy?"

They all see the logic of my solution. There really is no other choice. "By tomorrow?" Carver asks.

I wonder myself at the impossibility, given the damage, but somehow I'll have to make it happen. "Tomorrow," I say firmly.

Livvy says she will take care of notifying the Collective and they plan their exits before it gets any later. Right before they all leave, Xavier pauses at the door. "Just what did you run into down there?"

I see the gruesome images again. Human eyes with no lids, human mouths with no lips, discarded monsters of someone's twisted making, their birthplace a secret lab. Just like mine.

"Half-dogs, just like you thought. That's all," I answer.

Overdrive

Jenna doesn't leave with the others. She sends Miesha to stay at a small apartment she still keeps in the basement of her old brownstone, the upper floors now housing the Clayton Bender Art Gallery. She sends the others, including Livvy, on their way too. There's no arguing with her. She alone has the experience and expertise to get me back on my feet and that's everyone's common goal.

I sleep most of the day, restless sleep at first, haunted by shadowy images of LeGru, packs of creatures in tunnels, even images of Raine, her silhouette teetering on the edge of an endless black abyss, the Secretary behind her edging closer and closer. When I wake with a start, Jenna gives me something to sleep deeply and I finally do.

By late afternoon, I manage to get up and hobble to the mirror. I look at my naked self. Jenna really had her work cut out for her this time. It makes me think of my mother and all the bandaged knees, all the patched-up elbows, the frozen packs of peas on bumps, the sprains, scrapes, and bruises—nearly all of those for my brother. Rarely for me. I didn't take chances like he did. I played it safe. She'd be horrified if she could see me now. I'm not playing it safe anymore.

I step closer to the mirror and notice the healing has already begun, some due to Jenna's skills, some due to the properties of my BioPerfect, always programmed for repair. The surface scratches have already diminished. The dozens of lines crisscrossing my face and chest where the creatures' claws grazed me have gone from thin bloody red lines to pink ones. The gouges and gashes are another matter. The deep gashes on my right cheekbone and over my eye won't be healing overnight. My right arm, the one I used to shield myself that received the brunt of their attacks, feels like lead. Looking at it now, I'm mystified how I held on to that child creature so fiercely. My hip has a massive bandage over the gaping wound where they tore away my flesh. No wonder I feel like I've been hit by a truck.

I gently touch my side, feeling the familiar ache of cracked ribs too. I hit the concrete hard when they pounced on me. The ribs are almost the worst, making it difficult to take deep breaths. How quickly can I make those heal? Last time it took me a week, which is fast, but not fast enough for me now. I concentrate, not knowing how BioPerfect works. Can I will it to work at breakneck speed? If only I had a manual or there were buttons I could push, but it's all a mystery to me. Not unlike my original body.

I look like something out of a horror movie, but I don't regret my decision to follow LeGru. It erased all doubts I had that Karden was alive. I know it's based on nothing but a feeling, but it was so strong I felt like I could touch it. I'm not sure what that even means but I know I have to go back, except next time I'll have to find a way that won't kill me. An exact location is a good start.

I grab the sheet and wrap it around my waist, limp to the bedroom door and open it.

"Yes, Angel, I'll be home as soon as I can. Give Aunt Allys a hug for me. I love you too." I watch her sign off, her eyes lingering on the phone tab.

"Sorry."

Jenna whirls to face me, startled.

"I didn't know who else to call," I say. "I didn't mean for you to come all this way."

"That's what friends are for, right?"

I nod. Friends.

I limp to the closest chair, trying to camouflage my agony with a smile.

"You don't have to fake it with me, Locke."

I forgot she was reading faces long before I ever did. I allow myself to wince as I ease myself into the chair. I sit back carefully. I haven't seen what my back looks like, but by the feel, it probably doesn't look much different than my arm, something like shredded wheat.

Jenna sits on the sofa near me. "Now that you've rested and the others are gone, do you want to finish your story?"

I look at her confused. Did I babble a story while I was unconscious?

"Before passing out you told me he's alive," she says. "I assume you meant Karden. How do you know? Did you see him?"

At the time it seemed so clear. Almost like he was calling out to me. As if he knew I was searching. Even weirder, like our breaths were in sync. With sight and sound stifled in that dark tunnel, it was like I was sensing him in another way, maybe the way I sensed Kara when we were trapped in the dark. But explaining what I don't understand is impossible. I don't have words for what I felt, except for the word my dad laughed at whenever my mom mentioned it. *Intuition.*

I shake my head. "No, I didn't see him, or hear him, or touch him." I adjust my back against the chair. "Maybe I was just caught up in the moment."

"Tell me what happened."

I stare at the floor trying to remember. "Shortly before I was attacked I got this overwhelming sense. I felt close. It was like another part of me took over. Not my eyes. Not my ears. Something else. I was standing there in the darkness and . . ." It's ridiculous, but I say it anyway. "I just *knew*. Not very scientific, is it?"

Locke.

I look up, her silent voice reaching me.

"Lots of things aren't explainable. Yet. That doesn't make them unscientific. I remember before I destroyed the copies of you and Kara, I heard you both calling out to me, begging me to hurry. I didn't understand it, and my father said it was impossible, but it didn't make it any less real."

I remember Gatsbro telling Kara and me the same thing, that it was impossible for our voices to reach through our digital netherworlds to each other. But somehow they did and his denial didn't make it any less true for us.

Jenna leans forward, taking both my hands in hers. "Look what's happened to us, Locke. Our entire brains scanned. *Everything*. Even the farthest corners. Who knows what skills and senses left over from our Neanderthal days have become like a useless appendix because we haven't used them? Maybe some hidden dormant abilities—like a sixth sense—don't know they've been retired and now our Bio Gel has given them a second life." She smiles. "I believe you. Even if it isn't something you can totally understand or rely on, it still isn't something to ignore."

And that's the thing about Jenna.

In all the world she's the only one who understands what I'm going through. She's like me. I look down at her hands, still holding mine. She pulls them away and stands. "And now I need to get you some dinner. My job is to get you back on your feet so I better do it." She pauses halfway to the kitchen. "I'm sorry I yelled at you this morning. You *are* doing something important, Locke. Something that matters, just like you told Miesha. I know that means sometimes there are risks." She goes to the kitchen and I listen to her hum as water runs, cupboards open and close, and dishes rattle.

I'm about to call out to her to see if I can help when my iScroll ripples in my hand. *Come on, Carver, give it a rest for—*

I look at my palm. It isn't Carver.

It's Raine.

Panic hits me. She can't see me like this. But I want to talk to her. I need to, except I don't remember how to accept a call without the vidcast. I take a stab and say, "No video. Accept call." *Come on, Percel, help me out here.*

Raine's image looms in front of me. She looks confused.

"Locke?"

"Raine."

"I can't see you."

Thank you, Percel. "I just got out of the shower. Video's off."

"What's the matter with you?" she asks. "Your voice sounds strange."

Is it the medication Jenna gave me? Or do I simply sound weak? I make an effort to speak slowly and clearly.

"Must be the echo in the bathroom."

"I heard your mother isn't well. Is that why you didn't meet me last night?"

"That's right."

"And you can't come to the meeting tonight either? Is there something I can do?"

"No, it's only one of her bouts. She'll be fine. I need to stay home tonight and help her out but I'll be at tomorrow's meeting."

"I can't wait that long," she says. She's flustered. Her hair is in disarray around her shoulders. Her cheeks flushed. She's someplace dark, maybe a closet?

"Are you all right?" I ask.

"I—" She looks down briefly and then straight into my eyes, and even though I know she can't see them, somehow her gaze finds me and drills into me. "Locke, I'm skipping the meeting tonight and coming to see you instead. I hope that's all right. I need to see—"

"No, Raine. You can't—"

Her image disappears. She's clicked off. Or someone cut her off. I try to call her back but there's no answer. Did her father intercept her? Hap? I try to call again. Again, no answer.

What happened? My mind races with the possibilities. She doesn't even know where I live. Did she mean she would see me at the park? There's no way I can make it there. I barely made it from my bedroom to this chair without collapsing. Maybe if I—

I pull myself up. If I shower. If I get dressed. Maybe I—

I stumble and grab at the back of the chair, feeling woozy. *Do this, Locke. Figure it out.*

I walk with shuffling steps to my bedroom, concentrating on every move, trying to will my ribs and hip into compliance, and when I finally make it to my room, I decide I will have to skip the shower. Dressing will be challenging enough. I'm pulling my pants on when Jenna walks in. "What do you think you're doing?"

"I need to go out."

She laughs. "Look at you. How far do you think you'd get before passing out?"

"I'm feeling better."

"Oh, please." She rolls her eyes. "Whatever it is, it can wait until—"

We hear a knock at the door. My heart goes into overdrive. For once I hope it's Carver and he's pestering me again. But he wouldn't knock. He'd just walk right in.

"That must be Xavier," Jenna says. "I gave him a list of supplies." She's already headed toward the door.

I limp after her. "Jenna, stop. It might be—"

But she's already swinging it open.

Visitors

I watch the sharp intake of Jenna's breath as she looks at Raine. It tells me everything I already suspected. Raine is the mirror image of Karden. Probably all the way down to the obstinate tilt of her head.

"Hello, I'm Raine Branson," she says. "I'm here to see Locke. Is he available?"

Maybe even the timbre and cadence of her voice is the same.

Jenna blinks and takes another deep breath, trying to regain her composure. I wish there had been the time to tell her the truth about who Raine is. I watch Jenna's face, almost seeing the gears of her mind turn as she puts each piece together, and I pray she doesn't blurt out the name Rebecca. She clears her throat. "I'm not sure if—"

"Yes. I'm here." I know I should have ducked back into my bedroom before she saw me. I should have sent her away. I should have at least put on a shirt before I called out. But I didn't. The shakiness of her voice made all the shoulds disappear. I don't understand what Raine does to me—she makes me become someone else—someone who takes chances that I shouldn't. Jenna swings the door wider and Raine sees me standing in the bedroom doorway.

Her lips part and she looks like she's trying to suppress any reaction at all in front of Jenna but then she walks right past her over to me. "My God, Locke, what happened to you?"

"I—" I glance at Jenna, who shrugs and has no words to help me out. "I took a tumble. Down the stairs."

"But all the scratches, the cuts, the . . ."

The gashes. She stares at my bare chest. "There were cats involved. And glass I was carrying. Top of the stairs. It was dark. Late. Three cats I think. Feral." I keep piling on explanations, hoping one of them will stick.

Jenna begins to close the door, and a large golden arm reaches out to stop her. Hap enters the doorway. "You may not shut the door unless Miss Branson is on this side of it with me."

"Sorry," Raine says. "I forgot. May he come in too? I had to bring him."

I look at Hap. He looks at me. At least we have one thing in common—mutual distrust. "Sure," I answer.

Jenna lets Hap pass and she shuts the door. "I'll leave you two to talk. I have some things to take care of in the other room." She pauses as she passes me. "Left out a few details?" she whispers, and then adds, "I won't be far if you need anything." She obviously has her doubts about Hap too.

As soon as Jenna's gone, Raine puts her hand on my chest, touching the small raised lines, and gingerly moves to the thicker more tender ones that Jenna has woven back together.

Her hand drops to her side. "You lied to me."

I can't deny it. I hobble to the sofa and she follows. I've lied to her on so many levels, I don't even know for sure which lie she's talking about. We both sit, though it takes considerably longer for me to ease myself down than it does Raine.

I look back at Hap, who hasn't moved from his post by the door, but whose eyes haven't veered a centimeter from me. He looks like he's ready to finish me off. "What about him?"

She sighs. "Hap, privacy, please. Voices off."

"That's it?"

"It's not really necessary. But yes, that's it."

She waits for an explanation but I'm not sure which one she wants to know. I hate lying to her. Everyone has—for years. I don't want to be like everyone else. I want to be so much more to her. "What do you want to know?" I ask.

"Is it really that hard to figure out? The truth. Your mother wasn't having one of her bouts. You hurt yourself. Why did you make up a story? There's no shame in taking a tumble—unless that's not what really happened." She scrutinizes my chest again. Glass, cats, and stairs? There's suspicion in her eyes.

For her sake, I know I have to make this good, plus I'm not entirely sure Hap isn't listening in. "I did take a tumble, Raine. That's the truth. I was stupid and careless. I'm embarrassed about it. Don't tell anyone. Please." And then I go into a long explanation, pausing at all the right moments, looking away at all the right moments, using all the tricks I learned from Kara about being convincing, telling her how my father ridicules me for being careless, for not paying attention, if he got a whiff from the Collective about me missing meetings and why, well, I didn't want him to know, and neither did my mother, because arguments between us don't go well. They go very badly in fact. My father is strict and expects perfection—one reason my mother and I are both glad to be away from him for a while. I pile lie upon lie until I've painted a mirror image of her relationship with her own father, until her face goes from disturbed to sympathetic, and I hate myself when I'm done.

She reaches out and gently touches my cheek. Tears rim her lower lashes. Her fingers slide down to my lips, where one cut runs deeper than the rest. Her touch is velvet, barely there at all, but it's all I can feel, all I can think about. I don't deserve it, but I want more, more of Raine.

"Would it hurt too much if I sat close to you, Locke? Just for a few minutes?"

I lean back and pull her close, my arm around her so she's tucked in close to my left side, the one with intact ribs. She molds to me, like we've done this a hundred times, no awkward movements, just her and me, staring ahead at nothing at all. She tells me what brought her here in the first place, why she dared to skip tonight's meeting, something she's never done before, knowing the consequences she will have to pay if her father finds out. But as she speaks, I begin to grasp exactly what those consequences are. He was still furious with her about her inappropriate dress at our first meeting, so today he had technicians come. They strapped her down and scanned her, searching for what was wrong with her, trying to find the reasons, the damage, the deficits, anything at all that might explain her unacceptable behavior. And when they were finished, they scanned her again.

He's searching for numbers, Raine. Not damage. He's desperate for the missing half of the bank account numbers. Consequences have nothing to do with it. That's all your scans have ever been about. Nothing you've ever done.

She continues to tell me the details of the humiliating procedure. I wonder what the Secretary thinks, that she could be embedded with a time-sensitive biochip programmed to one day reveal itself? Would Karden have done that to his own baby daughter in the interest of safeguarding eighty billion duros? If he would, he's not a man I want to save. It's hard for me to listen. I want to react. I want to break something. Throw a chair against the wall. Do *something.*

"I cried," she continues. "I said I was sorry. He told me crying was unacceptable. He never has allowed it. Usually, for him, I can become that person he wants me to be, the one detached from my circumstances. After Mother died I tried even harder to be his perfect daughter. Proper. Unaffected. Prepared. The only time I ever strayed from his ideal was when I was alone up on my rooftop, or on one of my nighttime escapades." She lifts her eyes to look into mine. "I was good, Locke. For so long I was good for him. Somehow, it all worked, at least for a while. Now I feel like I'm walking a tightrope between two lives and I'm not sure exactly where I belong. . . ."

She looks at me, waiting, her last words more of a question than a statement.

She wants to know if my world is her world, but I don't know if it can be or if it even should be. I want to tell her that my world is so far from hers. I want to confess that I'm not who or even what she thinks I am—and she isn't who she thinks she is either. Xavier's words tear through me: *What would I be condemning her to? She'd be caught between two worlds, not fitting in anywhere anymore, not to mention what the Secretary might do with her.* What the Secretary might do. It makes my blood run cold. Maybe if I had kept my distance in the first place like I should have . . .

I look at the nugget-head. "Hap, privacy. Close your eyes."

He closes them. *I knew he was still listening.*

But now, being right is not as important as having a private moment with Raine. It's all I can do to keep from pressing my lips to hers. I want to erase the questions I can't answer, the worry, the doubt, but I know a kiss isn't the way to do it. I bring my forehead to hers, my eyes closed, feeling the warmth of her skin, the warmth of her breath on my face. I can't give her the answer she wants. "You have to go," I whisper. "It's not too late to make it to the meeting at Cece's. You can't risk it."

She pulls back to look at me, searching my eyes. "Locke, what are you afraid of? Tell me the truth. I've trusted you. Why can't you trust—"

"You should go, Raine. It's getting late."

"That's *all* you have to say?"

"That's all."

She stares at me, her jaw clenching. It's not the answer she wanted. It's an empty answer that holds no warmth, no future, and especially no trust. "You're right. I should go. I've risked far too much already."

"I'll see you tomorrow night."

"Of course. At the meeting." Her voice is flat.

"Raine, don't tell anyone about my accident. I don't want it to get back to my father."

"Right. The stairs and the cats." She stands, suddenly in a hurry to leave. "I understand too well. I won't say a word."

I stand to walk her out. "No, don't get up," she says. "Don't bother."

"It's no bother, Raine." I grab her hand so she can't leave without me walking her to the door.

Hap is already out and walking down the stairs ahead of her. She pulls her hand away from mine and pauses in the doorway. "It was nice of your mother to let me in. Tell her I said good-bye."

My mother? "Oh. Sure." I realize she means Jenna.

"She's very young looking."

My mind races, wondering how she could mistake Jenna for my mom, but I try to find a reasonable explanation for it. "Yeah, a lot of people say that. She's had some work done."

"I figured as much. But I can tell she's a good mother. I always notice things like that. She has that air about her."

Jenna? A motherly air? "You picked up a lot in just a few seconds."

Her eyes narrow. "Yes. I did."

I watch her walk down the stairway. Hap waits at the bottom watching both of us. When she's halfway down I call to her, "Raine, one other thing—how did you figure out where I live? I never told you."

She answers without looking back. "Hap told me."

Facing Plan B

It's already tomorrow. I watch the dim light that skirts the edges of my window shade grow brighter. I stared at my ceiling for half the night, trying to force my body to heal, trying to make it hurry. It seems like for the past year that's all I've been doing. Trying to hurry.

It's an irony that isn't lost on me. I had too much time for so long, years, decades, even centuries when there was no hurrying, when time crept by so torturously slowly that I begged for an end to it all, and now it seems there's never enough time. Hurry to get away from Gatsbro, hurry to warn Jenna, hurry to find Kara, hurry to live life, hurry to catch up. And now hurry because time is running out.

I roll to my side to get up and wince, my breath caught in my chest. I push up with my left arm, because my right is still too weak to use. I shuffle to the mirror. The outside is looking better, but the inside still feels like hell. *Hurry.* I hobble out to the kitchen, my bones and muscles feeling stiffer than the day before. Am I getting worse?

Jenna is surprised to see me up so early. She's even more

surprised when I pour myself a cup of coffee. "Lots of changes in just a short time," she says.

I try to straighten out my right arm. "Too many changes."

We ease into the morning slowly and once I've finished my first cup of coffee I begin telling her about Raine, explaining how I found out who she really is, and the kind of life she lives now with the Secretary.

"And she has no idea who her real parents are?"

"None. All she knows is that the Secretary saved her from some unknown Non-pacts who threw her in the trash."

"And no idea who you are either."

I shake my head.

Jenna sighs. "Poor girl. And I thought my life was a mess when I was her age."

"She thought you were my mother. Can you believe that? She said you had a motherly 'air' about you."

"Locke, I *do* have a motherly air. I'm a mother, after all."

"I don't see any air."

"Maybe that's because you're not looking."

She leaves to get the salves that Xavier brought during the night and begins preparing them at the kitchen counter. Whatever she used on me last time worked like a miracle, and I remember how Kara's bloody blisters disappeared almost overnight. She dabs it on my lip and face and then changes the bandages, noting how much I've healed on the outside already. "Your BioPerfect is definitely more advanced than any Bio Gel I've ever seen. Some of the smaller cuts are already gone. But this might speed the others along."

"What about the inside?"

"I can give you some pain meds, but your BioPerfect is on its own there as far as healing goes. Concentrate, Locke. It's all connected, your thoughts, the biochips, and everything you want them to do. Put them on speed dial."

I grin. Only Jenna would know that obsolete phrase. "Even the ribs?"

"Bioengineered with the blue goo?"

I nod.

"Then even the ribs."

I spend the next couple of hours concentrating as Jenna suggested, and while I think I might be seeing some improvement, it's still not fast enough. I promised everyone, including Raine, I'd be able to go to the meeting tonight.

By nine A.M. Livvy arrives, and a few minutes later, Carver and Xavier show up, both dressed in building maintenance uniforms. How many different kinds of uniforms do they have stashed away? They all acknowledge that I'm looking better, but when they watch me hobble from the kitchen into the other room like an old man, I see their faces drop.

"How are you possibly going to be able to go by tonight?" Livvy asks.

I have no idea, but I don't see that I have any other choice. "I will," I answer.

Carver lowers his shaking head into his hands. "This isn't going to work."

"We need to put it off another day," Xavier says.

Carver looks up. "We can't! We're running out of time! We've got less than a week before the money's gone forever and we still have no clue where Karden is!"

"Yes we do," I say.

They stare at me, their attention focused. "On the old west-bound track, about a hundred yards in, there's another tunnel, one of those unofficial tunnels that doesn't show up on any maps. There's probably hundreds of them down there but I had a feeling about that one and I went down it. I had only gone another thirty yards or so when I sensed something."

"Sensed what?" Livvy asks.

"Karden."

"What? Did you see or hear him?"

I shake my head. "No, no, I just sensed him. I knew I was close. He was there, somewhere. I know it."

Carver jumps up. *"Sensed? Somewhere?"* He throws his hands up in the air. "Is this what we brought you in for? So you could guess?"

Xavier stands too, shaking his head, rubbing his hand across his scarred cheek. "We need to rethink this."

"You're damn right we do. Maybe it's time to go to Plan B. He still has an in with Raine. All he has to do is lure her away from that big ugly chunk of metal that's always by her side, just long enough so we can grab her and then use her as a bargaining chip."

Lure? No. We can't go to Plan B. That one's no longer an option for me. "Wait. You're jumping to—"

"No. You wait." Carver points his finger dangerously close to my face. "The clock is ticking. A minute after the money's gone, Karden's a dead man."

Livvy nods in agreement.

"He's right," Xavier says. "We need to move on to—"

Jenna, who has remained quiet until now, steps forward. "You're all assuming that Locke won't be able to do what he says he'll do. He knows the situation with Raine and the Secretary better than anyone right now. Would it really be wise to prematurely abandon one plan in favor of another that has no guarantee of working either?"

They still aren't convinced. "Look at him," Carver says. "He can barely walk."

I stand. "I said I'd do it. I will. I get a little bit more information each day." I tell them about reading LeGru's lips and his going down there that night to prepare someone for scanning, and the faint red light that I saw in the distance, and the hum I heard.

"Why didn't you tell us about that before?"

"I'm telling you now."

Carver walks around the room rubbing the back of his neck like I'm directly causing a huge pain in it. He whirls to face me. "The end of the week. That's it. Three days. If you don't have a location by then, we go to Plan B." He heads for the door and then turns. "And that's assuming you pull it together by tonight and make it to the meeting. Those little *bits* you mentioned need to add up to something big *soon.*"

He leaves, his words *bits* and *soon* still hanging in the air. The room is quiet. Livvy sighs and goes to the kitchen looking for coffee. Like me, she didn't sleep much last night. Is she lying awake at night seeing the likelihood of her children becoming sixth-generation Non-pacts?

Xavier clears his throat. "Do you mind?" he says to Jenna.

She pauses, studying Xavier for several uncomfortable seconds, and finally stands, turning to me. "We should change your bandages and reapply the salve in another hour. I'm going into the other room to call Allys and Kayla, and maybe get some rest."

I nod and for the first time notice that Jenna's probably as tired as any of us. I wonder if she's slept at all in the past twenty-four hours.

She leaves but Xavier remains quiet.

"Go ahead," I say. "Get it out. Everyone else has."

He leans forward, his arms resting on his knees. "Just one question."

One question. But not *just*. "Okay."

"Why did you go? You were only supposed to get the location. You knew it was me who was supposed to go down into the tunnel."

"Sometimes plans change. The unexpected happens."

He stands and crosses the room, tilting the shutter blade to look out. "Yes, I suppose it does." He looks back at me and finally smirks.

"And?"

"The first time I met you I thought would be my last. We get a lot of violators trying to Escape. You and that girl were no different. We give Escapees new IDs and send them on their way. Most I never see again. I like to think they make it somewhere but I never know for sure. I always tell them we don't take repeats to scare them. I want them to try with everything they've got because this isn't a place with a lot of second chances. Not even firsts."

"Are you saying I've used up all my chances?"

"Not even close, kid. Just a simple statement. I never expected to see you again. I never expected that you'd be the one we'd ask to help us. I never expected that you and Raine—" He stops and snatches his maintenance hat from the table as he walks toward the door. "Let's just say, the next time the unexpected happens, call me. We're all running out of chances."

Needing to Know

Jenna and Livvy work with me throughout the day, walking me, giving me time to rest, helping me practice going up and down the stairs, and of course, changing bandages. The oozing has mostly stopped thanks to Jenna's skill, but more so than blood, there are still traces of the bright blue BioPerfect on the white bandage on my hip. Livvy tries not to act surprised but I see it in her eyes every time Jenna removes the bandage—blue evidence that I'm not one of them, but it doesn't slow her down in helping me to move from one end of the apartment to the other.

As I try to walk without limping I remember how I was so cocky at Raine's apartment that night—deftly slipping out of the room, sliding down the rope, learning the Secretary's and LeGru's secret plans, even heading off Hap with my smart-aleck cockroach excuse—and then heading down into the tunnels. *Don't let the enemy push you before you're ready.* But I'm not sure who was doing the pushing. I guess for that night at least, I did think I was immortal.

"Don't hunch," Livvy says. "Stand tall. It will help your ribs."

I'm not feeling immortal now.

By afternoon Jenna has reapplied the salve four times. That and my BioPerfect are working. Clothing will cover most of my wounds and Jenna says she can cover the fainter ones on my face and hands with skin paint, which is like makeup, but a couple of deep gashes on my right hand and the gash on my lip and cheekbone will still show.

"You'll have to make an excuse for those—or put off going for another day."

I shake my head. "I'll make an excuse."

"A better one than cats and stairs, I hope," she says, rolling her eyes.

Livvy raises her brows.

"Why don't you go home, Livvy," I say. "I'm doing better and I still have four hours before I have to go." I lift my arms and smile, trying to convince myself as much as her. "Look at my progress. And Jenna's here if anything comes up."

Livvy hesitates but leaves, glad to be on her way home to her family. When she's gone Jenna goes into the kitchen to check in with Allys and Kayla again and I go my room to—

I told Jenna I wanted to rest, and I'm lying on my bed so I suppose I am, but really I just needed to be alone. I close my eyes.

Cats and stairs.

And then the long convoluted story I told to go with it.

How stupid could I be to think she bought it? She was only waiting for me to come clean. She gave me trust but I couldn't give it back. How many notches have I slipped on her trust meter? But if I tell her about going into the tunnel, I have to tell her everything. She hasn't called again, and I hope the Secretary isn't putting her through another one of those scans. She described them as humiliating, but not as painful. How desperate could the Secretary be to get those numbers? If I had them I would give them to him just to make him stop. My head hurts thinking of all the possibilities—a good old-fashioned headache.

I try to put Raine out of my mind, concentrating on my hip, my back, my arm, trying to hurry the way Carver wants me to. Only a few days before the *bits* have to become something big. But every thought about the Favor and trying to figure it out drifts eventually back to Raine. And then, Shane. No doubt he was glad I wasn't at last night's meeting. Was he hovering over Raine? Letting his arm slip to her shoulder. Sliding his hand along her back. . . .

I sit up. I can't let myself do this. She asked me last night if my world was her world. I couldn't give her an answer then and I still can't. *Focus on the goal, Locke.* That's what I came here for. Not to—

Her expression flashes through my mind again, the way she looked just before she left last night. Retreating. Going back to the old Raine. The protective one. The one who keeps her distance. She didn't even turn to look at me when she answered my last question.

Hap told me. I've thought about her answer over and over again. How did Hap know? Does he simply have access to the Virtual Collective's files? Or has he been checking on me? Maybe on the Secretary's orders? Is he just waiting for the chance to get me alone and finish the job he started on my throat the first time he met me? I get the feeling he has the memory of an elephant.

186   I walk out to the nook in the living room where V-files and the

old crumbling paper plans are kept. I review them again, trying to see if there's anything I missed, but I have them nearly memorized now. The one file that is conspicuously absent is Karden's. No file at all in spite of him being what this is all about. I guess understanding him isn't as important as finding him, but I have to wonder how someone smart enough to orchestrate such a perfect heist had his plan explode into a full-blown disaster at the end, his wife sent to prison, his baby daughter stolen, and the money lost because of missing bank account numbers. He split up the numbers, which seems like a reasonable precaution with so much at stake, but he claimed he had sent the other half. If he did, what happened to them? Miesha said she had only been gone to the market a short time when she came back to the burning house. How did Security Forces even know Karden was there? I look at the note window that Carver wrote out for me the first night I met him.

$$797213672084$$

Twelve worthless numbers. Nothing to indicate even which country they might belong to, and there are thousands now. Just like the United States, other countries have split into factions. North and South Italy. Eastern and Western France. And at least a dozen new countries from China alone. Any of these countries would be happy to absorb eighty billion duros, and in a matter of days, they will.

I find myself back at Raine's file. The information contained in it is all useless to me now. I know the real Raine. I think I might be the only person who does.

"Your resting didn't last long."

I look up, startled. Jenna's been watching me from just a few feet away. Raine's face looms in the air between us. I quickly close her file. "I've rested long enough."

She tells me it's time to change my bandages again, and she reapplies the salve. Her fingers are gentle and she says I'm healing well but she's still concerned about a few of the deeper gashes. Even bioengineered skin can't be overstressed too soon. "It will tear open just like regular skin. No excessive movement or lifting for a few days."

"And I was just ready to go volunteer down at the docks."

She smiles and puts her supplies away. "I can't stay long, Locke. A week, maybe two at the most. The weather will be turning soon."

I look at her, realizing I had nearly forgotten about her first-generation Bio Gel and its limitations, but I'm overwhelmed by the thought of her leaving too. It's comforting having her close. Someone familiar. More than familiar. She's a piece of my past—and I had always hoped, my future. When I left California, that's what I held on to. That one day, after I had lived life the way she asked me to, I'd return. Jenna and I have history together. She's someone who knows everything about my past, including all of my mistakes, and still cares about me anyway. I get up from behind the desk. "Jenna, I'm sorry. I would never take a chance with your life. You know how much I care about you. I just didn't think when I—"

She puts her hands up to stop my apology. "Locke, I'm fine, but I can't take a chance on getting caught here in a freak early freeze. They still can't predict these things precisely—the weather can have a mind of its own. And Kayla does need me, but for another week or two I'll be all right." Her sky blue eyes fix on mine for a few seconds before she turns and goes into the kitchen, and I feel a strange twist in my gut. It had always been Jenna I loved. It was Jenna I was trying to hurry and live for, to catch up to her three lifetimes.

I walk to the kitchen doorway and watch her. She rinses a few dishes by hand, out of habit I suppose. Some things from our past we just can't leave behind. Her hair is still the beautiful silky blond it always was, still seventeen on the outside, even though there are lifetimes hiding on the inside. She's still the Jenna I always loved.

I walk up behind her and touch her arm. She turns to look at me. She would never let me kiss her before. Will she now?

"Jenna . . ."

She looks at me, confused. "What is it, Locke?"

I step closer to her, looking at her face, her eyes, her lips, all the memories of Jenna that I held on to when I was trapped in that hopeless world for so many years. For decades. Every eyelash that I counted to keep from going insane. Her hands, the slant of her nose, the way her hair fell across her shoulders, the glimmer of each blond strand in my imagined sunlight, the sound of her voice, every ripple of laughter I ever remembered played over and over again to mask the screams of Kara. Every memory of Jenna that helped keep me alive.

"I have to know, Jenna. Once and for all."

She exhales a slow deep breath. "Yes, I think you probably do." She reaches up and touches my cheek, pulling me closer, kissing me. Her lips linger on mine. I feel their softness, her tenderness, her warmth.

Slowly, I pull my lips away from hers.

Jenna.

But the reality isn't the same as the dream. It's different now. She's not the same girl I knew. I hear her words again . . . *None of us are who we once were.* How is it that she knew this all along, but I didn't? I do love her, but not in the way I thought I did. Not in the way I had always imagined. Our lives race past me. All the times before. All the times with Kara when we were three. *We held hands. We crossed a line. We made one another braver.* All the things that Jenna meant to me at a certain time in my life.

I search her face, not knowing what to say. "I—"

"I know. I love you too, Locke. There's a bond between us that won't ever be broken. But I don't love you in the same way I loved Ethan." She squeezes my hand. "And you don't love me in the same way that you love Raine."

I close my eyes. Hearing her say it out loud unhinges something inside of me I had locked away. I was afraid to even think it or believe it, much less say it. I have nothing to offer Raine. No life. Not even—

I blink, not sure I can even say it now. "Raine's not like me. She's different."

Jenna shakes her head, biting the corner of her lip. She knows exactly what I'm talking about. "There's nothing wrong with different, Locke. Get over your BioPerfect. Get over the technology. *Get over it.* Focus on what you have. She's like you in the ways that *matter.*"

I see Raine's eyes, glistening, looking into mine, wondering if my world could be her world. I remember the ache of wanting it to be so but saying nothing, hurting her, pushing her away with my silence.

The way I love Raine.

I need to tell her.

True Character

Wispy clouds cross the moon, thick cottony threads trying to become more, a new season trying to make its way into Boston. How many times did I ignore these subtle clues when I lived here before?

Raine is like me in the ways that matter. I learned that detail by detail, night after night, hour after hour, as one conversation rolled into the next, as time got away from us because we always had more to say. The devil isn't in the details. Raine is. She's every detail that inhabits my waking hours, and my sleeping hours too. Every step, thought, and breath of my day leads back to her.

As I pass the park, it's quiet. Whatever Security Forces crawled through it yesterday are gone now, and any evidence they found was packed up with them. How much of my BioPerfect did they scrape up from the ground in the park? How much did I leave behind, dripped in a blue trail through the tunnels?

I'm making it, step by step, block by block, standing straight, not hunched, counting my breaths until I see Raine. My hair is perfectly tousled over my eye to cover a cut that the paint wouldn't, my clothing loose and baggy to cover bandages, no excuse in mind yet for the gashes on my lip and cheekbone that still show. But none of that really matters to me now as much as seeing Raine and telling her the things I should have said before.

I'm early. A full forty minutes early. If the Secretary wants to haul me off to his office for another impromptu grilling session, I want to make sure there's still time to talk alone with Raine before the others come.

This time when I step out of the elevator, I'm greeted by Raine.

She looks at my face and then down at my hands, registering how much I've healed in just one day. I see the distance in her eyes. She wants to ask about my rapid recovery but then that would mean she cares. She's still angry. "Why are you here so early?" she asks instead. "I haven't even—"

I kiss her. She hesitates for only a second. "Someone might see—" but then her fingers are sliding along my chest, wrapping around my neck, sliding behind my head, through my hair, pulling me close. My hands gently cup her face, *Raine,* pulling her closer, sorry that I ever pushed her away, but finally that's what I have to do again, and I pull back. She takes a deep breath, her cheeks flushed.

"Raine, I have to talk to you. About last night. Is there somewhere we—"

"Not now. I have to get ready first. If my father sees me like this when everyone arrives, I'm not sure what will happen."

Her hair is loose, falling across her shoulders. She wears a thin loose-fitting white shirt with the sleeves rolled up and smudged pants like she just came from her rooftop garden.

"Give me twenty minutes," she says. "I have to shower and change." She walks away and then turns, looking at me sternly. "We won't have long. Make sure you have something to say this time."

I nod. Maybe I've only slipped to an eight on the trust meter.

She disappears down the hallway and I step into the living room to wait. It's less painful to stand than to ease myself in and out of chairs so I walk around the room, examining the artifacts the Secretary has collected. Maybe as I wait I'll come across one of those bits that Carver has instructed me to find fast, but it mostly looks like expensive things a designer has collected for him. Items are artfully arranged on shelves and in nooks, a Chinese vase, silver filigreed masks, an antique tortoiseshell letter opener, things with no personal connection other than being suited to his tastes like the antique sword hanging behind his desk.

In the far corner, on a shelf almost out of view, I find three beautiful leather-bound volumes that look like antiques too, but when I pull them out I see they're photo albums, not casual snapshots but professional photos taken for special occasions. Something personal at last. The first album has pictures of Raine as a toddler. The first photo is one of Raine dressed in a matching red dress and hat, held in the arms of a woman with auburn hair and a beaming smile. Raine's other mother. I turn the pages, one after another, some with Raine alone, many with her mother, but only one with the Secretary present. *He never did know what to do with me.* And yet, he saves these pictures.

I look at the next album, Raine as an older child, five, six, seven . . . always smiling with her mother. At least she had that much, an adoptive mother who cared about her. Was this woman really unaware of how the Secretary obtained Raine, or was she so desperate for a child that she didn't care? And finally the last album, beginning at about age twelve, only a quarter filled, probably because her mother died. The last picture is of the whole family, her mother, gaunt with a weak smile, Raine with a brave one, and the Secretary not looking directly at the camera but instead gazing somberly down at his wife and Raine. Worry or burden? Was he already wondering what to do with Raine once his wife was gone? Keep her or give her away?

"The Secretary doesn't like those to be viewed."

I glance over my shoulder to see Hap setting a tray of tea on a table. I flip another page. "Then why does he keep them?"

"I don't know," he says. "But before he returns home, I would advise you to put them back where you found them."

I turn around. "The Secretary isn't here?"

"There was a security breach two nights ago. His duties have required additional attention. But he's due back later this evening." A security breach? Just at the same time I went down into the tunnels? Since when did his duties include securing supposedly abandoned tunnels? This only confirms that the tunnels are home to more than half-dogs.

I place the albums back to where I found them. "Thanks for the tip." If there was ever a time I needed to butter up nugget-head this is it. "And thanks for the tea too. I don't need anything else. You can go."

He doesn't move.

"I won't touch any more albums if you're worried," I add.

"I'm not worried. For an Eater and Breather, you appear to be a fast learner."

Eater and Breather?

Besides Dot, I've never heard another Bot use that term. Dot used it in a soft, endearing way. Hap uses it with utter contempt. I know Raine is his priority, even above the Secretary. Is that what this is all about? He resents me and the way I've wormed my way into her life? He must have been aware of every single night she went down the rope ladder to be with me. He used to be her lone confidante. Now she has another.

I take a step closer to him. "I'm not trying to replace you, Hap."

"And that would be quite impossible, considering your abundant limitations."

I grin. "I'll remember that."

For the first time I see the expression on his nugget-head change, his eyes narrowing like a cat that's come to an understanding with a mouse, the closest thing I've seen to satisfaction on his face. He nods.

"Dorian has the night off," he says. "So I'll excuse myself now to finish preparing tonight's refreshments."

As soon as he leaves, I waste no time heading down to the lower level. How long do I have before Raine returns? Ten minutes? Fifteen?

The Secretary's office is in disarray, as though he left in a rush. Drawers and files are open. A half-finished drink still sits on his desk. His haste could be my gold mine. I race through the open files first, but there are only four memos that all seem to be standard bureaucratic transmittals. Trying to open up something else could be tricky, perhaps sending the whole system crashing, or setting off alarms if I touch the wrong file. Instead, I look through the drawers. Paper trails are rare these days, paper itself seldom used except for certain types of documents, and the only paper I find of consequence is a small handwritten note on a torn scrap of paper, yellow and brittle with age, that shows an address:

1407 Bridgemont, Cambridge

I compare it to notes on the Secretary's desk where he jotted down some random tasks, including an appointment at 7:00 with 195

LeGru. The handwriting doesn't match. He didn't write this note. I commit it to memory and put it back just as I found it, tucked in a corner of a lower drawer. I return to the files. I'll have to take a chance and hope I don't freeze or crash the whole system as I try to open additional files. My finger hovers over three possible folders identified with icons, no names. I briefly close my eyes. *Concentrate, Locke, which one?* I open my eyes and touch the one with a red triangle and hold my breath. A hundred subfolders spring into the air in front of me. *A hundred.* My eyes scan across them, bare titles that give little clue as to what's inside. There isn't time to hunt and peck. I zip my finger across the whole first row. A hundred more files fly into the air, the room a virtual littered mess of folders and files.

Time ticks wildly in my head. Seconds count. I scan as fast as I can and I'm almost to the end of the bottom row when I spot something. Blueprints for a lighting grid. I press it and a dozen more files open. Immediately I recognize the Old Library Building, but then something far more interesting—

"What are you doing?"

I look up. Raine is in the doorway.

What can I possibly say? I'm lost? Curious? I just stand there and she steps closer, her expression incredulous. *"What are you doing?"* she repeats.

"Raine, please, I can't explain right now. Keep your voice down. I just need another minute to—"

She comes at me, screaming, *"This* is what you had to tell me? You were going to snoop through my father's files? I can't believe this! Get out! *Get out!"* She swipes at the open folders and I grab her by the wrist.

"I know this doesn't look—"

"You're nothing more than a spy! That's all you ever were! Exactly what he warned me about! I was only a way for you to get to my father!" She reaches out with her other hand for the files but I pin her to my side.

"Please, Raine," I whisper into her ear. "I need this information. You have to trust me."

"Trust you? You've never done anything but lie to me! Let go! Let go of me right now!"

I miss half of everything else she's yelling as I try to maintain my grip on her with my injured arm and read the file that I need. Arlington station—a lighting grid, two pressure points, another grid down the main tunnel—

She stomps on my foot. Her elbow finds my already cracked ribs. I let go, bending over the desk trying to breathe. She jumps away from me and spins, a river of anger and hatred spewing from her mouth.

"It all adds up now! Your sudden entrance into the Collective, all the questions about my father, the—" Her eyes widen impossibly larger. "Oh my God. That little Non-pact girl. She knew your name because you're one of *them*." She steps back like the thought horrifies her and she shakes her head. "I *trusted* you. I gave you—"

She turns and runs out of the room.

I close all the files in one sweep and run after her, catching her midway on the stairs. I grab her hand from behind. "You have to listen to me, Raine! You owe me that much! I—"

"I owe you nothing! Now get out! Get out of my house and get out of my—"

"What's this?"

We both stop and look up. At the top of the stairs a crowd has gathered. Shane, Vina, Cece, Ian, Hap—and the Secretary.

Raine yanks her hand away from mine and continues up the last few steps. I follow her. The group ambles around us silently, the Secretary's eyebrows still raised waiting for an explanation. Neither of us speaks, so he does. "It seems that my daughter is throwing you out of our house," he says. He reaches out and pulls Raine to his side. I watch her stiffen under his touch. He never takes his eyes off me, zooming in on my gashed lip and cheekbone. "Was he inappropriate with you, my dear?"

Raine stares at me, her eyes large black pools, frightened and filled with fury all at once. *Please don't say it, Raine. If you mention the word* spy, *I'm a dead man.* She breaks her gaze with mine and looks down. "I don't want to talk about it," she whispers. "I just want him to leave."

The Secretary nods. "I understand. You're upset. We'll discuss this matter later in private."

"I'll throw him out. I'd be happy to," Shane says, taking a step toward me.

"I wouldn't," I tell him.

Shane stops. I don't know if it's the sound of my voice or my eyes drilling into him, but for once he makes a wise choice. He holds back. Vina, Ian, and Cece all stare, speechless, still trying to understand what just happened in the space of a few minutes.

"No need, Shane," the Secretary says. "I think my daughter has quite capably handled Mr. Jenkins already. Her message is clear enough. I'll walk him out."

I look at Raine one last time. She turns away and refuses to meet my gaze. I walk to the foyer, the Secretary following behind me. The elevator doors open and I step inside. I turn to face him. His smug smile returns and he touches his cheekbone in the same place where I have the deep gash on mine. I see his gears turning, wondering where I got it. "There was always something about you I found unsettling." His hand drops to his side. "I suppose one's true character is impossible to hide for long."

I look at him, returning his smug smile with one of my own. "And sometimes it's impossible to hide it at all," I answer, and the elevator doors close between us.

In the Tower

I return home and tell Jenna to go to the art gallery and stay with Miesha. *Now.* It's not safe for her to stay here anymore. As I expected, she argues the point with me, but I argue louder telling her this is my Favor, not hers, and she has to trust me. She must sense my desperation, and she leaves, with the caveat that if I don't check in with her she'd be back. As soon as she's gone I pack up all evidence of plans and the Network and destroy them. If it's not in my head, it's gone.

My arm and hip scream with pain. Holding back Raine from the files and then running after her took its toll. *Dammit! Hurry!* "I don't have time for this healing stuff!"

I check my bandages. The wound on my hip has torn, just as Jenna warned, and BioPerfect oozes from it again. I rummage through her supplies and find the tool that punctures and weaves the skin back together. I can't use anesthesia. I sit down on my bed and turn the tool on and then press it to the torn part of my wound. It penetrates my skin and I grit my teeth to keep from screaming. Sweat pours down my face, trickling down my neck. The only thing more painful than a half-human ripping your flesh apart is a laser needle weaving it back together. My hand shakes, and with every burning pulse, color explodes behind my eyes, blacking out the room, but I keep the tool in place until it signals that the job is complete. The tool drops from my hand to the floor and I fall back on the bed. I don't look to see if I did as good of a job as Jenna. I know I didn't. Just so it's closed, that's all that matters.

I wake with a start to find that I've slept for two hours. I listen for noise in the apartment, an intruder, but the only sound is the whir of an occasional car passing on the street. I pull myself up, leaving all the lights off, and go to the kitchen to look out the window, which has a better view of the parkway. Nothing.

The meeting must be over by now. I see Raine's face again, the shock and betrayal.

I close my eyes and brace myself against the kitchen counter taking several slow deep breaths. If only I had told her the truth sooner. Maybe then there would have been a chance. But by the time I admitted to myself that I loved her I had already lied myself into a corner.

We'll discuss this matter later.

Is the Secretary grilling her now? Is she telling him what she saw? How much longer before there's a knock on my door? Or maybe they'll just burn me out the way they did Karden.

My palm ripples. I jerk my hand up and check my iScroll, praying it's Raine, but it's only Carver. "Off!" I yell.

Percel appears. "It's an emergency, sir. I'm told to alert you at all costs."

"It's always an emergency with Carver," I shout. "I said *off!*" I can't recount the details of tonight's meeting with him right now. There are too many other things I need to do. I need to check the apartment for any lasting evidence in case someone comes. I need time to think. I need—

The Commons is quiet. Deathly quiet. Not even the smallest rustling of animals in the bushes. Is it the chill in the air, or something else? I don't sit on our usual tree. I hide in the shadows, afraid if she sees me she won't come down, but she doesn't come anyway. I wait hour after hour. The clouds thicken, weaving together until they block out the moon, and somehow that makes the silence even heavier.

Finally, near three in the morning she appears, a dark blanket wrapped around her shoulders so she's barely visible. She walks the length of the rooftop, maybe the only place where she still feels in control. She leans against the roof wall, looking out, not searching down below for me, but just staring out past the treetops, probably staring at nothing at all. Is she retracing every moment we spent together, imagining that it was all lies? It wasn't. She has to know that. What we shared . . .

I step out of the shadows.

I don't have much more to lose, and I walk to the clearing so I'm in plain view if she would only look down. She finally does, like she senses she's being watched.

She looks at me, and even from nine stories below and in the dark, I can see enough of her face to know the old Raine has returned. She has nothing for me. The blanket slips from her shoulders, forgotten, and she walks away, disappearing back into her father's domain.

Wreckage

There are still no knocks on my door. No fires to burn me out.

She didn't tell him. Yet.

But even not telling won't save me for long. It doesn't matter that I'm out of the Collective, and his daughter's life. I have no doubt the Secretary's still digging and has probably doubled his efforts to search my past. He spent far too long scrutinizing the injuries on my face, perhaps trying to match it up with the injuries a half-human might inflict. What throws him off, maybe even makes him lazy, is my age, my stature, my education, and my supposedly rich parents. I don't fit his profile of a Non-pact with an ulterior motive. In that respect, the Network knew exactly what they were doing in choosing me and creating my background. In the Secretary's mind I'm too much like the other kids in the Collective to be one of those animals he despises.

I'm out of the apartment early, taking the PAT to Cambridge. My three hours of sleep were short but determined. With the deadline looming and Carver itching to go to Plan B, there's no time to waste.

I didn't spend much time in Cambridge when I used to live here. I remember going to some bookshops with Jenna and Kara, looking for old volumes of poetry, and then hanging out at some outdoor cafés, sipping lattes and trying to outquote one another, but we never really ventured past the main streets.

Percel walks me through a maze of alleys and streets. He has no information about 1407 Bridgemont. No visuals, no history, only directions, but with privacy laws he says there's an opt-out provision so it's not unusual for this information to be unavailable. I remember Jenna telling me about the privacy laws . . . *the beginning of the personal privacy era . . . other than public space IDs, all personal tracking information and devices were outlawed.*

That must have really put a damper on the Secretary's extra-curricular activities.

"Left at the next corner," Percel tells me.

The street I'm on is like one from another time. My time. Quiet, lined with trees that are beginning to drop yellow leaves on streets that are cobbled. A market on the corner doesn't look that much different from the one my mother used to work at, small, with specials handwritten on placards in the window and silver pails filled with bunches of flowers near the entrance. I pause before I turn left, looking at the various bunches. Mums. Roses. Lilies. Lots of others I don't even know the names for. I wonder what kind Raine—

Roses maybe. But I'll probably never know.

"Left here," Percel reminds me.

I turn onto a long narrow street, one residence butted up to the next with an occasional business wedged between. There's nothing remarkable about the street other than it's quiet and pleasant. I begin to look at numbers from force of habit even though Percel has already informed me I have another twenty meters to go.

1401, 1403, 1405, and then nothing.

Between a two-story brownstone at 1405 and a one-story haber-dashery at 1409 is an empty lot. Nothing more than gravel and a few weeds. I look down to the corner to make sure we're on the right street but Percel assures me that the empty lot is 1407 Bridgemont.

I walk up the porch steps to the haberdashery next door and go inside, a bell on the door alerting them to my presence. They've really gone for the full quaint effect. A Bot who is cleverly made up as an old wicker dress form brings me back to the reality of where I am. I ask her about the lot next door.

"Not for sale as far as I know. It's been empty for years now."

"You mean it used to have something on it?"

She pulls back the black netting on her felt hat. "Yes. A home. It burned to the ground sixteen years ago during a raid. Two humans died." She tries to interest me in fabrics that would com-plement my eyes, but I'm already walking out, the tinkling bell and slamming door echoing with all the other thoughts swirling through my head.

Miesha and Karden's home. The Secretary had their address and has saved it all these years. It didn't come through an intelligence report, or through other official avenues. He got their address by way of a small handwritten note. A note that had no other identi-fying information on it. An anonymous note.

I'm just turning down the street to the apartment when Xavier intercepts me. I can't tell if he's angry or relieved but his expres-sion is wild. "Where have you been?"

"What's wrong?" I ask.

"It's Livvy. She's gone."

"What do you mean *gone?*"

He steps closer, lowering his voice. "There was a Security sweep last night. Carver tried to call you but couldn't get through. Security Forces went through Livvy's neighborhood grabbing anyone on the street. They got her and six others."

"But why? She wasn't even in public space."

Xavier's voice shakes as he explains that sometimes it doesn't matter. Sometimes they just want to send a warning message. Is it lawful? No. But who are Non-pacts going to complain to? Security?

I lean back against a gatepost, dazed, trying to make sense of it. "Is this because of me going down into the green tunnel?"

He says that may have triggered it, but that it's not the first time it's happened and it won't be the last. They do it periodically just to demonstrate that they're in charge. "And with the deadline drawing so near, the Secretary is probably breathing down the necks of every man on the Security Force. It's all about pecking order, and we're on the bottom."

"How long will they keep her?"

Xavier shakes his head, looking down at his feet, a mountain of restraint heaving in his chest. "They might let her go. The scare of the raid might be warning enough. Or she might already be on her way to the desert."

I can barely think, picturing Livvy and . . . "She's got kids," I whisper.

"You think I don't know she's got kids?" he hisses. "But she's already been tagged twice, if they count this as the third . . ."

Three strikes and you're out. Tagged like a dog. I search for the same restraint Xavier is able to dredge up on cue. "We'll get her back," I tell him. "Some way."

Xavier pushes his face within inches of mine. *"Stay the course,"* he says in a slow growl. "Her kids are who Livvy is doing this for. *Now*'s not the time to do something impulsive."

Like I did when I went down into the tunnel. He doesn't have to say it. I still hear him loud and clear. But sometimes staying the course can mean maintaining the status quo too, and look where that's gotten them. Nowhere.

I try to walk around him but he sidesteps in front of me. His eyes have gone from troubled to sympathetic. It makes my stomach tighten. "There's something else," he says.

He sighs, only making my gut squeeze tighter. "This probably isn't the best time to tell you this, but we gave you our word. We have some news about Manchester."

I thought they forgot about that. I had almost forgotten myself. "Did you find something?"

He nods. "They got into the labs. They had to burn the whole place down to cover their tracks, but they found something."

I close my eyes. I know what the something is. I'm not sure I can take any more bad news right now, not one more complication. "Are they bringing it to me?"

"It's here. Right now." He tilts his head gesturing behind him. "Over there."

A beat-up plumber's truck is parked outside the apartment. Jake stands next to it. I take a couple of deep breaths. *Hold it together, Locke.* "Have him bring it up."

"He can't." Xavier signals him and Jake rolls up the back door of the truck.

I'm not sure how long I stand there before I start hearing again; how long before I start seeing again. Xavier grabs my injured arm where a deep wound is still healing and the shooting pain brings me back to the present.

"They're labeled with two names," he says. "Kara Manning and Locke Jenkins. About a hundred of each."

Row after row of six-inch cubes all attached to battery docks, like houses on a city block. A whole city of nothing but Kara and myself.

"What should we do with them?"

A hundred possible Karas. Maybe one who is whole, or maybe a hundred who are the wreckage of an experiment gone wrong. A hundred Lockes, each one still trapped in a world of endless black corridors that have no beginnings or endings, still begging for a way out. A hundred Lockes listening to the tortured screams of Kara. But maybe one Locke who is more than me. Better than me. A whole city of uploaded minds—*spares*—that might have been forgotten for another two centuries on a storage shelf, or used as floor models all over the world. Hari still had dollar signs in his eyes even after Gatsbro's death.

"What do you want us to do with them?" he repeats.

I look at him, trying to understand his words. *Do with them?*

I always thought I knew what I would do. But a *hundred*. Maybe one that is—

I shake my head. I can't think. "You're right. This is a bad time."

Right now all I can manage to do is to stay the course.

Suspects

I walk around the small basement apartment, making my promised appearance, but also needing to ask Miesha something. The apartment takes up about half of the basement of the gallery. I look up at the small window that looks out at street level. Everything about the basement is different from when Kara and I used to hang out here with Jenna, except for the stone walls and the windows. "It doesn't look anything like I remember."

"It's been centuries. The whole house has been gutted and restored several times over," Jenna says. "It took some hits during the Civil Division too, and that had to be repaired. Only father's study on the second floor is still intact with all the original walls and contents—right down to the books in his library and the pen on his desk. I guess when you create something as groundbreaking as Bio Gel, people want to get a glimpse of the mind that created it. But most of the house is devoted to the art gallery now."

"It's strange to think you've been here before," Miesha says. "I keep forgetting how far back you two go." She walks over and brushes hair aside that hangs over my eye, like she's still my caretaker at Gatsbro's estate. "You're looking better than you did yesterday."

"What else would you expect?" I answer, trying to put her at ease. I even add one of my impish grins.

She balks. "Don't even try to use that on me. I know you too well."

I put away the smile and pretense. "You do know me, Miesha.

And there's something I need to know about you. But no questions asked."

She delivers a long slow blink, clearly not fond of conditional information, but waits silently for me to continue.

"When you lived in Cambridge with Karden all those years ago, who knew your address?" She looks startled and I tell her I'm only curious, trying to piece together the early activities of the Resistance. "I remember you told me that you and Karden lived under the radar and moved frequently, but you must have told some people where you lived."

She shakes her head. "I shouldn't have done it, but when we returned to Boston I contacted my parents. I wanted them to see their only grandchild. I thought if they saw Rebecca, that might change things between us, but they refused to come. They rejected her the same as they rejected me. They would never accept me being with Karden."

She pauses, looking down as her hand slides over her scarred forearm, the lasting proof that her long-ago nightmare really happened. Her gaze jerks back to me. "But if you're wondering how Security found us, it wasn't them. My parents had plenty of opportunities to turn me in before but they never did. They may have hated Karden but they didn't hate me. I told you before that Karden had been working on his next maneuver. We stayed in Cambridge longer than we had ever stayed anywhere before. Too long. I think Security must have traced his activity."

"And no one else knew your address?"

"Only a trusted few in the Resistance."

"Who were they?"

"You've already met them. Carver, Livvy, and Xavier."

I try to process what this might mean. Her estranged bitter parents versus three trusted members of the Resistance. "Was Karden close to the three of them?"

"Carver and Karden were childhood best friends." She shrugs. "But they all had a long history together."

"You don't seem to like any of them."

She steps over to a hutch that holds a few dishes for the tiny kitchen, checking a plate like she's just noticed a speck of dirt on it. "It has nothing to do with liking. It has to do with reminders. I can barely stand to look at them because when I do all I see are memories." She pauses, rubbing her thumb across the plate. "They make me remember all the nights I lay on my cot in prison, staring at the ceiling and wishing it had been them and their families in the burned rubble instead of mine. Every ugliness in myself and every horror from that day are what I see when I look at them." She pulls a towel from the drawer and begins wiping down each plate and restacking them. "When I saw you yesterday . . ." She shakes her head. "I thought, they have no right to do this to me again. No right."

I walk over to her and pull the towel from her hands so she has to look at me. "They aren't doing anything to *me*, Miesha. I'm here because I want to be. I don't know how all these things work, how any person ends up in a place where they never expected to be, but maybe sometimes we find ourselves in exactly the wrong place at the wrong time and then maybe there's just as many of those other times too when we're in exactly the right place just when we need to be there. I'm hoping *this* is one of those other times."

She's silent like she's trying to weigh the odds. "Me too," she finally whispers, and then dismisses me in her trademark Miesha way, snatching the towel back from me and wiping a final plate.

When it's time for me to leave Jenna says she'll walk me out. Miesha and I don't say good-bye, as we never do. Maybe some scars last forever.

When we're in the dark stairwell that leads up to the street, Jenna pulls me closer and whispers, "Did you tell Raine?"

She already knows. I hear it in her voice. I shake my head. "No."

"Why? Are you afraid?"

"No. I just didn't get the chance."

"That's probably the poorest excuse I've ever heard for not telling someone that you love them."

Yes. It probably is. But I can't begin to tell her all the reasons why speaking to Raine is no longer an option, so I just nod in agreement and walk up the stairs to the street level.

I hide in the shadows, watching my apartment from across the street. I wear my black government charity coat as camouflage, but maybe for other reasons too. I remember when I saw land pirates wearing them, filled with swagger. The first time I put one on that's what I needed, swagger and to feel dark and dangerous the way Miesha described Karden. That was my purpose then, to feel strong enough to survive. I know a coat doesn't make someone into something else—it's only a symbol of what you want to be— but it's a good reminder too.

I know who I am and it's not a rich kid living in a luxury apartment going to school with rich kids. It's freeing not to have to play that role anymore, even if it makes me a target. *I suppose one's true character is impossible to hide for long.* On that much, the Secretary and I agree.

My palm ripples and my chest catches. I jerk my iScroll up, hoping and praying Raine has had a change of heart, but the caller is unidentified. Anonymous. I hesitate, wondering if I should accept, but before I can the call ends. "Percel, who was it?"

"Sorry, sir, it was an unregistered source. No caller ID."

Who besides Raine and the Network knows my code? And why did they terminate the call before I could answer? Is someone trying to figure out where I am?

I look back at my apartment. I deliberately left the shutters open and the lights on so I could check for unusual activity when I returned. I don't want to be ambushed. Security patrols on the street are more frequent, slowing down as they pass my apartment, but at least they don't stop. The Secretary seems to be employing cheap intimidation methods with a clear message: Stay away from my daughter.

Even though I can't see my front door from my position, I open it with the remote code anyway, hoping it will trigger movement inside if anyone is there. It remains still. When I decide that everything is reasonably clear I return to the apartment, lock the door behind me, eat a leftover chunk of cheese, and wash it down with some water. I've hardly eaten today.

Next I call Carver, trying to dispel my guilt over not taking his call last night, wondering if I could have made any difference for Livvy. He sounds and looks drained, as though he hasn't slept in days.

"I'm sorry about Livvy," I say. "Any news?"

He shakes his head. "No. Any news on your end?"

I want to give him at least a glimmer of hope. "I was able to duck into the Secretary's office last night for a few minutes and got a quick glimpse of some blueprints. There's a lighting grid down in the tunnel. I think it must lead to something."

His face brightens. "You're going back tonight?"

Apparently the Collective wasn't notified. The Secretary must assume that I have the good sense not to show up. Maybe that's the purpose of the increased patrols. At least that's one worry off my mind—Xavier and Carver don't know yet that I was thrown out. "Yeah, going back tonight," I tell him.

"Good," he says. "Find out more. If I hear any news about Livvy I'll let you know."

"Thanks."

He's about to sign off but I stop him. "About last night—I'm sorry I didn't take your call. I was—"

"No need to explain. You're making progress. We desperately need that now."

It *was* progress—until I was caught.

A Deadly Walk

I stay in the cover of the trees this time. I don't want to drive her away with my presence.

I just need to see her and know she's still okay.

The experimental scan that awaits Karden—and possibly Raine too—haunts me. I imagine all the ways it's more painful and risky than a standard scan.

While I wait for her to show, memories of all our nights together begin to surface, the times on the PAT taking turns choosing destinations, laughing together as we chose Hawaii, or Paris, or Moscow, and PAT repeating over and over, *Not a valid destination,* but it delayed our departure, and that was really all we wanted—more time to be with each other.

I think about the miles and miles we walked for all the prescribed hours that the Secretary slept, using up each minute because we had so much to talk about, so much to share, the places we wanted to visit, the things we wanted to see. It didn't matter that we were born in different centuries—there were so many things that were amazingly timeless between us. And then I think about the times the conversation turned and I ached because I had to share a different version of myself.

I think about all the nights we lay under the stars in each other's arms, and I listened to her breaths like they were my own. I think about our first kiss and all the ones that came after, the times I traced her lips with my finger, traced the profile of her face, the times my finger slid down her throat and across her collarbone and I thought she was too perfect to be true. The times I told her the truths I could, how I was mesmerized by her from the first time I saw her even though I wouldn't admit it to myself, and she told me the truth of the night we danced in the graveyard, that all she could think about was me dancing with Vina and wanting to replace that memory with one of us dancing together instead. And I told her it worked. The truth.

But I did use her.

That's one truth I can't change.

At 2:15 she appears. Like the first night I saw her, she climbs onto the edge of the rooftop wall and dangles her legs over. The wind is brisk and blows strands of hair across her eyes. She turns her face to the wind and stands. Her gown snaps in the wind. I stand too, holding my breath. *Raine, get down.* But she walks the length of the wall, one foot over another, her arms poised at length for balance. *Get down. Please.* I don't dare call out and draw her attention away from her footing. Her movements are fearless and graceful. Confident. But my God, she's nine stories up on an old building that may have loose stones. When she gets to the end she jumps down onto the rooftop and disappears back into the shadows. Gone for the night. A short but potentially lethal appearance, like she has to push her limits in new ways.

I step from the shadows, angry at her for taking such risks, angry that she could throw so much away without even an explanation, but then I see movement again on the rooftop. I'm about to move back where it's dark, but before I can, Hap steps to the edge and looks straight down at me as if he knew I was there all along.

Bitter Pill

I sneak in through the door that Raine showed me—the one that's never locked—like they know some poor souls must always be in need of sanctuary if they're only smart enough to find their way in. The hinges groan as I open the heavy wooden door. I don't worry at the sound. Very little sneaking is actually involved. Like every time I visited here with Raine, the cathedral is empty, void of priests, caretakers, nuns, and even those in need of middle-of-the-night confessions. I'm not sure anyone comes here anymore but Raine and myself.

And now, maybe just me.

I walk up the center aisle, imagining all the times I walked up it so long ago, barely seven years old, barely able to see over the pews in front of me, my stomach rumbling, thinking about the doughnut with colored sprinkles that my mother promised if I behaved myself, which meant no sliding to the floor, no picking my nose, no putting my feet on the hymnals. I nearly always got the doughnuts with sprinkles afterward, because I nearly always behaved. And the truth was, I would have behaved even without the doughnuts. I liked the order of the whole mystical affair, the standing up, the sitting down, the touching of fingers to lips, the passing of peace, the ringing of bells, the swinging of incense, and especially the organ that vibrated to the core of my bones. It made me feel connected to everyone there. Maybe to the whole universe. I felt safe.

Is that why Raine comes?

I listen to whispers from the stained-glass saints. . . . I pretend I'm somewhere in heaven. Maybe that's why she *used* to come. I doubt she'll be back. She may never descend from her rooftop tower again—unless she trips on a ledge and falls from it. And we all fall sometime.

I reach the end of the aisle. The last time I went farther than this it was as an altar boy. I'm light-years from that altar boy now. Light-years in every way, from lost innocence to a lost body. From here it's seven stairs and seven footsteps to the altar. I still have every inch memorized. I remember how I trembled with each step, how I feared the supremely inconsequential—tripping and shaming God and my family.

The things I know now that I wish I had known then.

Sanctuary.

Refuge.

Asylum.

A piece of Raine's heaven.

I walk up the steps and turn, staring back at the empty church, the white stone balcony above the entrance doors, and the towering gold pipes of the organ above that. Everything just as I recall.

The world's changed, Locke. It's always changing.

At least some things don't change.

I sit down on the last step and look down at my hands. The gashes are gone. When I wasn't looking, wasn't paying attention, wasn't trying to hurry it along, the BioPerfect did what it was programmed to do. It repaired me just as my own skin would have done—but faster and better. Hundreds of small changes that took place right in front of me to add up to something bigger and whole.

I run my finger across my lip. That gash is nearly healed too. I listen to the sounds of the church, the ghosts of another time, rosary beads squeezing in my grandmother's hand, the shuffle of the repentant on their way up the aisle to accept communion, the collective amens that were like notes of music, as clear as yesterday but lifetimes ago. So much has happened since then—a jarring kaleidoscope of events I never planned, one piling onto the next, changing me into someone else more than any blue gel beneath my skin ever could. . . . The accident, being trapped for centuries, running for my life with Kara, nearly killing Gatsbro with my bare hands, carrying the remains of Dot in my arms, leaving Jenna and California for the unknown, the Favor, and then—

I stand. There were so many things I never could have foreseen. I walk back down the center aisle and step out the side door into the night. I adjust my coat against the chill. All these people, all these things, all these changes for better or worse, are the truth of my life. I wouldn't change any of it because it's what led me to Raine, and she's what changed me the most of all.

I remember her sarcastic words to me on the first night we met. *The truth's a bitter pill.*

Yes, Raine, I'm afraid it is, but sometimes we all have to swallow it.

Affairs in Order

I wake up early. It's going to be a full day.

My first stop is a meat market near my apartment. I order a dozen whole raw chickens. The clerk raises her brows. "Large party?"

"Something like that. Just wrapped in paper, please."

I carry the two bags straight to the public gardens. As I pass I look at the ground where I lay four nights ago, leaving a trail of blue goo. It's not there anymore. I pace back and forth, passing time until a couple holding hands walks away, and then I slip through the bushes to the makeshift entrance of Arlington station. I carefully make my way down the steps of rubble, allowing my eyes to adjust completely before I step into the cavern. I set the bags down and touch the wall next to me, sliding my hands along it until I find what I'm looking for. I press it and simultaneously a dim red light in the distance illuminates an area of about fifty feet in front of me and a high-pitched hum echoes through the cavern. I pick up the bags and walk to where the red light is and feel the wall, again searching until I find what I need and press again. Another hum, another fifty feet of dim red light.

I dump out the bags on the walkway above the abandoned track. "These are for you!" I yell. "I know you're hungry. Come and get them."

I leave, repeating my process, touching hidden panels to illuminate my way back, but more importantly sending the high-pitched hum echoing around me. That's how LeGru managed to navigate these tunnels unscathed. Like bats in a cave the half-humans depend on sonar to help them navigate the black tunnels, which explains their screeches, and the high-pitched hums temporarily disorient them. If only I knew where every hidden panel in the grid was, but I was only able to pinpoint two before Raine elbowed me and I had to abandon my search. I emerge from the bushes back into the gardens. Maybe the chickens will provide a little cheap insurance.

Next I search the city for a hardware store. I know that nearly everything is ordered via cybermarts now but surely there are still stores for those who can't wait for deliveries. I find one tucked down an alley off Commonwealth Avenue. It claims to be the oldest hardware store in Massachusetts—and I'm guessing, maybe the only one. Like the haberdashery in Cambridge, they play up the quaintness factor with a Coke machine in one corner that would have been an antique even in my day, and wooden barrels that hold merchandise—but most of it is unrecognizable to me—building materials that even my father couldn't have guessed at. I go to the counter and ask for rope.

"How much and what kind?" the clerk asks.

I eyed the amount I would need earlier today but I throw in a few extra feet for good measure. "Sixty feet. And whatever kind of rope will hold me."

The clerk looks at my build. "That would narrow it down to about everything we have."

"Something lightweight that throws easily," I add.

"That helps." He leads me to a wall of spools and pulls one out that has a thin flexible rope—but it's bright orange. I tell him I need something less conspicuous and he pulls out a spool of lightweight black rope that is perfect. I leave with sixty feet of rope tucked into my pack and head for my next stop.

The Information Exchange on State Street is a secure place for the exchange of sensitive information. An Information Bot asks me to peruse the menus as I wait in line before I engage a Service Kiosk. Births, Deaths, Real Estate, Taxes, Banking, Utilities, Licenses, Transportation Applications, the list goes on and on. I look at the various occupied kiosks and I can see people who look like they're talking to themselves. Virtually nothing is visible other than the customer. Even sound is secure within the invisible boundaries of the kiosk. When it's my turn, I request Banking and I'm directed to a kiosk with a Virtual Representative. A woman, who appears to be a real woman in some other reality, sits in front of me.

"I'm here to inquire about foreign banking accounts."

"You wish to open an international bank account, sir?"

"Not exactly. The thing is, when my aunt died she left me some numbers to an account, but they weren't complete. She lived all over the world. Can you tell me anything about these numbers?" I pass the note window to her with the twelve numbers.

She looks at it and shakes her head. "It appears you have only the last twelve numbers, and the IBAN identifiers for country and branch are within the first twelve numbers. Without the first half of your IBAN, it's impossible to trace the account."

"So this is the last half of the numbers?"

"Yes. Do you know which countries she resided in?"

I shake my head, explaining she lived just about everywhere.

"Well, you may want to search her belongings for the other half. It's not unusual to see foreign account numbers split up this way. The objective of most of them is secrecy for one reason or another. I've heard of customers finding account numbers in the most unlikely and unsecured places—slid between the pages of a treasured family book, tucked in socks, even engraved on the inside of wedding bands."

I know for a fact that Miesha doesn't wear a wedding band, and their belongings were destroyed in the fire, including Karden's socks. Besides, if the Secretary had found anything among the belongings before he burned the place down, we wouldn't be in this race right now.

But at least I know I have the second half of the account number. "Do you have a list of the country codes?" I ask.

She brings up a list and flicks me a note window containing 179 countries and their respective four-digit identifiers. "But without the missing numbers, this won't do you any good. Searching through her personal belongings is your best bet. If it's a significant amount of money, you can be sure she left more information somewhere."

I glance at the ridiculously long list of countries and their codes—countries I didn't even know existed—and I slip the note window into my pack. I thank her, saying I'll search through my aunt's socks. She disappears and the private walls of the kiosk vanish.

Socks, wedding bands, books. Or maybe a time-sensitive biochip hiding somewhere inside Raine waiting to be procured as LeGru suggests. The thought makes my pulse race, but I move on to my next task. Staying the course as Xavier would say, but this is *my course.*

I head for the PAT.

"Need a lift?"

I look at the CabBot who has offered the ride. As convenient as a cab would be, I need the rest of the money on my card for my next stop. I wave him on. "No thanks."

"No charge," he says. "For you."

He's not a CabBot I recognize. He seems to notice my hesitation. "I hear you can tell a good story," he adds.

So word *has* gotten around. Dot has friends who are passing along her story. And they're obviously pointing me out.

I accept his offer and he takes me to a market where I buy as many groceries as my card allows. Fresh oranges, strawberries, chocolate peaches, fresh kale and squash, bags of nuts and beans, slabs of brisket, and on a last impulse, four dozen animal cookies, the kind that make animal noises. I carry the groceries to the waiting cab and give him directions to Xavier's neighborhood.

"I don't understand," Xavier's wife says as I unload bag after bag of groceries and set them on a table in the center of the courtyard.

"Where I came from, people reciprocated," I say. "I'm afraid I'm never going to get the chance to cook for everyone here—which is probably lucky for you—but this is something my parents drilled into me. You're never too young or too old to reciprocate. They liked that word a lot."

Children flood out of the surrounding buildings. I pull the box of cookies from the cab. "May I?"

She nods, and I pass out the cookies. The courtyard becomes a barnyard of noise and squeals. I leave a few cookies in the box and point to the rest of the groceries. "Will you see that some of this goes to Livvy's family?"

"Of course, but—" She pushes back a strand of hair from her forehead and frowns. "You act like we might not see you again."

After today, it's quite possible that they won't. "I just wanted to take care of something while I still have the chance." Before I run out of chances.

Some lessons I learn later rather than sooner.

Unmasked

I sit in my apartment waiting for darkness, wishing I could fast-forward the clock, anger simmering in me as the time gets closer, good fuel to sharpen my focus. I empty my pack out onto the kitchen table. I'll have to travel light—only the essential things I'll need—and I sort through the contents. I rewind the rope so it will unfurl with a single throw and place it back in the pack.

Karden's knife could be useful and I put it back in too. I look over the note window the clerk gave me, skimming over the countries and four-digit codes again. I look at them again and again, trying to memorize them in case I come across any similar numbers, and then set it in the pile with the other things that will be staying behind.

I shuffle through the other contents and pick up the eye of Liberty. *Let's find the other eye of Liberty together. . . .*

I squeeze the green sea glass in my fist. So much can change in just a few days. She wants nothing to do with me now but I throw it into my pack anyway. I slide the note window that Carver gave me to the no-go pile but then stop to look at it. I already looked at it several times today when I was showing it to the clerk, but something about it stops me this time. I examine the numbers again, hastily handwritten the first night I met him, but they still mean nothing to me. I've looked at too many numbers today. I shove it back into the no-go pile. I won't need it for where I'm going. Now there isn't anything left to do but wait.

You're nothing but a spy. No, I'm so much more than that, Raine, and somewhere down deep you know it too. Or you will. You're just too wounded to admit it.

A cloudy night. I couldn't ask for better to muffle light and sound. I stake out a section of the north wall that's hidden from the street, analyzing the best path to the top. I find a dark section with no footholds more than three feet apart. I begin my ascent, finding hand- and footholds between the stones, on broad window casements, and on the narrow three-inch stone ledge marking the lines between floors of the seven-story office building.

Another ledge, another casement, carefully making my way to the top until I finally hoist myself onto the roof. Roosting pigeons are disturbed by my presence, flutters rising into the air, but they quickly go back to their bird dreams.

The roof tiles are steep and slick with fungus. I crouch low as I move across to the rooftop edge and I eye the chimney of the building next door looming another three stories above me. I walk farther up the steep roof trying to get the best angle I can until I'm nearly at the peak. I'm about to pull the rope from my pack when a tile slips loose beneath my foot and I find myself sliding down the roof toward the edge at breakneck speed. I frantically grab at anything, my fingers digging in but only catching mold, my feet, my knees, every part of me trying to stop my deathly descent, and finally, just a few feet from the edge, my right hand catches a vent pipe. I barely reach out in time with my other hand to grab my pack as it slides past me. The loose tile falls to the ground seven floors below, a dull thud on the soft earth.

With a desperate grip on the vent pipe, I carefully pull myself back up. Half-humans couldn't stop me, but a simple loose roof tile nearly did. Sometimes it's the smallest and most innocent things that you have to watch out for.

I retrace my steps back to the peak, crouching even lower this time, and pull the rope from my pack. I need to be there before she is. I throw the looped rope, missing the top of the chimney by a good twenty feet. I rewind and throw again, closer but still missing it. I widen the loop and try again, this time hitting my mark. I pull the rope taut, testing it, hoping the old chimney stones hold and that I can pull myself up to the roof garden without detection.

I grab tight and am just about to make the swing to the wall when I see something falling from the rooftop above me. I stop breathing, fearing the worst, but then I see it's only Raine's rope ladder swinging directly in front of me, like a wagging invitation. I'm not sure what to think. It's not where Raine would normally drop it. Did she see me coming?

I look at the ladder. Regardless of her motivations for dropping it here, it's an invitation and I swing to the wall with my rope and climb it. When I'm almost to the top I look down at the staggering distance to the ground and I'm jolted by all the times Raine has taken this risky path. I crawl over the ledge and look for her but no one's here. "Raine," I whisper.

Hap steps out from behind an arbor.

"You," I say.

"Yes, me."

"Where's Raine?"

"Still inside."

I look around, wondering if the Secretary is watching from the shadows. "So this was only a trap." I let my pack slip from my shoulder to my hand and reach inside for the knife.

"Yes, a trap," Hap confirms. "But probably not the kind you're imagining."

"A trap is a trap. And I bought it. But if you think I'll go easily, you're wrong."

Hap eyes my hand in my pack, like he's amused at whatever defense I might be reaching for. "This trap isn't for you," he says. "It's for Raine. She'll be coming out soon. I suggest you conceal yourself until I can lock the door behind her. That way she'll be forced to stay and listen to whatever you have to say. And I assume you have a lot that needs to be said." He waves me to a dark corner.

I don't move. He's trying to help me?

"Why so surprised?" he asks. "Who do you think carried you up to your apartment the night you were injured?"

I shake my head. It makes no sense. "Why?"

"Word gets around."

Hap has an odd weakness for talking to other Bots.

Like CabBots?

"Dot isn't the only Bot who has ever dreamed of Escape, Mr. Jenkins," he says. "However, Raine is my priority. My assigned task is to guard her, but even for a being such as myself, assigned tasks can develop into something else. My task as guard has evolved into protector, and sometimes that even requires protecting Raine from herself. I'm not doing this for you. I'm doing it for her."

I can't quite believe what I'm hearing. It's more than loyalty. He *loves* Raine. He loves her like a protective uncle. I shake my head, still in disbelief. "Why do you portray yourself as such a hard-ass?"

"That's my job. I'm not a chatty Tour Bot the way Dot was. And if you must know, I don't have the ability to smile. It was not considered a necessary add-on for my job—rather, a hindrance. But trust me, it's far more debilitating than having no legs, especially when one comes to care for the Eater and Breather one is assigned to look after. But you above all others should know about limitations."

If he carried me up the stairs, he saw the BioPerfect oozing from me. He knows everything, including my unique limitation.

He could have turned me in at any time and gotten me out of the way. But *word gets around*. I never would have guessed that he was a Bot like Dot, one with hopes for being more, maybe even with hopes for Raine to have more.

"Now I suggest you hide yourself because Raine will be coming through that door in approximately twelve seconds. I hear her on the stairs. If she sees you before I can lock the door, she'll run, and there won't be a second chance to arrange a meeting like this."

I move, hurrying to a black corner just a few feet from the rooftop door.

The door swings open and Raine emerges.

"Hap, what are you doing up here?"

He tells her he was checking her ladder for wear and then dismisses himself, exiting through the door she just came through. She hears the click of the lock and pulls on the door handle but it doesn't budge.

"Hap?"

This is my cue. I step from the shadows.

"Hello, Raine."

She spins around, her eyes wide, her mouth open as she catches her breath. She turns and lunges for the door, hitting it and calling for Hap. I grab her from behind, pinning her against the door to quiet her. She struggles under my grip.

"Ten minutes," I whisper in her ear. "That's all I ask. Ten minutes to explain. Are you afraid to give me even that?"

"I owe you nothing. Not even ten minutes. You're a liar."

"Are you sure, Raine? Are you one hundred percent sure about everything? You said you wanted the truth. I think that's what you're really afraid of. The truth. Because I'm willing to give it all to you right now. Everything." My lips touch her ear, slide to her cheek, my breath warm against her skin. "Do you really want the truth?" Her chest heaves. Seconds tick past. Her arms relax beneath my grip.

"Ten minutes," she whispers. "That's all."

I release her and she turns to face me. I motion to the seat beneath the ivy-covered arbor. "I'll stand," she says.

"Fair enough." I walk over and take the seat myself, dropping my pack at my feet.

She stands there, waiting and rigid, but even in the dark I can see her eyes fighting to maintain distance. She's still walking a tightrope, trying to keep her balance in her safe little rooftop world. I wonder which way the truth will push her.

"Why are you wearing that coat?" she asks, her voice dripping with disdain. "You look like one of those—"

"You said you wanted the truth—here it is. This is me, Raine." I pull the collar up around my neck to drive the point home, the way the land pirates would. The way I imagine Karden would too. "This is the *real* me. Warts and all. And this is only a fraction of what I was afraid to tell you. I hope you can handle all of it."

She looks at me, unresponsive, still waiting in her usual defensive style like nothing can penetrate her armor. We'll see.

"You were right. I'm a spy. A Non-pact. One of those animals you're afraid of. I was sent here by an underground Resistance movement to get information. Everything about me is fake. My background. My family. That apartment isn't even mine. All a ruse to get in good with you because your father has information the Network needs."

"You used me."

"Yes, I did. And I'm not proud of it. But I had a good reason."

"*A good reason?*" she snaps. Her top lip lifts in disgust. "The things you said and did. You use someone like that and—"

"*My ten minutes!*" I snap right back at her. "The truth is hard to hear, *a bitter pill*, right? Do you want to hear it or not?"

She lifts her chin and is silent. I continue. "I had good reason because there's a man the Secretary has imprisoned—"

"My father's sent a lot of people to prison. He's the Secretary of Security in case you haven't heard."

"This man's in a secret prison, Raine. He stole some money. *A lot* of money. Not for himself but to fund the Resistance. And there are a lot of people who want that money, including the Secretary and LeGru. But the money all disappeared into a foreign account before anyone could get their hands on it, and with half the account numbers missing, no one can find it. *That's* why they're keeping him. They're still trying to get it out of him. He's been in that secret prison for *sixteen* years. It's an unofficial one hidden beneath the city that the Secretary—"

"Why do you keep calling him the Secretary? The Secretary! He's my father, for God's sake!"

I stand and step toward her. "No, he isn't! And you know he's not! Not even in the loosest sense. And that's another truth I didn't want to tell you. He's your captor, Raine. Your warden. You weren't a piece of trash. You never were. He didn't save you—he stole you. You once had two parents who loved you. He threw them both in prison, burned down their house, and then took you like you were a piece of confiscated property because he thought you might have information he needed. That's what all those scans have been about. He wants the account numbers just like the Resistance does."

She puts her hands over her ears. "You're lying! Stop! It's all lies!"

I grab her hands and force them down. "You're going to listen, and you're going to listen to it all."

Her hands tremble.

"Your mother's name is Miesha. She has scars all across her arms from where she shoved them through a window trying to save you from the fire. They told her you were dead and threw her in prison for eleven years for being part of the Resistance.

"Your father's name is Karden. Everyone thinks he's dead too. He's the one who's being held by the Secretary in a secret location. That's how I was hurt. Not cats and stairs. I went looking for him, but there are animals down in those tunnels that the Secretary counts on to keep people away. They nearly killed me. That's what I was looking for in his office. A safer way in.

"Your father—" I shake my head, not sure she can even fathom the importance of what I'm about to tell her. *"Your real father* was the leader of the Resistance. Without him to lead it, the Resistance died. People need him. Like all those Non-pacts you visited. Non-pact children who laugh and play and cry and have dreams and hopes just like any other child. Children just like the child *you* would have been."

I watch everything in her struggling to maintain control, from the faint tremor of her fists, to her frozen pinpoint pupils. "Rebecca," I whisper. "Your real name is Rebecca."

I watch her eyes change, her pupils growing to large black circles, like she's been drugged by the memory of another time   231 when that name was whispered in her ear. A sound that's vaguely familiar. She shakes her head and brushes past me, stopping at the arbor, almost hanging on to it, and then she turns, slowly sliding to the seat as if her legs will no longer support her.

I step back, wondering how I'll tell her the rest, but it all has to be said.

She looks up at me, defiantly, waiting, like she's regained her footing, found her way back to the old Raine who believes in nothing but distance, who has found a way to survive by not believing in anything at all. "Your time's almost up," she says.

"You wanted truth, Raine. And this is the rest of it. I don't want you to say anything. I don't want you to respond. I just need you to listen, because I may not get another chance to say it. I'm telling you all of this because—

"Because something went wrong. Something happened. Something I never planned or anticipated. I was only traveling from one side of the country to the other trying to find a life. Trying to rebuild a life that was stolen from me. Because there's another secret about myself that you need to know, maybe the biggest reason I never told you the truth, the thing I've always been terrified to reveal because I was afraid it would change your feelings about me."

I pull the Swiss knife from my pack and pull out the largest blade. It's the only way she'll ever really believe what I'm about to tell her. I yank up my sleeve and swipe it across my arm, first blood, and then blue BioPerfect trickles from the wound. I hear her gasp. "This is the real me, Raine. Illegal in every possible way."

Her mouth opens but she doesn't speak. I tell her the whole

story, my prior life, my years trapped in limbo, my new body, Kara, Jenna, being on the run, and Dot, who had more humanity in her than most humans I know. I tell her how I was trying to come to grips with my old life that had vanished, and understand the new one I had to live, the life I was trying to find here, until I finally come full circle, back to where I started. "But something went wrong." I go well beyond my allotted ten minutes and she never moves, never blinks. I wonder if she's even hearing me anymore, but when I finish she closes her eyes like she's blocking me and the world out.

"Raine," I whisper. I step closer, like I'm pleading for my life, pleading for *us*. "I didn't plan it. I didn't even want it. It was the worst possible thing that could happen, but it did happen. I fell in love. With you. That part of me was never fake. That's probably the only real thing I have. I love you, Raine. *I love you.*"

She opens her eyes. I look at her face, every angle, every eyelash, every muscle struggling to hide what she's feeling, but I still see it, so much pain, so much anger and fear, such a whirlwind of emotions that I can't tell if there's anything left in her for me. Her eyes glisten. I step toward her but she puts up her hand to stop me and shakes her head, unable to speak. Like if I take one more step she will crumble.

"I know I blew it. That's a phrase from my time that means that I ruined the best chance I ever had of being happy, but that's because even though I have BioPerfect beneath my skin, I'm still not perfect, just like I never was, and never will be. But if I could do everything over again, I would. Almost everything. Some things I'd want to stay exactly the same."

I stare at her, waiting, hoping. Her eyes are fixed on mine, seconds passing, a tightrope, a lifetime of decisions churning in them.

She looks away, and my throat swells. It wasn't the answer I wanted.

·I walk over and grab my pack from the ground. "I'm still committed to what needs to be done. I'm not going to live my entire life on the run. I'm going down in that tunnel tomorrow night, with or without the information I need, with or without your help."

"You might be killed."

"That's right. But time's running out and there's a man down there who believes in the same thing I do. We all have to believe in *something,* Raine. Even if it means there's a risk. But our risks have to matter. If the only risk you ever want to take is walking on the ledges of rooftops, I guess that's your choice."

"How do I know everything you're saying right now isn't a lie too? Just to get what you need from me? Like before?"

I look in her eyes and shake my head, hoping she'll look long enough and deep enough to see something in me that isn't artificial and manufactured. More than anyone else in the world, I need her to see that. "I don't know," I say. "I don't know how you can know anything for sure. It's a risk. Something only you can figure out. If you don't believe me, call the Secretary. Turn me in. Maybe I won't even make it off this rooftop tonight. But at least I tried. I gave something I believed in a shot."

I reach in my pack and throw her the eye of Liberty. Her reflexes are still fast, like the trained athlete she is, and she catches it. "Keep it," I say. "It's yours. I don't want to find the other one without you."

She doesn't say anything, just grips the piece of glass in her fist.

"I guess my ten minutes are up," I say.

"Yes," she agrees. "They are."

I leave, taking my rope from the chimney, her eyes following my every move, and I scale down her ladder, wondering if the truth is what she really wanted to hear at all.

The Smallest Things

Jenna looks up at the sky. "I wish I could stay. I actually miss the snow terribly. It's one of those things you don't realize you'll miss until you can't have it." She looks back at me. "I'm sorry I have to go. I know it's bad timing for—"

"You need to leave. I want you to. We all have our limitations. You have your Bio Gel, and I'm . . . I'm missing that magic ten percent of original human goo that would make me legal. We have to deal with what we have."

She squeezes my hand and pulls me closer. "The world will change, Locke. Laws change . . . *people* change."

I hear the inflection in her voice. I told her about Raine. She knows what's eating at me more than anything else. *People change.* But sometimes not in the ways we had hoped.

"I'll be okay," I tell her.

This time it's me leaving her at the train station. A low-pressure depression is sending an unseasonal arctic blast to Boston in two days. She called me early this morning. She has to leave before it comes.

"I wish you'd take Miesha with you. It's not safe for her to be here."

"She won't leave, Locke. I can't force her. Besides, you need to tell her about Rebecca. She deserves that much. It's her right."

It may be her right but it's also a connection that could kill her. "Not yet. It's too dangerous for her right now. In a few days the account will expire and then the Secretary won't have any use for Miesha. I'll call for her to come back then, but if she should find out about Raine before that—"

"She'll stay put at the apartment. I told her she'd jeopardize your Favor and maybe your life if she didn't. She doesn't give a hoot about the Favor but she does care about you."

She'd give a hoot about the Favor if she knew what it was all about. But I do wonder, if I'm even able to get Karden out of that hellhole, after so many years apart, will he and Miesha only be strangers? Will there be any love left between them? How long can . . . I take a deep breath. *Raine.* How many years does it take to stop loving someone?

"I'm sorry, Locke. I know how much this hurts. But maybe she'll—"

I put my hand up in the same way Raine did last night to stop Jenna from saying more.

"I told you, I'm okay," I say firmly, and I smile, determined not to let thoughts of Raine show on my face again. "Say hello to Allys and Kayla for me. I'll call as soon as I can."

"Be careful," she says.

I nod. "Always."

She kisses my cheek and turns to leave but I stop her one last

time. I hesitate, feeling foolish, maybe even afraid to hear her answer, but she's the only one I can ask. "Do you ever get used to it, Jenna?"

"What's that?"

"Not being who you once were . . . not being like everyone else?"

She looks at me, staring for the longest time, and finally reaches up, raking her fingers through my hair and then pulling a strand over my eye, exactly where my cowlick used to be. She frowns. "Being like everyone else is highly overrated."

She turns and leaves. I watch her walk down the stairs to meet her train, my eyes never leaving her until she's swallowed up by other travelers, and I wonder when and if I'll ever see her again.

It's still early, barely past breakfast, and I stroll through Quincy Market, most of the shops still closed, again wishing I could fast-forward the clock, wondering how I'll fill the whole day waiting for night to come. But everything I told Raine last night was true. With or without her help, I'm going down tonight, down before Xavier and Carver think it's time to implement Plan B, down before LeGru uses a scan on Karden that he might not survive. Down because if I can't get any more information from the Secretary, there's no reason to wait. All I'm doing is giving him more time to beat me to what we both want. I'll have to use the little information I was able to get and trust my instincts for the rest.

I pass a bakery and am caught off guard when the shopkeeper waves me down, remembering me from my visit with Livvy.

"Hello, Locke. Nice to see you again. How's your mother?" I open my mouth to answer but then notice that one of her fingers is torn away, the digital coils glowing. I had no idea she was a Bot. She's as realistic as they come, imperfect, wrinkled, plump around the middle. She sees me staring. "Little accident. Reached too far into the mixer. Bot Repair comes tomorrow." She smiles, but there's nothing *more* about her. Her eyes are focused and bright, but dead. She is perfectly programmed. Friendly, efficient, but nothing beyond that. How does the *more* happen with some and not others? How did it happen with Dot? *We dream. We imagine.* Dot's voice is still clear in my head, a unique voice that was hers alone. It's a voice I desperately needed to hear right now, to remind me of the whole meaning of the Favor.

The Bot waits politely for my response. "My mother's fine, thank you," I reply.

She offers me a curly protein sample and tells me they're on special, two for one. I pass and move on.

It's way too early for lunch but I remember the Italian sub I had here a few weeks ago—a taste of home, something real, comfort food—unfortunately I have no money left to pay for one. I sit down at an empty outdoor table and rummage through my pack. Could I barter with the two unused phone tabs? I notice the knife in the bottom. I should have given it to Raine last night. It's the only thing left of her father's—

I freeze.

I don't even have to look.

He carried that thing with him everywhere he went. . . . His father gave it to him. . . . It's the one Karden left at my house the day before he disappeared.

Karden did have a backup plan and Carver had it all along.

I grab the knife and instinctively pull out the smallest blade. *Sometimes it's the smallest and most innocent things you have to watch out for.* I run my finger across the tiny engraved numbers that might pass for a product code.

Carver and Xavier need to be told right away. I flip my palm to call when it ripples. I'm about to swipe my iScroll, thinking that for once Carver finally has good timing, but then I see it isn't him.

It's Raine.

I hesitate, almost afraid to know why she's calling, but I swipe anyway, more afraid to miss a chance to talk to her.

I immediately see desperation in her eyes.

"My father's leaving for an appointment in twenty minutes," she whispers. "He'll be out of the house for two hours. Come and get the information you need. I don't want your death on my hands. I'll have the front desk let you up."

She clicks off before I can say a word. It all happens so fast. A few seconds and she's gone. Breathless instructions that leave me breathless too.

I don't want your death on my hands. These last few words reverberate louder than anything else she said. Was she calling only out of a sense of duty, or is she trying to protect something she still cares about?

Twenty minutes. I throw the knife back in my pack and run at breakneck speed, dodging cars and pedestrians, my coat flapping behind me like black wings. I make it to the Commons in fifteen minutes, gasping for air. From a hidden vantage point, I watch the apartments. Just as Raine said, in a few minutes I see the Secretary's car emerge from the garage and drive away.

I call Carver and Xavier. I talk fast, not giving them a chance to speak. "It's happening today. Now. I have to move fast. The Secretary's gone and Raine's giving me access to his office. I've found the missing account numbers too. They were on Karden's knife. Meet me at the entrance to the Arlington station. I don't know what kind of shape he'll be in when I bring him out."

Assuming we make it out.

They sputter and try to ask questions but I don't give them a chance. I sign off and tell Percel, no calls. *None.* From here on out, I don't want a single moment of distraction.

After racing across town in the crisp air, the elevator ride is slow and suffocating. The nine floors up seem like nineteen. It's only paranoia setting in, I tell myself. It's all happening too fast.

But really, it isn't fast. It's been months and years in coming. It's happened in skipped meals, sacrificed freedoms, crumbled homes, and slivers of hope clutched in broken hands. And because of these past weeks I've spent with Raine, for me it's been a lifetime.

The elevator finally stops.

One, two, three endless seconds.

And the door slides open.

Calculated Control

She's there.

Waiting.

Her eyes are as wide and open and beautiful as I've ever seen them. No distance. Her brown irises as deep as night, shadowed by lashes that refuse to blink. The green eye of Liberty is cupped in her hand, like it hasn't left that spot since I threw it to her last night. She doesn't have to say a word. I know. She didn't call me just because she doesn't want my death on her hands. I step out and she takes a hesitant step toward me. I shake my head, unable to say more than a hoarse "Raine."

She falls into my arms, hugging me so tightly, I think that she'll never let go. I don't want her to. Not ever. I squeeze her back just as fiercely, my face lost in her hair, breathing in every lost moment. "I'm sorry," I whisper. "I'm sorry."

She says the same thing to me through tears, and then she's kissing me, her cheeks and lips salty and wet. She finally pulls back, her wet lashes clumped together, her eyes fixed on mine. There's so much more to say, but there isn't time and we both know it. She grabs my hand and pulls me toward the stairs that lead down.

Midway on the stairs, she stops abruptly and turns. "Locke, my mother—my *adoptive* mother—wasn't part of it. She didn't know what he did. She really did love me. I know she did. All she ever wanted—" Her voice cracks and she swallows. "All she ever wanted was a baby and she said I was her answered prayer. A gift from heaven." Her eyes glisten with tears she forces back. "She was a *good* mother."

I know she needs to hold on to the good in her life, just like I hold on to memories to validate my past. It can't all be a waste. I squeeze her hand and nod understanding. She grips my hand tighter, letting out a deep cleansing breath, and we continue down the stairs. The house is unusually still and quiet. The only sounds are the creaks of our steps in the hallways. "Where's Hap?" I ask.

"No one's home. Father sent Hap on an errand."

"An errand? Isn't he supposed to stick by your side?"

"Usually. But Father needed something and he had already given Dorian and Jory the day off."

We reach the Secretary's office and I push the door open. Unlike the last time I was here the office is in meticulous order, but conveniently one file has been left open, which is good news for me. It means the whole system hasn't been shut down and hopefully I can access the folder with the red triangle again—the one with blueprints for the lighting system in the tunnels.

I walk around to the desk. Raine waits on the opposite side as I explain what I'm looking for. With one touch after another, folders open and files fill the air, including the blueprints.

"I've got it," I say. I read the map, finding the third and fourth light pads in the tunnel, when something begins happening with the files. One by one they converge back into a single pile, like they're on autopilot. I try to grab them out of the air, spreading them back out again, but in seconds, they're stacked into one unreadable pile—and finally a note flutters to the top. A handwritten note.

The hairs on my arms rise.

Raine must see something on my face and she races around the desk to see what I'm looking at.

We both stare at the note.

Welcome, Locke.

"Step behind me," I whisper to Raine. She doesn't move. *"Step back,"* I say again, using my arm to push her behind me.

The office door swings open. LeGru enters, flanked by two Security Force officers, one of them heavily armed with a gun that looks like it could take down a whole army with one blast.

The Secretary walks in behind them. He smiles. "So much more convenient for you to come to me instead of me having to hunt you down. I suspected my daughter hadn't cut off communications with you. Now, if you'll come out quietly from behind that desk and take a seat." He motions to the guards who take another step toward us.

Raine grabs my arm, trying to stop me. "It's okay," I say. I look at her, trying to convey how deadly our situation is. This is no longer just her father who might discipline her for acting out. He's a cunning and desperate man who will not lose eighty billion duros at any cost. "Just stay here," I tell her. "Trust me, *please.*"

I walk to the other side of the desk. The guard raises his weapon, showing he's ready to use it. I take a seat as I'm told. The Secretary walks over to his rightful place behind his desk, just inches from Raine. He touches her chin, and she flinches away. "He's filled you with lies already, hasn't he? Who to believe?" He pushes Raine down into his chair.

He explains he doesn't have time to waste. He knows I'm not who I say I am, that every record and document submitted to the

Collective turned out to be fake. "But who are you? No question that you're part of some resurging Resistance faction trying to acquire the same thing I am. But as you well know, time is running out. I don't have days on end to interrogate you until you break. Whatever is in your head, I need it now."

He looks back at LeGru and raises his brows.

I feel a stab in my neck, and a flash of heat pulses out to my fingertips. Almost instantly I lose focus. The room spins and my vision doubles, triples, my limbs going numb, garbled voices surrounding me. I can't even be sure I'm still sitting in the chair, but then something strange happens. As quickly as the disorienting wave hits me, it begins to subside. I know what's happening. I *feel* it happening. Whatever they injected me with, my BioPerfect is attacking it, disabling it, like a virus that's invaded my system. Just as BioPerfect repairs cuts and gashes on the outside, it works for survival on the inside too. *Survival* is its prime objective. The dizzy wave dissolves, my focus returning with heightened clarity, and I listen to the Secretary drone on with his smug explanation.

"And as it turns out, this also gives us an auspicious opportunity to try some new technology out on you. Unfortunately for you, the scan is quite painful, but well worth the—"

LeGru abruptly walks over to the Secretary, interrupting him and showing him a device in his hand. "Something's wrong," he says. "It's not working. The nanobots are all . . . *disappearing*."

LeGru slowly looks from the device in his hand to me, his lip pulling up in a disgusted sneer.

"Am I making your skin crawl, LeGru?" I ask, knowing he's figured it out. "The same way you made my skin crawl from the moment I met you?"

The guard standing behind me knocks the back of my head with the butt of his gun.

LeGru shakes his head, his sneer widening as he turns to the Secretary. "His body's not even—"

I recognize my chance and won't wait for a second one. I jump to the side, grabbing the smaller unarmed guard, swinging his body to deflect the armed guard who is already coming at me. The smaller guard flies across the room, smashing into the wall, and falls unconscious to the floor.

The armed guard regains his footing, but before he can come at me again I lunge, both of us wrestling for control of his weapon, flailing through the room, overturning tables and smashing into the Secretary's precious artifacts. When we tumble into a chair, the guard breaks free, aims the weapon at me, and fires, but not before my leg swings up, knocking him back, and his aim is thrown upward, blowing a hole through the ceiling.

Plaster rains down around us. I lunge again, trying to grab the weapon from him, but his grip on it remains secure, which helps me when I swing him around and send him flying through the air—straight toward the window. He crashes through it, disappearing along with his gun, the shatter of glass blending with his scream as he falls nine stories. I catch my breath, wiping blood from my mouth where the gun hit my lip, and I spin, ready to take on LeGru and the Secretary next, but the Secretary already has me beat.

He holds Raine, his arm crooked tightly around her neck, so tight that a sudden jerk could snap it.

I put my hands up, showing him I'm backing off. "Don't—"

"Shut up! Sit down in the chair. *Now*."

I look at Raine. He's holding her so tightly she can't speak, but I see her eyes, angry, telling me in a million ways not to do as he says. But I have to. I can read his face even more clearly than hers. I slowly move to the chair and sit and he instructs LeGru to get the body cuff from the guard who lies unconscious on the floor. LeGru grabs it from the guard's belt and places it over me and the cuff contracts, snugly pinning me to the chair. Once I'm secure, the Secretary loosens his hold on Raine and pushes her back in his chair. "So, my daughter got mixed up with some sort of lab beast, or at best, a cyborg."

"Fully human," I say. "More so than you."

"Who do you work for? You couldn't have pulled this off on your own."

Raine jumps forward. "Don't tell him anything, Locke!"

The Secretary spins, hitting Raine's face with the back of his hand, sending her sprawling back into the chair. I strain against the cuff but it holds me tight. Blood dribbles from the corner of her mouth. She wipes it away. "Don't tell him," she says, glaring at him, daring him to hit her again.

He turns back to me. "Sadly, it looks like you've infected her with your lies, but worse for you and her, you may have told her what it is I need to know. Our experimental scan may have failed on you, but it won't fail on Raine. Are you going to force me to use it on her?"

"I haven't told her anything."

He turns to LeGru and tells him to inject her. LeGru prepares another injection and walks toward Raine.

"Wait!" I say. "I have what you want."

The Secretary turns, raising his eyebrows. "And just what is that?" he asks. "Don't stall. I won't give you a second chance."

I have no doubt that this once, he's a man of his word. I look at my pack lying on the floor, the knife—his golden fleece—only inches from his feet. But it's not nearly as valuable to me as Raine is. I look at her sitting in the chair just behind him. Once I give him what he wants, I'm dead, but he'd have no more reason to harm her.

"I have the missing numbers."

I watch his face transform, like now he's the one who has been injected.

"They're at your feet," I tell him.

"Don't play with me, boy. I know games and lies when I see them. I warned you—"

"In my pack. On the floor. There's an old knife that had belonged to Karden. The only thing of his that you didn't burn in the fire. The missing numbers are engraved on the smallest blade."

He glances down at the pack, sixteen years of greed and hunger spreading across his face. "For your sake, I hope you're telling the truth." He reaches down and grabs it, but like lightning, Raine is moving, snatching, spinning, and before he even straightens back up, the tip of a sword is at his throat. He looks with horror at the empty display behind his desk, his prized silver sword now firmly in Raine's hand.

"Don't move," she says. "You know I could sever your jugular and be out of this room before your body even hits the floor."

He swallows carefully. "But, Raine, I'm your father."

She presses the tip of the sword harder against the tender skin at the base of his throat. I watch her struggle, but only briefly, the mere flutter of an eyelash, as the hatred, betrayal, and trained devotion are overtaken by the calculated control she learned from him. "And that's why I haven't already killed you." She motions with her head to me. "Release him," she says to LeGru.

LeGru looks at the Secretary for confirmation. He carefully nods, obviously seeing Raine teeters on the edge of slashing his throat anyway. "Hurry," he whispers.

LeGru loosens the cuff and pulls it off me. I get out of the chair, pushing him down where I was sitting, and I back another chair up to his. "Your turn," I tell the Secretary. Raine carefully walks him over, the sword never leaving his throat. He sits and I place the cuff over both of them, securing them back to back.

"It won't do you any good," he says. "You've dispatched two Security Officers. It will be only seconds before more are swarming all over this building."

I grab my pack from the floor. "Then we'd better go." We head for the door.

"Raine!" the Secretary screams, raised veins furious at his temples. "Don't you dare leave me like this! You'll be sorry if you walk out that door! You'll become a hunted criminal just like him! I'm giving you one last chance—"

Raine spins, thirsty rage in her eyes, her chest heaving, the sword cutting the air and then balancing in her hands like she's testing it, eager to plunge it right through his heart. "You're giving *me* a last chance?" She steps closer until the sword is dead center between his eyes.

"Raine," I whisper.

She stares at him, her gaze frigid and her hand brutally steady. "The only thing I'll be sorry for is if I don't walk out that door right now." She lifts the sword. "And *you*, Secretary Branson, will never make me sorry for another thing as long as I live."

We hear sirens, then doors slamming, and we run.

Betrayal

"The roof," Raine says. "They'll be coming up the elevator and stairs."

We race to the roof and look over. Dozens of Security vans have converged on the two streets below. We tie down the rope ladder and throw it over the narrow alley walkway on the other side. Raine goes over first, the sword still in her hand. "Leave it behind," I say, afraid she'll lose her grip.

"Not a chance," she answers, and begins her descent. I tell her I'll follow once she reaches the ground, worried that Hap's handiwork won't hold us both at the same time. She balks, saying there isn't time and she won't continue unless I come along right now. I do, praying with each rung that the carefully woven twine will hold, and relieved when the last few rungs are finally in sight. We jump the last few feet to the ground just as Security Officers round the corner and spot us. They yell for us to stop and aim their weapons, the red target lights already centered on our chests. We freeze, both of us lifting our hands into the air, but then someone else rounds the corner behind them.

Hap.

He silently reaches out, grabbing both by the necks, lifting them off the ground. We hear them scream but we don't wait to see what else happens. Hap has given us our chance to run and we do, because we know more officers will be right behind them in pursuit. We turn down alleys, duck between buildings, and take cover in stairwells.

I hear Raine's ragged breaths but she never lags, pulling me into shadows and crevices I didn't know existed, more familiar with these alleyways than I am. We pull flat against a wall as a Security van races past hunting for us, and we stop breathing when forces on foot run down nearby passageways, guns in hand.

When it's safe, we escape from one dark corner to another, trying to gain some distance between us and them. After a full minute passes with no sight of them, we make a break for the Commons across the street, running low through cars that slam on brakes to avoid us, and we don't stop running until we reach the public gardens and the hidden entrance to Arlington station. We go halfway down the steps and finally stop, taking a moment to catch our breath.

"I've got to go in to get him now," I say. "It won't be long before the Secretary's free and he figures out where we're headed." I look down the steps trying to see into the cavern. "Someone was supposed to meet me here. He must still be on his way. Wait here. It's not safe for you to go farther."

Raine grabs a fistful of my sleeve, stopping me. "Hold on just a minute," she says sarcastically. "You're not going anywhere without me."

"Raine, you don't understand. It's dark down there and—"

"And I'm pretty damn good with this sword. I seem to recall *you* telling me there's safety in numbers and it doesn't hurt to have someone who cares about you covering your back. Your pearls of wisdom don't work both ways?"

"But—" I look at her face. She's an easy read right now, the obstinate tilt of her chin, her eyes wide, resolute, and unblinking, and I know it's useless. There's no arguing with her. I've more than met my match. I bend down and kiss her. "Don't say I didn't warn you."

We make our way down the rest of the steps and as we go I explain to Raine where the four light panels are but that I don't know if those four are enough to get us all the way to where Karden is. The files started closing before I pinpointed them all. "Stick close," I say.

"Right on your back," she answers.

I find the first light panel, which is deftly camouflaged in the streaked concrete near the entrance, and I press it. The distant red light and the hum radiate the prescribed distance, but then I hear another noise behind me. Raine and I both spin. Carver steps out of the shadows.

I straighten from my crouched position where I was ready to spring. "You shouldn't sneak up like that. I almost—" I look around. "Where's Xavier?"

"On his way. You said you had the knife." He puts his hand out, waiting for it.

"We're going in for Karden now. There isn't a lot of time."

"You're taking *her*?"

Raine doesn't know Carver from Adam and bristles at his tone. "I'm his daughter. Why not?"

251

Carver shakes his head. "Do whatever you want," he says, like he's suddenly stopped caring about details, as though he's forgotten how hard we've all worked toward the goal of saving Karden. He stretches his hand out farther. "But give me the knife," he says again, this time with urgency. His coolness is gone. The hunger, the need, the sharp pinpoints of his eyes—it all has new meaning.

That's when all my nagging thoughts tumble into order. The note window that Carver gave me on the first night we met; the aged piece of paper in the Secretary's desk; the address of the house that burned down that was oddly familiar even though I had never been there before; the numbers I recognized though they were new to me. Almost. All handwritten. Notes written years apart. But all with the exact same handwriting. *Lesson two: You may never know precisely who the enemy is.*

I step closer to him. "You're going to burn in hell, Carver."

He looks at me like I'm crazy, but just as quickly I see him grow tired of the game. Feigning denial is too much work and apparently not necessary anymore now that he thinks he has what he wants. He pulls a gun from his pocket and aims it at me. "Hand it over."

"It was you all along. You're the one who turned him in."

"It was the heist of the century. It was going to change the face of the Resistance. Karden wasn't fit to lead it. I had to get him out of the way."

"And get complete control of the money."

"He knew nothing about compromise. He was little more than a focused brute."

"But a brilliant one. The only one who could pull off something like this."

He shrugs. "He was good at some strategies. That was it."

I step in front of Raine. "While you weren't good at any. You thought he had already sent you the whole account number when you delivered his address to the Secretary."

"I admit, it was a premature move."

I laugh. "Premature? That's a slight understatement."

Watching the frustration rise in his face, I continue to mock him, comparing his stupid actions to Karden's brilliant ones. He loses patience, waving the gun. "Give me the knife!" he yells. His voice echoes through the station. I talk right over his demands, belittling his intelligence, enraging him further.

"Give me the knife, you filthy lab mutt! You worthless glorified Bot! Give it to me!"

As he screams I lean close to Raine and whisper, "Go to the red light in the tunnel behind us. Don't stop until you reach the second panel. Press it. I'll catch up. Go."

Raine moves away and Carver hardly notices. He's only focused on me and my pack, which contains the knife. He stops screaming and holds the gun straight out, like he's ready to fire.

"If you shoot me, you'll never get Karden back."

"A justified casualty for a bigger cause. Money is what this whole world's about, and I'm tired of not having it."

I try to stall for time, knowing I need only a few more seconds. "Money makes things happen," I answer. "No denying it. But it's not the biggest thing. Not by a long shot. It's people that make the difference."

"Not in my world," he says. "Last warning. Toss me the knife."

Lesson one: Never give the enemy a warning.

I pull the knife from my pack, smile, and act like I'm going to toss it to him, then stop. "Not a chance, asshole." I begin stepping back into the tunnel, the dim red light closing in around me. "Come and get it."

Even if he gets a lucky shot in and kills me on the first try, he's still going to have to venture to where I am in the tunnel to retrieve it—a tunnel that will plunge back into darkness again in just another second or two. I know he's too much of a coward to do that. He shoots, grazing my arm, the hot sting of the bullet slicing my skin. The timed light turns off, cloaking me in blackness. "Be gone when I come back," I tell him. "Run as far and as fast as you can."

I turn and run deeper into the tunnel, shots ringing out around me, Carver screaming for me to come back, promising to split the money with me.

Without the protection of the hum from the first panel, I'm fair game for the half-humans. I run as fast as I can through the darkness, and thankfully I make it to the next panel and Raine. She's already pressed the second light and I know it will turn off in seconds too so I grab her hand and we head for the third panel. We hear distant screeches, like the packs of half-humans are alert to our presence. I hope they're retreating to deeper tunnels away from the sound of the high-pitched hum. We reach the third panel and press it, moving on to the fourth, now so deep in this labyrinth of tunnels it's a wonder that anyone or anything has ever found its way out again. With the dim red glow, I can see scattered sticks along the abandoned tracks and I finally realize they aren't sticks but bones. We're moving so fast, I hope Raine doesn't notice them.

We reach the fourth panel and rest before we press it.

"This is where he's been all this time?" Raine asks, looking around at the grim reality of this modern-day dungeon.

"There are no guarantees, Raine. He could be dead, but when I was down here before, I sensed something. I think it's him and I think he's alive."

"How will we know who he is? Do you know what he looks like?"

I shake my head. "I've never seen him. But I think we'll know."

She tilts her head to one side not understanding what I'm saying.

"He'll look like you," I tell her.

She braces an arm against the wall and looks away. "I don't know if I'm ready for this part. I'm afraid. . . ."

I pull her close. "You? Afraid of anything?" But I know the feeling of trying to take in so much change so fast, and meeting a long-lost parent, especially under these circumstances, would have my head spinning with trepidation.

"Ready?" I ask.

She presses her lips together and nods.

I push the panel and we continue, another hundred feet of dim red light, and high-pitched humming. Halfway down the tunnel I stop and close my eyes, concentrate, trying to get past the distraction of the hum, trying to sense if we're getting closer.

Something.

"Let's keep moving," I whisper to Raine.

When we round the curve of the tunnel, the reach of the light ends. We search for the next panel but can't locate it. Raine and I look at each other, assessing our next step. We don't know what lies ahead other than darkness.

"You can still go back," I tell her. "You saw what happened to me the last time."

She shakes her head. "We've come this far." She raises her sword, ready to strike, and I pull the eighty-billion-duro knife from my pack.

"Back to back," I say. I explain to her about my eyes and their ability to see faint images even in complete darkness and tell her I'll go first. She'll be a lot more graceful and adept at walking backward than I would be and I'll be better at guiding us in the right direction. "If you hear *anything*, slash and stab." Step by step I walk her through the tunnel, telling her when to step left or right to avoid an obstacle. We advance a good fifty feet and I think we're going to make it without incident when we hear a screech close by and I see movement to our right. I can hear Raine's sword cutting the air.

"I'm slashing!" she calls frantically. "What's there?"

I see the outline of the pack. My knife is out, poised, but nothing is coming at us. I force my eyes to pull in every molecule of scattered light, and then I see more. A large half-human at the front of the pack, keeping the rest back, snarling, a small creature at its side. The one I let go? It appears this half-human is letting us pass—at least this once.

"We're here to get a friend," I say. "We'll be passing back this way one more time and then we won't bother you anymore."

A flurry of yelps and screeches echo through the tunnel. They growl and they snap and I have no idea if they can understand a thing I said. But beneath the slime, the scabs, and the grotesque lipless mouths, their lidless eyes are still completely human. It makes them even more horrific, trapped in bodies and minds at odds with each other, not even knowing they're abandoned experiments. I'm glad Raine can't see in the dark.

"Move slowly," I whisper. "Stay close. I think they're letting us pass."

The pack follows us as we move until we finally reach a point where the tunnel curves again and we see light. White light. The pack scatters in the other direction. We cautiously move forward. Up ahead the tunnel ends and it opens into a large brightly lit chamber with four doors on either side. A Security guard walks past, disappearing down an adjacent hallway.

Raine and I look at each other and nod, our wordless signal that we're ready. We advance to the chamber, hugging the wall in case the guard returns. I gently ease open the first door, to find an empty room that looks like an office. We move on to the next door, carefully gauging the fall of our footsteps. The second door only reveals a supply room. We both take deep silent breaths and move on to the third door. It has a lock on it, easily opened from this side. As soon as I touch the door, I know. There's someone inside. "Wait here," I whisper. "If you hear someone coming, signal me." I open the door and enter.

The room is antiseptic white, void of any warmth. In the corner, a man lies on a thin ragged mat facing the wall.

"What now?" he asks.

I step closer. "I'm here to take you out."

He rolls over. "Get out of—" He eyes my clothing and his face sparks with suspicion. "Who are you?"

"The Network sent me. I'm here to take you out."

He stands, wincing, like the effort pains him. Scars wind across his arms, his neck, another across his jaw and forehead—I

257

assume failed attempts to escape through the tunnels. I notice fresh bruising on his cheekbone. He's very thin but muscular, clearly still a soldier in his army of one. I can't believe the legend is standing right in front of me.

"Which game are you playing this time? I've seen them all."

"No game, Karden. This is the real deal. We have to hurry."

He shakes his head and smirks and then turns away to lie back down on his mat.

"I have your knife," I say. "Miesha gave it to me."

He spins. *Dark and dangerous.* His eyes cut through me. I toss him the knife. His reflexes are fast, like Raine's. He examines the knife, a pained furrow growing between his eyes, as though he's remembering Miesha. He throws it back to me, disgust crossing his face. "There's a million knives out there like this one."

"No, none quite like this one," I say. "Especially not like the smallest blade."

His eyes narrow. I have his attention. "You need to trust me," I tell him. "We don't have a lot of—"

The door swings open and Raine steps inside. "There are footsteps coming down—"

She freezes, her eyes fixing on Karden.

The air is sucked from the room. Karden looks at her and then back at me, his eyes glassy and wild like I'm playing another trick on him. They see themselves in each other. The striking resemblance is impossible to miss. It's probably only a few seconds but it feels like a century that each of us waits for someone else to speak.

Finally, I'm the one who has to break the silence. "It's the real deal," I say again.

Raine looks away, overcome. "We need to go," she whispers.

Karden nods, like he finally believes it. "There will be two of them bringing me dinner. Stand behind the door. Now."

Raine and I move to positions behind the door just as it swings open. The dispatching of two more guards is nearly uneventful, Raine holding her sword to the throat of one before he can draw his weapon, and me grabbing the other from behind, holding him by the neck. They're both young guards, frightened, pulling the lowest rank of duty. We take their weapons and lock them in the room, warning them to remain silent or we'll come back and finish them off—or worse, we'll disable the lights so the creatures of the tunnel take care of our work for us. I quickly check the remaining rooms, praying that Livvy might be in one of them, but they're all empty. We're only a few feet out of the chamber when I notice Karden's severe limp.

"You're injured?" I ask.

"A bad ankle. The interrogations have been more intense these last few weeks. I can make it, though."

He won't make it. Not as far as we have to go. Not to mention the man is malnourished and hasn't run anywhere in sixteen years. I grab his arm and pull it around my shoulder, taking on the bulk of his weight. "Who are you?" he asks.

It's a question that's haunted me ever since I got my life back. A question that Jenna yelled at me as a challenge—it made me leave California, searching for the answer. The original Locke? A fine replica? Bot or man? Or as Kara said, *Only a memory housed in a look-alike body.* Right now the answer is as important as a glass of water in a five-alarm fire.

"A guy in a hurry," I tell him. "Let's go."

Yellow Sea

By the time we make it back to the first panel, Karden is hardly walking at all. He downplayed his injuries. It went far beyond a bad ankle. More likely broken. I suspect some internal injuries too. His breathing is labored. We barely made it through the first stretch of darkness. With only a few days left until the deadline, LeGru and the Secretary apparently stopped caring about the extent of injuries to their golden goose.

On the return trip, the half-humans only stayed at bay for a short time, breaking past the larger creature that held them back. Without Raine we wouldn't have made it at all. She took out several with her sword before being slashed on her shoulder. We made it to the light panel just in time, sending them scattering.

The dim red light and hum guide us on the last stretch through the tunnel. We emerge into the station like ragged soldiers dragging ourselves the last few steps to home, Karden still trying to hobble along on his one good foot, coughing like fluid is filling his lungs. Raine's shoulder is drenched with blood though she insists she's okay.

As soon as we enter the cavern of the station, the distinct salty scent of fresh blood hits us. Even in the suffused red light, we can see the grisly spatter of blood on the walls and floor. The half-humans got something. "Don't look," I say. "We're almost out of here." But it quickly becomes a moot point. A hand that's missing three fingers lies in the path in front of us. And just a few feet past that, part of a scalp, the tuft of hair mostly red with blood. I recognize it. He must have run after me, more crazy with greed than with fear at that point, too close to the goal to let it slip away from him.

I hear a muffled gasp from Raine. She recognizes it too but says nothing. For Karden it has been too long to even suspect that these sparse remains are his childhood friend. And as much as I think Carver probably got what he deserved, there's no satisfaction in the loss. I shouldn't even compare him to Kara. He chose his own path and Kara didn't, but still when I glimpse the remains of Carver, I see what was left of Kara, plunging over a cliff.

Up ahead where light floods down the steps at the entrance, I see the silhouette of a man. Karden's chin lifts. He sees him too. A shuddering breath rattles his chest. "What took you so long?" he calls as we continue to limp forward.

The man doesn't move. When we get closer his features come into view. The tough grumbly man who is liberal with scowls and spare of words shakes his head, unable to speak. "These things don't happen overnight, you know," he finally grumbles back, his voice cracking.

We stop, just a few feet away. Xavier and Karden stare at each other.

"You've put on a few pounds," Karden says.

"And you've lost a few."

Karden pulls away and stumbles forward, the two men embracing, Xavier's face wrinkling as he holds on to his friend. He finally pulls back, swiping his eye with the heel of his hand. He looks Karden over again like he can't quite believe he's really here. "Living the cushy life all these years, huh?" he says.

"Yeah, the accommodations were great."

Xavier takes a deep breath and tilts his head toward Raine. "You've met her?"

Karden turns around to look at his daughter. "Barely." He takes a shaky step toward her. "Rebecca—"

"My name is Raine now," she says, correcting him.

Karden shows no sign of offense. There are no illusions that this will be an easy reunion. He's a stranger to her, and her past experience with a father is not a positive one. "You need to have that shoulder looked at, Raine," he says and puts his arm on Xavier's shoulder for support. "You don't want to end up a scarred buzzard like the two of us."

She bites her lip and nods. "I will." I can see she's relieved at the space he's giving her, maybe even relieved that he's nothing like the Secretary. I watch the two of them, eerie mirror images of each other, even down to the way they narrow their eyes as they look at each other. Alike in ways they don't even know yet, both risk takers, evident from the first time I saw Raine sitting on a rooftop edge dangling her feet over the side, maybe both of them slaves to a gene that craves an adrenaline rush, a balance of power, justice. Maybe both just as subject to their DNA as I am to my BioPerfect.

"But there's nothing wrong with a few scars," she adds. "We all have them, even if they don't show."

Karden nods, his eyes grim, like he's remembering all the taunts from the Secretary claiming Rebecca as his own daughter, like he's imagining what kind of life his daughter has had to live all these years with the enemy.

"We need to go," she says. "My father—Secretary Branson—is probably loose by now. He'll stop at nothing to get you back."

"And you," I add. The Secretary may want Karden for money,

but I saw the wild fury in his eyes as we walked away. He wants Raine for something even more dire. Betrayal.

We make our way up the steps, Xavier holding Karden, who by now has little strength left at all. I step out from the bushes first, seeing if it's safe. Xavier has a CabBot waiting not far away. I ask Raine to stay with Karden and I wave Xavier out so I can talk to him alone. I tell him about Carver. He squints, a mixture of anger and horror pressed across his face. I know the two of them didn't get along, but it's obvious he never expected such blatant betrayal, especially when he learns it was Carver who turned in Karden in the first place. We both agree that now is not the best time to tell Karden.

"There's only room for the two of you in the cab," I tell him. "We'll take the PAT." I slide the knife into his hand. "Two for two. Karden and the account," I say. "We did it."

He looks in my eyes, for once not in a hurry to look away. "Favor," he answers. "You asked me what the *F* stood for in Mr. F. Favor. Only a code name but not friendly like your friend suggested."

I grin. "Yeah, I knew it couldn't stand for that."

He grins. "I underestimated you, kid."

"We're not home free yet," I answer. "You still have to get back and get that account secured—and hide Karden. The Secretary will be turning this city upside down looking for him."

Raine comes through the bushes, supporting Karden with her good shoulder. "He's getting weaker," she says. "He needs to go."

Xavier swings Karden's arm over his shoulder, tightens his grip, and when we're sure there are no Security vans in sight, makes a run for the cab.

When they're gone, Raine and I step out, heading for the PAT station, but from out of nowhere a Security van cuts us off, its sirens piercing the air. We run for Beacon Street and the maze of alleys just beyond it that might give us an escape, but another van cuts us off. They converge from all directions, sirens screaming, another, and another, trapping us in the intersection, leaving us nowhere to go, but almost as quickly, yellow cabs invade the spaces between them, a small fleet darting into the intersection, filling it, recklessly ramming vans, stopping, jamming traffic, ten, twenty, thirty, an army of yellow cabs snug against van doors, blocking all possible exits from the vehicles. I see the Secretary in one of them, pounding on the window, trying to disengage it, screaming, his shoulder banging on his door to force it open against the cab that wedges him inside, his face spasming with rage at his inability to stop us when we're within his sights. I recognize the CabBot crashed up against his door—Bob, the first one I told Dot's story to.

"What's happening?" Raine asks.

"A Favor," I answer. I grab her hand, and through the chaos and snarl of crashed vans and cabs, we escape.

Sanctuary

I savor the silence, a different kind, not the nervous silence that listens for footsteps, or an alarm to ring. Just silence that is warm, slow, gentle to breathe, calm as a summer sea. The kind of silence where small sounds are welcome, the murmur of prayers below, the rumbling roost of pigeons on nearby window ledges, the occasional whispering groan of the ancient organ like it's still settling in.

It wasn't possible to go all the way across town. The city was crawling with Security Forces looking for us, and Raine's bloody shoulder was a flag drawing attention. But we did find safe haven. Father Emelio bandaged both of our wounds and gave us a place to clean up. He's one of many priests who are part of the Network. He had always been aware of our midnight visits to the Cathedral but never made himself known until he saw us in trouble. Word had spread quickly.

Raine emerges from behind the crimson velvet curtain, her hair still wet. He brought us brown friar robes to wear while our clothes are cleaned and repaired. Raine's robe is several sizes too large and hangs off her shoulder.

It's the first time we've been alone and not running since all the secrets between us were revealed. She steps into the organ gallery, the dim light of dusk washing through the stained glass casting us both in a jeweled glow.

She steps closer, no words, only our breaths, our hands barely grazing each other's arms, our lips slowly meeting, mine sliding across her shoulder, along the crest of her collarbone, the faintly beating hollow of her neck, lifting her hair, kissing the creamy blade of her back, not in a hurry, breathing in each inch, our lips finally sliding closer until they meet again and linger, savoring the moment.

"You already told me how you feel, but I never got to tell you," she whispers. "I love you, Locke. *I love you.* I've wanted to say that from nearly the first time we met."

I pull back so I can see her eyes. "Even now, knowing what you know about me? What's beneath my skin . . ."

Her eyes grow impossibly deeper and warmer. "Especially now, with everything I know about you." She reaches up, smoothing back hair that's fallen in front of my eyes. "We've both had something taken from us," she says. "Lives we never got to live. I want to start living mine now—with you." Her lips part and a worried sigh escapes. "But I'm not going to deny I'm terrified. I don't know what will happen—"

I pull her close, staring over her shoulder at the nave of the church below us. "I don't know either." No one knows better than I do that it's impossible to predict the future. I squeeze her tighter, closing my eyes. "I never could have predicted *this*, that I'd be standing here holding you right now." I lower my head, whispering into her ear, my lips brushing her earlobe. "We'll be okay. We have each other." Her heart pounds against my chest. She's giving up far more than I am—the only life she's ever known. And like the Secretary said, if she stays with me, she'll be a hunted criminal. I pull away and tilt her head up to mine. "Are you sure about this?"

She nods and even manages an impish grin. "No question. I didn't plan it. I didn't even want it. It was the *worst* possible thing that could happen, but it did happen. I fell in love. With you." I smile as I listen to her mock my words from last night, complete with eye-rolling, but at the same time, a warm rush fills me.

Her grin fades and she grows serious again. "Just like you, I'm not perfect, Locke, but I'm not stupid either. I'm not going to ruin the best chance I ever had of being happy—because these last weeks with you are the happiest ones I've ever known."

She steps away, looking over the balcony. "And there *are* other risks I want to take. Ones that matter. I need to know the truth, not just about myself but about other people, like those Non-pact children I met, the ones leading lives that I might have led." She spins to face me. "I know after everything that's happened this is crazy to say but I think in some warped way he did love me. Maybe just for my mother's sake, I don't know. But I could never be exactly the daughter he wanted me to be because I had Non-pact blood running through me. That was the one thing even he couldn't change."

"You're still a Citizen," I say. "You could go back. He can't take that away from you."

"There's no going back. Ever. It shouldn't matter what's running through my veins—or what's beneath your skin," she says, and steps closer. "No going back, Locke. Get that straight right now." She pulls my face close, our lips touching, breathing each other's breaths, nothing between us anymore, no lies or secrets. I ache inside in a way I never have before, in a way that makes me feel hopeful, in a way that makes being part of someone else's dusty forgotten inheritance part of another lifetime. Not this one. Not the life I'm living now.

It turns out we have to spend the next few days in the organ gallery above the church. Father Emelio keeps us updated. The whole city is thrown into a Stage 10 Alert because of a security threat. The public is never told what the threat is but we know it's us. All highways out of the city are in lockdown, which means extensive searches of every vehicle leaving the city. City streets aren't much better, but because Boston is still billed as the home of a revolution that birthed two nations, tourism refuses to be shut down. But IDs are being checked and double-checked and no Non-pact in his right mind is leaving his home.

I don't mind this time being holed up in the gallery with Raine. There are worse places to be. Much worse. I know, I've been there. In fact, in some ways I wish this time would never end. It's surreal, day turning to night, night to day, the world outside almost ceasing to exist, the colored light of stained glass creating a new world for us, our world, Raine and me lying on blankets the father has brought us, our arms wrapped around each other, dozing, sleeping, touching, waiting to leave, but in so many ways not wanting to. A small piece of heaven. Our heaven.

Raine sleeps in my arms now. I look at the large round stained glass window above us. The exact same window I looked at so long ago when I was an altar boy and I should have had my eyes closed in prayer. Maybe even then I didn't like the black world inside my head.

The world changes. It stays the same.

I ease my arm from beneath Raine's head, replacing it with a folded blanket, and slip through the velvet curtain to the steps leading to the nave of the church.

As I walk down the center aisle, I feel the timeless power of it, a world that moves forward but stays the same too. My bare feet are cold against the marble floor. I'm all alone except for flickering candles, dancing shadows, and soft lights illuminating the altar. I stop midway, in the center of a world that refuses to stop spinning and it carries me along with it. I swallow. The immensity presses down on me.

It's a journey, Locke. A long one.

Even my father never would have guessed that a journey could be this long, but all those years are a part of who I am now—even those 260 spent in a voiceless vacuum. If not for them, my life would never have intersected with Raine's.

I saw and heard, and knew at last / The How and Why of all things, past. My past echoes around me. Glimpses. Ghosts. A world gone by, but still kept alive in this new one by me. My throat swells and I lower my head and bend my right knee the way my parents taught me before entering a pew, my right hand brushing my forehead, my heart, each shoulder in turn, and finally my lips. I see my mother nodding approval, my father touching my shoulder, and I step into the pew and sit, my hands resting on the seat in front of me, hands unlike any kind this church has ever known before. Just below them, cradled on the back of the pew, are a hymnal and a Bible. Real books. I pull the Bible from its slot, trying to recall something from my catechism days, and I flip through the pages until I find it. A Psalm. I linger on the words that seem to be written just for me.

> *O Lord, you have searched me and known me.*
> *You know my sitting down and my rising up;*
> *You understand my thought afar off.*
> *You comprehend my path and my lying down,*
> *And are acquainted with all my ways.*
> *For there is not a word on my tongue,*
> *But behold, O Lord, You know it altogether.*

I touch my fingers to the paper, feeling the words somewhere inside me.

My frame was not hidden from You,
When I was made in secret,
And skillfully wrought in the lowest parts of the earth.

My fingers slowly trace one line.

I will praise You, for I am fearfully and wonderfully
made;

Fearfully and wonderfully made. I stand and exit the pew, repeating the practiced liturgy, and return to Raine. She smiles as I pull an extra blanket up over us and put my arm around her waist. There are all kinds of definitions for life. I have my own now. And that's all that matters.

I'm startled awake with another blast of sirens in the streets outside the church. Raine's eyes flutter open. We wait for them to pass and they do. We know this is only a brief respite, and not even a safe one. They're still searching. How long before they search here?

I closed down my iScroll before I came here, not knowing if the Secretary had learned my code when Raine called me, so our outside communication has been limited. I use the phone tab if I have to talk to anyone. I briefly spoke with Miesha, telling her to stay put until I call her.

When I finished the call Raine repeated the name with wonder, *Mee-sha*, and asked me about her birth mother. I told her as much as I could, especially about our time running across the country with Dot. Oddly, I smile remembering those times, even though I wasn't smiling then. I remember fuming in the back of the land pirates' truck when Miesha wouldn't tell me about her past, eating a disgusting oily tuna sandwich beneath a smelly tarp. Time has already softened so many memories. I tell her about the two of us pulling Dot from the cab, neither of us willing to leave her behind, because Miesha knew as well as I did that there was something different about Dot. I tell her how Miesha struggled to tell me about Rebecca's and Karden's deaths, how she felt like she had lost everything and there was no point to life.

"And then she found you?"

"Small consolation, huh?"

I tell her she saved me, driving off with me in Gatsbro's limo while he banged on the windows for her to stop. "She's a brave and strong woman, but I'm not sure what she'll do when she finds out about you."

Because of the lockdown, I haven't told Miesha yet. I'm afraid she'll leave her apartment and head straight for us without any regard to safety, or even confront the Secretary herself, ready to tear him to shreds with her bare hands. I remember how crazy Jenna got when Kayla went missing. There's something about a parent that you just don't want to mess with.

With only twenty minutes on the phone tab, I've had to keep my calls short but I've also stayed in touch with Xavier. The account is secure. Eighty billion duros are now safely transferred into the hands of the Resistance, but the Secretary has no way of knowing that yet and is probably still trying to beat the deadline. He also says Karden is recovering. The broken bones, ribs and ankle, have been attended to and are healing. But the damage from malnutrition will take longer to mend. He knows about Miesha and wants to see her but is willing to wait until it's safe. I guess after waiting this long, a few more days is tolerable.

Raine stirs, nestling closer to my side for warmth. We kicked the blankets aside during the night. I'm just about to pull the blanket back over us when the phone tab vibrates. It's Xavier. The lockdown is lifted. It's presumed that the "dangerous suspects" escaped before the lockdown was in place. But we know the real reason for the lift—today was the deadline. It's over. I picture the Secretary, crazed with defeat, still trying to track us down, still believing we are the key to his lost billions. It's gone. He'll never get it back now. But that won't stop him from trying. Or exacting some sort of revenge. Some of that has already begun.

Xavier tells me that every CabBot involved in the traffic jam has been recycled. Every single one. Gone. And a few who weren't even there were recycled just for good measure, CabBots like Dot who had become something more but were willing to risk what they had for Escape. There's still no sign or word from Hap. I fear he's met the same fate.

"It's time for you to go, Locke, while you can, before someone spots you. It's a small city. At least now it is. Everyone knows who you are," Xavier says. We discuss what our options are and I tell him I need to run them past Raine first, and finally we make plans to meet up tomorrow.

Everyone knows. Does that include Shane, Vina, and Ian? I imagine each of their responses was different, Vina probably enjoying a vicarious thrill by the revelation, Shane mimicking his father's rage, sputtering at his failure to be Raine's perfect match, but it's Ian's response that interests me the most. It was his idea to help the Non-pacts. He thinks differently than many Citizens do. Maybe one day soon he'll be in a position to help even more.

I roll over and kiss Raine's forehead. "Time to wake up," I whisper. "I'm going to make you another protein cake for breakfast."

She smiles and stretches, her eyes still shut. "Hmm, yummy, I was hoping we'd have another one of those tasty morsels."

"Plain or plain this time?"

"Extra plain," she says. "With you on the side."

Liberty

I frightened Miesha, showing up at the basement apartment with no notice, but that was the plan.

"Get your things," I tell her. "You won't be coming back."

At least I hope she won't be coming back. None of us know for sure how this will play out. Miesha does her usual balking. I'm mesmerized watching her. The way she waves her hands, the way her lips purse with annoyance, the subtle rumble of certain words. I'm seeing the smallest details of Miesha with new eyes.

"What's the matter with you?" she asks.

"Nothing," I answer, but my heart pounds in my chest.

She's still using her cane for stability. I take it and offer my arm instead. It's midmorning and the streets are busy. Crowds are an asset, but I pull the hood up on my coat before we exit the building just in case.

I planned to tell her in the cab, to prepare her, but she keeps rattling on, filling the silence the way Miesha has always been prone to do. I keep waiting for the right pause but it never seems to come.

"Miesha, I need to tell you something!" I finally blurt out awkwardly, interrupting her midsentence. She stops. She sees the magnitude of what I need to say in my face; I see the painful expectation in hers. I never thought telling her something like this would be so hard. Now time is running short. We're already driving down the alley.

"Miesha, I'm sorry I couldn't tell you this before, but I just didn't know how things would play out. I didn't want you to be hurt all over again."

Her chest rises in slow careful breaths. "What are you saying, Locke?"

The cab stops in the courtyard. Xavier and a small crowd are waiting, standing close to the bonfire in the middle for warmth. Miesha looks out the window, and then her eyes dart back to me, suspicious. "Why are we *here*?"

"This is what I was trying to tell you—"

The cab doors swing open. Miesha steps out and I run around to the other side to help her. I hold her arm as she walks slowly toward the group. "Miesha, the Favor they brought me here for was about saving someone. Someone that you—"

The crowd parts. Miesha stops walking. There's nothing left for me to say.

Karden stands there staring at her.

I feel Miesha lean harder against me, like her joints have gone slack. "What kind of trick is this?" she says, her voice a shaky whisper, but Karden hears it just the same.

"No trick, Miesha," he says and steps closer, hobbling on a crutch. "I've been a prisoner. Your friend rescued me."

Hearing his voice, her knees buckle. I grab her around the waist and she straightens her legs. Her whole body stiffens like she's forcing strength back into it. She steps away from me and walks silently toward Karden until they're face-to-face. They stare at each other for the longest time, a space of time that makes the rest of us grow uncomfortable, like they're both taking in the lines and toll sixteen hard years apart has brought. Finally, they whisper words to each other that none of us can hear. My fear that there would be nothing left between them vanishes. He reaches up, touching her face, and she melts into him.

The rest of us step away to the other side of the bonfire, giving them space, the moment too intimate even if it's in the middle of a courtyard, but even through the crackle and hiss of the fire I hear Miesha's sobs, something I've never heard from her before. And just that quick, suddenly the Favor is not about me trying to find a life, not about justice or a resistance, or anything large and global, it's about something as basic as air and gravity, something as basic as the love between two people.

I look up and see Raine's face in the window of Xavier's home. Waiting. I see the fear in her eyes. Meeting Miesha is different from meeting Karden. She loved her adoptive mother and for her entire life had been told that her birth mother was an animal. I can't make Raine wait through this any longer.

I walk back over to where Miesha and Karden are standing and I tug on her arm, turning her to face me. "There's someone else you need to meet," I say softly.

I intend to walk her inside the building but when we turn, Raine is already standing in the doorway. Miesha spots her. I hold her tight, waiting for her to breathe again, fearful that this final shock might make her collapse completely, but something else happens instead. She takes a deep breath, visibly becomes stronger right before my eyes, her chin lifting, pulling away from me, seeing the utter terror in Raine's eyes just as I do, and for her child's sake she keeps it together, becoming the steel-strong mother who plunged her arms through a window and into a burning building trying to save her baby so long ago.

"Her name is Raine now," I say.

Miesha nods. "Raine," she whispers to herself. She swallows. "Let's go inside and meet, Raine."

The four of us, me, Raine, Karden, and Miesha, sit in Xavier's modest living room for an hour. At first I talk, telling Miesha about the Favor, then Karden talks about his time in prison, the Secretary taunting him with stories of his wife and child that nearly broke him. Miesha keeps it together, the only clue that a storm rages within her is whenever the Secretary's name is mentioned and the knuckles of her fist whiten. Finally Miesha asks Raine if she remembers anything about her and Karden.

Raine shakes her head.

"No, of course you wouldn't," Miesha says apologetically. "You were too young." For the first time her voice cracks. She takes a shallow clattering breath. "And your adoptive mother? She was good to you?"

"Yes," Raine whispers.

The creases fanning out from the corners of Miesha's eyes deepen and her lower lip trembles. I watch the sixteen years that she missed with her own child race through her eyes, precious years that she can never get back and for the first time I think it's possible for her sixteen lost years to be far more than the 260 that were lost to me.

Miesha bites her lip to stop its trembling, and her head tilts to the side slightly. "May I—" She blinks, trying to force back tears, but one trickles from the corner of her eye anyway. "May I hold you?" she asks.

Raine nods, and Miesha leans forward, holding her daughter for the first time since she was a baby cradled in her arms, her shoulders shaking, her eyes squeezing shut. Raine's eyes close too, her lashes wet. I watch her fingers curl into Miesha's sweater, at last gripping the mother she searched for in her late-night walks.

I look at Karden, and even for someone as wiry and tough and self-disciplined as he is, someone who has survived years of isolation and who knows what else, this proves too much for even him and he looks away, tears flowing down his cheeks.

Xavier appears in the doorway and knocks softly on the wall. "Sorry," he whispers. "But their car is here. It's not safe for them to linger too long."

Time. It seems there's always too much. Or not enough. But we know we have to deal with what we have.

Miesha seems to understand this too. We explain to her where we're going. A safe house in New York. It's a good town to get lost in for a while. And we need to get good and lost, at least until the money can start helping us, opening some doors and closing others. Plus, there's someone else there, someone who needs a Favor. Xavier's promised me it's nothing of the magnitude of this last Favor, just enough to keep me "out of trouble," as he describes it. Karden will be staying here and recovering until he's better able to travel. It's not safe for him to stay in Boston either.

We walk outside and Xavier points to a narrow place between two buildings where a truck is wedged, almost hidden from view.

The plumbing truck. "One last thing before you go. We need to do something with them. Did you decide?"

I think I decided almost the minute I saw them. I just needed to be able to do it myself. I finally understood Jenna's long-ago actions in that moment, knowing why she threw our copies in the pond. Until we face an impossible decision ourselves, we don't ever really know for sure what we would do. I know now. A life gets one chance, maybe two if we're lucky, but a hundred chances reduces what is precious to a product—a product whose only purpose for existence is to replace that which is lost.

Not everything can be replaced. Kara's gone. If anything's left, it's only her shell, the one Gatsbro tried unsuccessfully to fill and use for his own greedy purposes. No one will have that chance again.

One by one, I disconnect the cubes from their battery docks and pass them to Xavier, and others who quietly offer their help, and they take them to the bonfire. Cube after cube labeled with LOCKE or with KARA, a hundred Lockes, a hundred Karas, one by one, gone. No more wandering through an endless, timeless void. No more searching for doors that don't exist. Finally, I come to the last cube, but it's labeled differently from the rest.

Gerald Gatsbro.

My blood runs cold and I hesitate. Xavier waits, his hand outstretched, ready to carry it off with the others. I stare at the cube, a second chance to give Gatsbro what he deserves. I'm inclined to keep it, walk away to one of the many abandoned buildings that surround us and tuck it away into a dark corner. Leave it there. Let it sit for centuries. Or longer.

Raine appears at the rear of the truck. "Locke, are you okay?"

I inhale sharply, focusing on her face, her eyes bright, ready to leave her past behind. I look back at the cube, my last chance for revenge for everything he did to me and especially to Kara. "Yes," I answer. "I'm fine." I disconnect Gatsbro's cube and hand it to Xavier.

The copies are finally all gone, their journey over, and now only one Locke remains, the Locke reaching for Raine's hand, ready to begin a new journey.

We walk across the courtyard to the car the Network has given us for our Escape, a beat-up wreck but still an extravagance by Non-pact standards. Xavier shows me the basics. I tell him that I never learned to drive, but he assures me there's nothing to learn. The car will do it all. "But if you ever need to break the rules—and I have no doubt that you will—a simple Override command will take care of it."

I see the weight in Xavier's eyes. He had tried to talk me out of taking Raine. *This isn't a life she's used to,* he had told me. *There are other places we can hide her.* What he doesn't know is it's not a life I was used to just a short time ago either. But life changes. We adapt. We have no other choice.

He tries to reason with me one last time. "Are you sure you want to take her? It's not going to be an easy life on the—"

Miesha steps forward, tucking a strand of hair behind Raine's ear, worry in her eyes too. "She'll be fine," she says. "She's a strong young woman."

Raine smiles. I know it's hard for her to say good-bye too. A relationship barely begun will have to wait again. She reaches out, this time initiating her own embrace with Miesha.

Karden reaches into his pocket and holds out his Swiss knife to me. "I hear it's gotten you out of a few scrapes. Take it," he says.

I look into his eyes, dark and deep like Raine's, the fire and focus still there, never giving up. I reach out to take it from him and he grips my hand with both of his, squeezing it hard, his gaze locked on mine, an understanding. A nod. A silent *thank you.*

We get into the car and I begin to pull the door shut when a large golden arm swipes through the air blocking me from closing it. Raine and I both suck in startled breaths.

A familiar voice booms in our ears. "You may not shut the door unless Miss Branson is on this side of it with me."

Xavier grins. "Sorry, kid. Forgot to tell you."

I turn and look behind me. I face a perpetual stern scowl, but now I know what lies behind it. Something more. "Get in, Hap," I say. "*Back* seat."

Raine and I hold hands in the front seat. We've been on the open highway that hugs the coast for an hour now, the windows down, the brisk autumn air blowing through our hair. We both wear our government-issue charity coats for warmth, a symbol of shameful poverty for so many, a symbol of hope for us. Are the odds with us? Probably not. Two kids out to change the world. Two kids being hunted by a still-powerful man. Not good odds. But the odds have never been with me, and yet, here I am.

With Raine.

She spots a wide sandy beach and pulls the frosted green glass of Liberty from her pocket, still in need of its lost mate. "Do we have time?"

Never enough. Always too much.

But now, as I look into her eyes, the time seems just right.

Thirty Years Later

I hear a soft knock and I pause, listening to see if it came from upstairs. Is one of the boys rapping on the wall? Another weak knock but this one is clearly coming from the front door, which seems unlikely because of the late hour and the drifts of snow that are piling up by the minute. Perhaps a neighbor in need of something?

I cross to the foyer, startling as I swing open the door. "What are you doing out there? For God's sake, you shouldn't—" I reach out to pull Jenna inside but she steps back and shakes her head. "Jenna, you can't stay out there in the cold. You know—"

"I've been walking all day, Locke. That's why I'm here. To walk."

"But you can't—"

"It's time, Locke," she says forcefully, cutting me off. I finally understand what she's saying. This isn't just a walk.

My mouth opens, but no words come out. She's a Jenna I've never seen before. The calm, serene Jenna she's always been, but a very weary one too. I see it in her eyes, still crystal blue, forever stuck at seventeen, but a fire has left them.

She reaches out, smiles, touching my temple where my hair is tinged with gray.

"I guess you were right," I say. "It's all connected. The Bio-Perfect got the message that I want to grow old with Raine. It's making sure I do. I can't bear the thought of—" I realize what I'm saying and stop.

"That's the advantage of progress," she says. "I, on the other hand, have a first-generation Bio Gel that's never gotten that message—only the survival one."

"Jenna, please—"

"Kayla's in Africa with her husband. She's so happy, Locke. She loves her work there. She called me last week and I saw she has a hint of gray at her temple too." Her smile fades. "She's getting older, Locke. Before I have to face the day that—" She shakes her head. "I'm tired, Locke. No one can live forever and it already feels like I have. I've outlived Allys, Ethan, everyone I've ever known, but I refuse to outlive my own daughter."

Her gaze drops to her hands laced together in front of her. "My parents couldn't face it. Neither can I." She looks back at me, her eyes hopeful. "No parent wants that. I always knew that one day . . . one day I'd return to Boston for a last walk in wintertime." She takes both of my hands and squeezes them with icy fingers. "Now is that time. And I want to share this last moment with someone who knows me—someone who knew me from the beginning. Someone who always made me braver. That's you. Please, this one last time, come walk with me."

"Locke? Who's there?"

I turn to see Raine walking in from the kitchen, large with our third child. She stops when she sees Jenna out in the cold. She knows what that means too. She tries to persuade her to come in, but Jenna is firm in her decision.

"It's already done. I've been outside for hours. I just need a little time with an old friend." Her voice is fragile.

Raine touches her belly, perhaps understanding more than I can, and walks over to hug her. There are no more words between them, just an exchanged look of understanding. I grab my coat and give Raine a kiss. "I'm not sure when I'll be back. You'll be okay?"

"Hap's upstairs, and Mother and Father are right next door if I need anything," she says, and she pushes me toward the door and Jenna.

The wind has stopped like the world has sucked in its breath for Jenna, and snowflakes flutter as delicately as white butterflies in no hurry to land. Jenna hooks her arm into mine as we walk, leaning on me more with each step. We're the only ones on the street, the only ones with a reason to be out late in weather like this.

"You and me again," she whispers. "Just like in the old days. Almost."

Kara's name doesn't have to be said. She's always present.

She sighs, serene and content. "Such lives we've lived. Lives we never could have imagined."

An understatement. "Never," I agree. "My imagination isn't that good. But we're probably not so different from anyone else. We all envision one life and live another, don't we? I'm probably lucky my other imagined life never came to pass."

She laughs and pulls my arm closer. "You've done a lot of good, Locke. Your parents would be proud."

I smile. "I didn't exactly become the president or scientist they had hoped for."

"Better," she says.

Change came relatively fast by most people's standards but never fast enough for me. Jenna was right, it was molded over time by people who refused to give up. I was one of those people. I pushed and pushed and realized I had become a member of the

Resistance. A leader even. Raine and I together, along with Karden, Miesha, and Xavier. It wasn't easy, but I guess things of worth rarely are.

Raine and I lived on the run for the most part, just about everywhere, even in the room under Jenna's greenhouse for a while, but we didn't have to wait ninety years for change the way Jenna did. The money helped our voices be heard, but it was still people who made the biggest difference. Each one made sacrifices, some contributing in large ways, others in small, everyone helping as much as they could, but all people who never lost sight of the goal.

Ian proved true to his character, and years after we had last seen him at a Collective meeting, he became part of a core Citizen group who helped push through legislation. He worked closely with Xavier and other key Non-pacts to draft the final wording of the bill.

Ten years from the time we began running, the country was reunified and the whole class of Non-pacts ceased to exist. After a lifetime of living on the fringes, Non-pacts were now Citizens like everyone else and could openly walk wherever they chose. Raine and I were both overcome with emotion the first time we saw Karden and Miesha walking hand in hand toward us through cheering crowds at Faneuil Hall for the official signing, two new people in so many ways.

A short time later that freedom was extended to all sentient beings like the one Dot had been. They were given basic rights, the circumstances of their existence no longer tied to their worth. *We even dare to dream that those worlds could be ours one day. Escape is not about moving from one place to another but about becoming more.*

Life it seems is precious, no matter how you come by it. In

appreciation for the work I'd done, they allowed me to name the bill that secured these rights, now known as the Dot Jefferson Act.

We never found Livvy. The Reformation and Reassignment camps were disbanded. She wasn't in them. There were trials for crimes against humanity—LeGru was tried and sentenced to life imprisonment—but the Secretary escaped the trials, enough of the old system still in place to protect him. A pardon. He retired in disgrace, an old man on a government pension, absolved of his crimes by an outgoing president. My only consolation is that he's utterly alone in a prison of his own making, still holed up in his rooftop fortress, knowing that the child he stole—his daughter—helped to topple his secret empire, and a lab beast like me was his final undoing.

Like Karden and Miesha, Xavier became a new person too, refocusing his energies on employment and decent housing for former Non-pacts. Because of him, the abandoned tenements on the south side of Boston have been cleaned up or bulldozed, and every man or woman willing to work is paid a fair legal wage. But there's always more to do.

The world has changed. It's gotten better. It's gotten worse. After all these years, Jenna's words still echo in my head, *just as one problem is solved, a new one is created.* The work never ends. If there's one thing you can always count on in this world, it is change. I don't fear it the way I used to. I try to be ready for it. One day, maybe, all the changes will be only for the good. I can dare to dream. I can always hope for more.

We turn the corner. The Commons is just ahead, but I watch Jenna's strength ebbing, her steps slowing. I know that Allys's death a few years ago was a blow to her. True to form, Allys had married again, this time to an adventure seeker. Allys said seven was her lucky number, but on one of their ocean adventures near the tip of South America they were both drowned at sea. At least we all knew she died doing what she loved and was with someone she loved when it happened. Jenna's arm shakes in mine, and with a sudden wild desperation I'm ready to sweep her into my arms and run, save her, keep her, turn back a clock that always moves forward, but the unthinkable stops me. What if I outlived every-one that I love? *Raine. My boys.* I wouldn't want it for myself. I can't force it on her.

"Can you make it?" I ask.

She nods. "Remember when we used to come here when we were supposed to be in seminar?"

"Hiding behind the Washington Monument. How could I forget? This was the first place I was ever kissed. By *you.*"

She laughs. "But it certainly wasn't the last."

"No." I smile, thinking of Raine, my first kisses with her not far from this spot. "Not the last by a long shot."

"Even with all the hard times, we have a lot of good memories."

"It doesn't have to be over, Jenna. There's still time—"

She looks at me sharply with strength I didn't think she still possessed. "Yes, Locke. It's *over.*" And then more softly, "Death isn't a curse. It's the shadow that gives life its form, and that shadow's whispering to me now."

Her shoulders slump like the burst of energy has drained her. Still, she lets go of my arm and walks onto the lawn of the Commons, snow swallowing her boots, her arms shaking as she lifts her hands and face to the sky.

"I had forgotten how snowflakes felt on my face," she says.

"They sting," I say.

"No, it's more of a flutter. Almost like wings brushing my cheeks."

I lift my face, trying to see the snowflakes as Jenna does. I've become immune to them, so many winters in Boston now. I remember winters as a child, racing to get my sled at first snowfall, the excitement and fear of hitting my brother dead center on his back with a snowball, the times I tried to capture the quarter-sized flakes to put in our freezer, wanting to preserve the fragile crystals forever, and more recently, sharing the first-time wonder with Raine as our toddler son caught the tiny treasures in his own small hands and licked them away.

"And so light," she says. "A lacy wing that melts away. It's a miracle."

A miracle. That's the look I saw in my son's eyes too. And though I knew all the explanations of how snowflakes form, in that moment I ached inside with the mystery and miracle of it all.

A cough wrenches Jenna's lungs and her steps falter. I hurry to her side, holding her, my arm around her waist.

"It's time, Locke," she whispers. "I can feel it."

"No, Jenna, not yet—"

Her legs fail and I catch her, falling to the ground with her.

"Jenna, what can I do?"

"Nothing. . . ."

> *Locke*
>
> *Jenna*

A mysterious connection that can never be explained.

A connection that will never be broken.

She coughs, her shoulders shaking in my arms. I spread my fingers beneath her head, supporting her, looking at the girl, still every bit seventeen but over three hundred years old.

"So many others are already gone. It's my turn."

She stares into my face, the last thing she'll ever see, staring until her crystal blue eyes don't see me anymore, snowflakes gathering on her lashes. My hands tremble as I reach up and close her lids. I pull her close to my chest, holding her, rocking her, the world hushed, saying the word it took me more than a lifetime to learn. *Good-bye.*

Snowflakes fall silently around us, fluttering white butterflies.

No, Jenna . . . never gone.

Some things last forever.

Acknowledgments

I owe thanks to so many remarkable people who have made the Jenna Fox Chronicles happen.

First, thank you to the many writers who have held my hand through the course of these books and shared the "writing life" with me and all that it entails. Special thanks to Marlene Perez and Melissa Wyatt who listened to my questions and ramblings and offered much wisdom as I worked my way through this final book. Writing a series, I've learned, is not for the fainthearted.

Thank you to all the smart and hardworking people at Macmillan and Henry Holt. Jean Feiwel for support and inspiration, helping the ending crystallize while on tour! Rich Deas who made the puzzle come together perfectly with his breathtaking jacket designs; Laura Godwin for being a beacon of encouragement and calm; Rebecca Hahn for taking care of infinite details, and special cheers to the marketing, publicity, and sales staff for getting Jenna's and Locke's stories into the hands of readers. I am deeply grateful to the whole talented Mac-team.

My editor, Kate Farrell, is simply the most perfect editor any writer could dream up. Thank you, Kate, for your wise counseling, creative nudging, and boundless enthusiasm throughout this trilogy. Jenna and Locke's story wouldn't be the same without you—they'd probably still be stuck in a cube! You *are* the best.

I've said it before but it still bears repeating: My agent, Rosemary Stimola, is smarts, wisdom, savvy, and friend all rolled into one *brilliant* package. If she doesn't already have a star named after her, she should—or a whole constellation. Thank you, Ro. I am one blessed writer.

I am grateful to and for my children, Karen, Ben, Jessica, and Dan, They continue to inspire me and bring me so much joy. Without them there would be no stories. They are also my constant cheerleaders, always wanting "more." Which means I need to get back to work, but not before I mention:

As always, my infinite love and gratitude to my husband, Dennis. He makes everything that matters to me happen, sometimes just by walking into the room.

GO**FISH**

MARY E. PEARSON

What were your inspirations for the future world of the Jenna Fox Chronicles?

I was inspired, surprisingly, by history and past worlds. Since *The Fox Inheritance* and *Fox Forever* are so far in the future, I had a lot more freedom with what I could include, but like *The Adoration of Jenna Fox*, I wanted it to be as realistic as possible—a future that could really exist. So I looked at our political and social pasts and how we've progressed—or not—over the centuries, and I used those as a model for the political and social world of the future. Some things get better and, unfortunately, some things don't.

For the advanced technology, I again did research, found out what scientists are working on and predicting for the far future, and incorporated a lot of that. Artificial intelligence and human-like robots were one of the fun things I included.

Do you think our future will look like the world you created?

Yes, very similar I think, barring any unexpected natural or man-made disasters, which are always a factor that can change the world in the blink of an eye. In *The Fox Inheritance*, I had a "mini disaster" when a monster volcano blew some decades earlier and wiped out a large portion of the population, which in turn gave rise to more human-like robots to replace the workforce. But in truth, a monster volcano erupting at full force could have even more dire consequences, eliminating humans from the earth entirely.

What is one aspect of the digital world that you can't live without?
Only *one*?! My laptop. That's where I write my stories.

What was your favorite part of your futuristic world that you wish we could have today?
I developed a soft spot for a certain compassionate and childlike Bot in the story. If there could be Bots like her helping us to see our world through newer and gentler eyes, I would love that.

Tell us about your writing process. Where do you write? When? What do you eat/drink while crafting a story?
Ah, it always comes back to food, doesn't it? I am not much of a snacker—usually the only thing you will find sitting on my desk is a glass of water—but I do admit that at certain times of the year when I have really good dark chocolate in the house, I will freely set it next to my keyboard when I am gnashing my teeth over a scene or deadline and indulge at will. And of course it is all medicinal so I can do it guilt-free, right? As far as the writing itself goes, when I begin a project, I open a file, give it a working title, and from that point on the file is open on my computer. Except for a power outage, it's never closed. And then from morning, until I go to bed, I write. Not continuously, of course. I will sit down in the morning,

reread what I wrote the day before, rewrite a bit, and then try to make progress with new territory, go take a shower, go back to write more that came to me while in the shower, and so it goes throughout the day. I have daily goals of so many words—the ones I call keepers. In one day I may write 3000 words to end up with 250 that I feel are right.

As for where I write, I have a bedroom in my house that has been converted to an office. It is the darkest, quietest corner of the house, with a pretty view out the window of trees in my yard and very often I have birds outside my window looking in. Maybe that's why birds have made appearances in my last two books.

When did you realize you wanted to be a writer?

I think it was in high school. Before that I had always loved writing, but the actual "job" of being a writer hadn't occurred to me. I remember reading *The Outsiders,* my first book that really seemed like it came from my generation, and I thought, this is the kind of book I could write. Before that, while I had loved the literature I had read, it always seemed like it was from another time—authors long dead, the classics and such—so joining those ranks seemed distant and unattainable.

How did you celebrate publishing your first book?

When "the" call came, I still remember jumping up and down in the kitchen with my daughters squealing. That was all the celebration I needed.

Which of your characters is most like you?

When I finished *The Miles Between,* I thought that one of the secondary characters, Mira, was a bit like me. She is perky and cheerful and always trying to make everyone get along, but beneath that perky exterior she has some more serious motivations. I've known for years that I have a "peacemaker" personality, so I was a bit surprised to see some of those qualities emerge in Mira.

As a young person, who did you look up to most?
My sister. I was five years younger and I tagged along behind her incessantly and she was always nice to me and always included me. Of course, during our teen years we had a few arguments—mostly over the bathroom—but other than that we have always gotten along great. She is a strong, even-tempered, salt-of-the-earth kind of person and I still look up to her.

What was your worst subject in school?
Math. I am not a numbers person. I can barely remember how old I am—which is sometimes convenient.

What was your best subject in school?
English, but not when it came to dissecting sentences. I hated that part. I think because I was an avid reader I internalized what made a sentence correct, rather than memorizing the "rules" of proper sentence structure. I think rules and memorization are for left-brainers, and I am an intuitive right-brainer all the way.

Are you a morning person or a night owl?
Definitely a morning person, but I am married to a night owl, so I have learned to sleep in a little more. But my body clock still tries to wake me at the first sign of dawn.

What's your idea of the best meal ever?
Um, food! The best meal ever would be a huge bowl of steamers—mussels or clams or both!—a little butter to dip

them in, a loaf of hot sourdough bread, a nice buttery chardon-
nay, and a big slice of mud pie—with extra fudge—to finish it
all off. And if I am sitting outside on a patio or at the beach on
a warm night while I eat it, I would be in sheer heaven.

Which do you like better: cats or dogs?

I'm a dog person. I've always had dogs, or maybe I should
say they have always had me. First, Rags, who was a shaggy
mutt, and then Duke and Buddy, who were both golden re-
trievers. Now we have two more goldens, Brody and Hunter,
who are completely spoiled. We even let them on the couch
(gasp!), which we never did with our other dogs. If I wasn't al-
lergic, I think I would really enjoy cats too. My sister-in-law
has three cats that are pretty darn cute—and a lot less hairy
than my dogs!

What is your worst habit?

Laughing at inopportune moments. I suppose it is nervous
laughter, but my husband has already told me that I can't attend his funeral.

What is it that you like best about yourself?

I can forgive and forget. Maybe it is just a bad memory. Maybe
it was my mom saying, "Don't cry over spilled milk." In other
words, move on, life is too short to worry about the past.

Where do you go for peace and quiet?

My patio or deck—especially at twilight. I love that time of the
day. Everything, including the breeze, seems to quiet down.

What makes you laugh out loud?

Tom Hanks in *The Money Pit*. Every time.

What are you most afraid of?
Potato bugs. Luckily I rarely run into them because they creep me out more than anything. Ick—those buggy eyes!

What time of the year do you like best?
Summer all the way! Bare feet! Shorts! Juicy peaches! Warm evenings! Eating outdoors! It doesn't get any better than that. Also, I think somewhere deep down inside, I still associate summer with that wonderful free feeling of summer vacation and no school. I can still hear my childhood friends calling me outside to play kick-the-can.

If you were stranded on a desert island, who would you want for company?
My husband. He is my best friend, makes me laugh, and is one of the smartest people I know. He'd figure out a way to "unstrand" us—that is if we even wanted to get off the island. Being stranded on a desert island with him doesn't sound so bad. Sort of a forced vacation. Can we have a pile of books too?

What do you want readers to remember about your books?
There's a hundred different answers to that depending on the book and the reader but a few thoughts . . . I hope that perhaps they will remember seeing themselves and feeling less alone, or remember stretching to ponder new ideas or viewpoints, or remember walking in someone else's shoes and gaining a new perspective, or perhaps simply remember a fond few hours where they were able to escape into a different world where they shared a journey with me.

What was your favorite book as a teen?

I loved poetry—Dickinson, Frost, Cummings, Yeats—anything I could get my hands on. A few books that I loved and reread many times were *The Outsiders* by S. E. Hinton, *A Tree Grows in Brooklyn* by Betty Smith, and *The Good Earth* by Pearl S. Buck. As a younger teen I remember loving anything written by Ruth M. Arthur. A while back I managed to get my hands on an old copy of *Requiem for a Princess,* which has long been out of print. I reread it and was happy to see that I was as impressed with her writing now as I was then.

What would your readers be most surprised to learn about you?

That I love to laugh. I can be very serious and my books tend to be on the very serious side, but laughter is the necessary balance to it all. My husband makes me laugh every day, and when I get together with my sister, I become impossibly silly.

Thousands of years in the future, a new America is built on the ashes of our present. The rebellious Princess Lia is on the run, little knowing that her jilted prince and a hired assassin are in hot pursuit.

Turn the page for a sneak peek of

THE KISS OF DECEPTION

MARY E. PEARSON

1

Today was the day a thousand dreams would die, and a single dream would be born.

The wind knew. It was the first of June but cold gusts bit at the hilltop citadelle as fiercely as deepest winter, shaking the windows with curses and winding through drafty halls with warning whispers. There was no escaping what was to come.

For good or bad, the hours were closing in. I closed my eyes against the thought, knowing that soon the day would cleave in two, forever creating the before and after of my life, and it would happen in one swift act that I could no more alter than the color of my eyes.

I pushed away from the window, fogged with my own breath, and left the endless hills of Morrighan to their own worries. It was time for me to meet my day.

The prescribed liturgies passed as they were ordained, the rituals and rites as each had been precisely laid out, all a testament to the greatness of Morrighan and the Remnant from which it was born. I didn't protest. By this point numbness had overtaken me, but then as midday approached, my heart galloped again as I faced the last of the steps that kept here from there.

I lay naked, facedown on a stone-hard table, my eyes focused on the floor beneath me while strangers scraped my back with dull knives. I remained perfectly still even though I knew the knives brushing my skin were held with cautious breaths. The bearers were well aware that their lives depended on their skill. Perfect stillness helped me hide the humiliation of my nakedness as strange hands touched me.

Pauline sat nearby watching, probably with worried eyes. I couldn't see her, only the slate floor beneath me, my long dark hair tumbling down around my face in a swirling black tunnel that blocked the world out—except for the rhythmic rasp of the blades.

The last knife reached lower, scraping the tender hollow of my back just above my buttocks. I fought the instinct to pull away, but I finally flinched. A collective gasp spread through the room.

"Be still!" my aunt Cloris admonished.

I felt my mother's hand on my head, gently caressing my hair. "A few more lines, Arabella, that's all."

Even though it was offered as comfort, I bristled at the formal name my mother insisted on using, the hand-me-down name that had belonged to so many before me. I wished that at least on this last day in Morrighan she'd cast formality aside and use the name I favored, the pet name my brothers used, shortening one of my many names to its last three letters. Lia. A simple name that felt truer to who I was.

The scraping ended. "It is finished," the First Artisan declared. The other artisans murmured their agreement.

I heard the clatter of a tray set on the table next to me and whiffed the overpowering scent of rose oil. Feet shuffled around to form a circle—my aunts, mother, Pauline, others who'd been summoned to witness the task—and mumbled prayers were sung. I watched the black robe of the priest brush past me, and his voice rose above the others as he drizzled the hot oil on my back. The artisans rubbed it in, their practiced fingers sealing the countless traditions of the House of Morrighan, deepening the promises written upon my back, heralding the commitments of today and ensuring all of their tomorrows.

They can hope, I thought bitterly as my mind jumped out of turn trying to keep order to the tasks still before me, the ones written only on my heart and not a piece of paper. I barely heard the utterances of the priest, a droning chant that spoke to all of their needs and none of my own.

I was only seventeen. Wasn't I entitled to my own dreams for the future?

"And for Arabella Celestine Idris Jezelia, First Daughter of the House of Morrighan, the fruits of her sacrifice and the blessings of . . ."

He prattled on and on, the endless required blessings and sacraments, his voice rising, filling the room. And then when I thought I could stand no more, his very words pinching off my airways, he stopped and for a merciful sweet moment silence rang in my ears. I breathed again, and then the final benediction was given.

"For the Kingdoms rose out of the ashes of men and are built on the bones of the lost, and thereunto we shall return if Heaven wills." He lifted my chin with one hand and with the thumb of his other hand he smudged my forehead with ashes.

"So shall it be," my mother finished, as was the tradition, and she wiped the ashes away with an oil-dipped cloth, "for this First Daughter of the House of Morrighan."

I closed my eyes and lowered my head. *First Daughter.* Both blessing and curse. And if the truth be known, a sham.

My mother laid her hand on me again, her palm resting on my shoulder, maybe offered as a gesture of comfort, but my skin stung at her touch. Her comfort came too late. The priest offered one last prayer in my mother's native tongue, a prayer of safe-keeping, which oddly wasn't tradition, and then she drew her hand away.

More oil was poured, and a low, haunting singsong of prayers echoed through the cold stone chamber, the rose scent heavy on the air and in my lungs. I breathed deeply. In spite of myself, I relished this part, the hot oils and warm hands kneading compliance into knots that had been growing inside of me for weeks. The velvet warmth soothed the sting of acid from the lemon mixed with dye, and the flowery fragrance momentarily swept me away to a hidden summer garden where no one could find me. If only it were that easy.

Again, this step was declared finished and the artisans stepped back from their handiwork. There was an audible gathering of breath as the final results on my back were viewed.

I heard someone shuffle closer. "I dare say he won't be looking long upon her back with the rest of that view at his disposal." A titter ran through the room. Aunt Bernette was never one to restrain her words, even with a priest in the room and protocol at stake. My father claimed I got my impulsive tongue from her, though today I'd been warned to control it.

Pauline took my arm and helped me to rise. "Your Highness," she said as she handed me a soft sheet to wrap around myself, sparing what little dignity I had left. We exchanged a quick, knowing glance which bolstered me, and then she guided me to the full-length mirror, giving me a small silver hand mirror that I might view the results too. I swept my long hair aside and let the sheet fall enough to expose my lower back.

The others waited in silence for my response. I resisted drawing in a breath. I wouldn't give my mother that satisfaction, but I couldn't deny that my wedding kavah was exquisite. It did indeed take my breath away, the ugly crest of the Kingdom of Dalbreck made startlingly beautiful, the snarling lion tamed on my back, the intricate designs gracefully hemming in his claws, the swirling vines of Morrighan weaving in and out with nimble elegance, spilling in a V down my back until the last delicate tendrils clung and swirled in the gentle hollow of my lower spine. The lion was honored and yet cleverly subdued.

My throat tightened and my eyes stung. It was a kavah I might have loved . . . might have been proud to wear. I swallowed and imagined the prince when the vows were complete and the wedding cloak lowered, gaping with awe. *The lecherous toad.* But I gave the artisans their due.

"It is perfection. I thank you, and I've no doubt the Kingdom of Dalbreck will from this day forward hold the artisans of Morrighan in highest esteem." My mother smiled at my effort, knowing that these few words from me were hard won.

And with that everyone was ushered away, the remaining preparations to be shared only with my parents and Pauline, who would assist me. My mother brought the white silk underdress from the wardrobe, a mere wisp of fabric so thin and fluid it melted across her arms. To me it was a useless formality for it covered very little, as transparent and helpful as the endless layers of tradition. The gown came next, the back plunging in the same V so as to frame the kavah honoring the prince's kingdom and displaying his bride's new allegiance.

My mother tightened the laces in the hidden structure of the dress, pulling it snug so the bodice appeared to effortlessly cling to my waist even without fabric stretching across my back. It was an engineering feat as remarkable as the great bridge of Golgata, maybe more so, and I wondered if the seamstresses had cast a bit of magic into the fabric and threads. It was better to think on these details than what the short hour would bring. My mother turned me ceremoniously to face the mirror.

Despite my resentment, I was hypnotized. It was truly the most beautiful gown I had ever seen. Stunningly elegant, the dense Quiassé lace of local lace makers was the only adornment around the dipping neckline. *Simplicity.* The lace flowed in a V down the bodice to mirror the cut of the back of the dress. I looked like someone else in it, someone older and wiser. Someone with a pure heart that held no secrets. Someone . . . not like me.

I walked away without comment and stared out the window, my mother's soft sigh following on my heels. In the far distance I saw the lone red spire of Golgata, its single crumbling ruin all that remained of the once massive bridge that spanned the vast inlet. Soon it too would be gone, swallowed up like the rest of the great bridge. Even the mysterious engineering magic of the Ancients couldn't defy the inevitable. Why should I try?

My stomach lurched and I shifted my gaze closer to the bottom of the hill where wagons lumbered on the road far below the citadelle, heading toward the town square, perhaps laden with fruit, or flowers, or kegs of wine from the Morrighan vineyards. Fine carriages pulled by matching ribboned steeds dotted the lane as well.

Maybe in one of those carriages, my oldest brother, Walther, and his young bride, Greta, sat with fingers entwined on their way to my wedding, scarcely able to break their gazes from each other. And maybe my other brothers were already at the square, flashing their smiles at young girls who drew their fancy. I remembered seeing Regan with dreamy eyes whispering to the coachman's daughter just a few days ago in a dark hallway, and Bryn dallied with a new girl each week, unable to settle on just one. Three older brothers I adored, all free to fall in love and marry whomever they chose. The girls free to choose as well. Everyone free, including Pauline, who had a beau who would return to her at month's end.

"How did you do it, Mother?" I asked, still staring at the passing carriages below. "How did you travel all the way from Gastineux to marry a toad you didn't love?"

"Your father is not a toad," my mother said sternly.

I whirled to face her. "A king maybe, but a toad nonetheless. Do you tell me that when you married a stranger twice your age, that you didn't think him a toad?"

My mother's gray eyes rested calmly on me. "No, I did not. It was my destiny and my duty."

A weary sigh broke from my chest. "Because you were a First Daughter."

The subject of First Daughter was one my mother always cleverly steered away from. Today, with only the two of us present and no other distractions, she couldn't turn away. I watched her stiffen, her chin rising in good royal form. "It's an honor, Arabella."

"But I don't have the gift of First Daughter. I'm not a Siarrah. Dalbreck will soon discover I'm not the asset they suppose me to be. This wedding is a sham."

"The gift may come in time," she answered weakly.

I didn't argue this point. It was known that most First

Daughters came into their gift by womanhood, and I had been a woman for four years now. I'd shown no signs of any gift. My mother clung to false hopes. I turned away, looking out the window again.

"Even if it doesn't come," my mother continued, "the wedding is no sham. This union is about far more than just one asset, and the honor and privilege of a First Daughter in a royal bloodline is a gift in itself. It carries history and tradition with it. That's all that matters."

"Why First Daughter? Can you be sure the gift isn't passed to a son? Or a Second Daughter?"

"It's happened but . . . not to be expected. And not tradition."

And was it tradition to lose your gift too? Those unsaid words hung razor sharp between us, but even I couldn't wound my mother with them. My father hadn't consulted with her on matters of state since early in their marriage, but I had heard the stories of before, when her gift was strong and what she said mattered. That is, if any of that was even true. I wasn't sure anymore.

I had little patience for such gibberish. I liked my words and reasoning simple and straightforward. And I was so tired of hearing about tradition that I was certain if the word were spoken aloud one more time, my head would explode. My mother was from another time.

I heard her approach and felt her warm arms circle about me. My throat swelled. "My precious daughter," she whispered against my ear, "whether the gift comes or doesn't come is of little matter. Don't worry yourself so. It's your wedding day."

To a toad. I had caught a glimpse of the king of Dalbreck when he came to draw up the agreement—as if I were a horse given in trade to his son. The king was as decrepit and crooked as an old crone's arthritic toe—old enough to be my own father's father. Hunched and slow, he needed assistance up the steps to the Grand Hall. Even if the prince was a fraction of his age, he'd still be a withered, toothless fop. The thought of him touching me, much less—

I shivered at the thought of bony old hands caressing my cheek or shriveled sour lips meeting mine. I kept my gaze fixed out the window, but saw nothing beyond the glass. "Why could I not have at least inspected him first?"

My mother's arms dropped from around me. "Inspect a prince? Our relationship with Dalbreck is already tenuous at best. You'd have us insult their kingdom with such a request when Morrighan is hoping to create a crucial alliance?"

"I'm not a soldier in Father's army."

My mother drew closer, brushing my cheek, and whispered, "Yes, my dear. You are."

A chill danced down my spine.

She gave me a last squeeze and stepped back. "It's time. I'll go retrieve the wedding cloak from the vault," she said, and left.

I crossed the room to my wardrobe and flung open the doors, sliding out the bottom drawer and lifting a green velvet pouch that held a slim jeweled dagger. It was a gift for my sixteenth birthday from my brothers, a gift I was never allowed to use—at least openly—but the back of my dressing chamber door bore the

gouged marks of my secret practice. I snatched a few more belongings, wrapping them in a chemise, and tied it all with ribbon
to secure it.

Pauline returned from dressing herself, and I handed her the
small bundle.

"I'll take care of it," she said, a jumble of nerves at the last-
minute preparations. She left the chamber just as my mother returned with the cloak.

"Take care of what?" my mother asked.

"I gave her a few more things I want to take with me."

"The belongings you need were sent off in trunks yesterday,"
she said as she crossed the room toward my bed.

"There were a few we forgot."

She shook her head, reminding me there was precious little
room in the carriage and that the journey to Dalbreck was a long
one.

"I'll manage," I answered.

She carefully laid the cloak across my bed. It had been
steamed and hung in the vault so no fold or wrinkle would tar-
nish its beauty. I ran my hand along the short velvet nap. The
blue was as dark as midnight and the rubies, tourmaline, and sap-
phires circling the edges were its stars. The jewels would prove
useful. It was tradition that the cloak should be placed on the
bride's shoulders by both her parents, and yet my mother had returned alone.

"Where is—" I started to ask, but then I heard an army of
footsteps echoing in the hallway. My heart sank lower than it

already was. He wasn't coming alone, even for this. My father entered the chamber flanked by the Lord Viceregent on one side, the Chancellor and the Royal Scholar on the other, and various minions of his Cabinet parading on their heels. I knew the Viceregent was only doing his job—he had pulled me aside shortly after the documents were signed and told me that he alone had argued against the marriage—but he was ultimately a rigid man of duty like the rest of them. I especially disliked the Scholar and Chancellor, as they were well aware, but I felt little guilt about it since I knew the feeling was mutual. My skin crawled whenever I neared them, as though I had just walked through a field of blood-sucking vermin. They, more than anyone, were probably glad to be rid of me.

My father approached, kissed both of my cheeks, and then stepped back to look at me, finally breathing a hearty sigh. "As beautiful as your mother on our wedding day."

I wondered if the unusual display of emotion was for the benefit of those who looked on. I rarely saw a moment of affection between my mother and father, but then in a brief second I watched his eyes shift from me to her, and they lingered there. My mother stared back at him, and I wondered what passed between them. Love? Or regret at love lost and what might have been? The uncertainty alone filled a strange hollow within me and a hundred questions sprang to my lips, but with the Chancellor and Scholar and impatient entourage looking on I was reluctant to ask any of them. Maybe that was my father's intent.

The Timekeeper, a pudgy man with bulging eyes, pulled out

his ever-present pocket watch. He and the others ushered my father around as if they were the ones who ruled the kingdom instead of the other way around. "We're pressed for time, Your Majesty," he reminded my father.

The Viceregent gave me a sympathetic glance but nodded agreement. "We don't want to keep the royal family of Dalbreck waiting on this momentous occasion. As you well know, Your Majesty, it wouldn't be well received."

The spell and gaze were broken. My mother and father lifted the cloak and set it about my shoulders, securing the clasp at my neck, and then my father alone raised the hood over my head and again kissed each cheek, but this time with much more reserve, only fulfilling protocol. "You serve the Kingdom of Morrighan well on this day, Arabella."

Lia.

He hated the name Jezelia because it had no precedent in the royal lineage, *no precedent anywhere* he had argued, but my mother had insisted upon it without explanation. On this point she had remained unyielding. It was probably the last time my father conceded anything to her wishes. I never would have known as much if not for Aunt Bernette, and even she treaded carefully around the subject, still a prickly thorn between my parents.

I searched his face. The fleeting tenderness of just a moment past was gone, his thoughts already moving on to matters of state, but I held his gaze, hoping for more. There was nothing. I lifted my chin, standing taller. "Yes, I do serve the kingdom well, as I should, Your Majesty. I am, after all, a soldier in your army."

He frowned and looked quizzically to my mother. Her head shook softly silently, dismissing the matter. My father, always the king first and father second, was satisfied with ignoring my remark because, as always, other matters did press, and he turned and walked away with his entourage, saying he'd meet me at the abbey, his duty to me now fulfilled. *Duty.* That was a word I hated as much as *tradition.*

"Are you ready?" my mother asked when the others had left the room.

I nodded. "But I have to attend to a personal need before we leave. I'll meet you in the lower hall."

"I can—"

"Please, Mother—" My voice broke for the first time. "I just need a few minutes."

My mother relented, and I listened to the lonely echo of her footsteps as she retreated down the hallway.

"Pauline?" I whispered, swiping at my cheeks.

Pauline entered my room through the dressing chamber. We stared at each other, no words necessary, each of us clearly understanding what lay ahead of us, every detail of the day already wrestled with during a long, sleepless night.

"There's still time to change your mind. Are you sure?" Pauline asked, giving me a last chance to back out.

Sure? My chest squeezed with pain, a pain so deep and real I wondered if hearts really were capable of breaking. Or was it fear that pierced me? I pressed my hand hard against my chest, trying to soothe the stab I felt there. Maybe this was the point of cleaving. "There's no turning back. The choice was made for me," I answered. "From this moment on, this is the destiny that I'll have to live with, for better or worse."

"I pray the better, my friend," Pauline said, nodding her understanding. And with that we hurried down the empty arched hallway toward the back of the citadelle and then down the dark servants' stairway. We passed no one, everyone either busy with preparations down at the abbey or waiting at the front of the citadelle for the royal procession to the square.

We emerged through a small wooden door with thick black hinges into blinding sunlight, the wind whipping at our dresses and throwing back my hood. I spotted the back fortress gate, used only for hunts and discreet departures, already open as ordered. Pauline led me across a small muddy pasture to the shady hidden wall of the carriage house, where a wide-eyed stable boy waited with two saddled horses. His eyes grew impossibly wider as I approached. "Your Highness, you're to take a carriage already prepared for you," he said, choking on his words as they tumbled out. "It's waiting by the steps at the front of the citadelle. If you—"

"The plans have changed," I said firmly, and I gathered my gown up in great bunches so I could get a foothold in the stirrup. The straw-haired boy's mouth fell open as he looked at my once pristine gown, the hem already sloshed with mud, now muddying my sleeves and lace bodice and, worse, the Morrighan jeweled wedding cloak. "But—"

"Hurry! A hand up!" I snapped, taking the reins from him.

He obeyed, helping Pauline in similar fashion.

"What shall I tell—"

I didn't hear what else he said, the galloping hooves stampeding out all arguments past and present. With Pauline at my side, in one swift act that could never be undone, an act that ended a thousand dreams but gave birth to one, I bolted for the cover of the forest and never looked back.

Once there were three—three friends who loved one another—
and after a terrible accident destroyed their bodies, their three
minds were kept alive, spinning in a digital netherworld. . . .

Follow Jenna, Locke, and Kara in Mary E. Pearson's stunning trilogy,

THE JENNA FOX CHRONICLES

"What will hold readers most are the moral
issues of betrayal, loyalty, sacrifice, and
survival." —*Booklist*

The Adoration of Jenna Fox
ISBN 978-0-312-59441-1

"Gripping, urgent, and highly appealing."
—*School Library Journal*

The Fox Inheritance
ISBN 978-1-250-01032-2

"A more-than-satisfying conclusion to a
thought-provoking trilogy."
—*School Library Journal*

Fox Forever
ISBN 978-1-250-04005-3

macteenbooks.com SQUARE FISH